MQ WEBB

When you're Dying

TBR
PRESS

For my mom, who read countless drafts and still had the enthusiasm to read another x

1

Chapter 1

Then

"Where are you going?"

It was him, his voice deep and insidious. He was close, moving across the rooftop tiles behind her, the sound of his footsteps cutting through the rain. She was afraid to look—if he reached out, he could almost touch her. The edge of the roof loomed high. If she fell, there was only the ground to stop her.

The thought was dizzying, and she almost lost her footing, somehow fighting the vertigo so she could ready herself for the attack. He was angry, and it would probably come fast and heavy, his fingers clawing at her, propelling her closer to the guttering and what awaited her below.

Up here, the smell of fresh rain overpowered the mildew on the rooftop tiles. There was no chimney, just a few solar panels that looked as if they'd give out if she grabbed on to them. If he pushed her from the roof she would fall to her death, but being up there faced with her own mortality has made her realize something important. She isn't ready to die.

She looked out at the darkened sky, the rooftop gritty against her bare feet. The humidity of deep spring hit like a force of its own as the east coast sky threatened to open with electricity, warming her cheeks and filling her lungs with turbulent energy.

She had nowhere left to run, and without turning around, she knew he was blocking the way back inside through the loft window.

He'd grown quiet, but the sudden silence didn't fool her. He was playing a game. When she turned he'd use her changing balance against her and send her sprawling. He stalked silently now, trying to elicit fear. She wouldn't give him what he wanted no matter how high her heart rose in her throat.

The roof tiles were slick with layers of rain, making it difficult to stay out of his reach as he closed in behind her. A peal of thunder took her by surprise as she approached the edge. Was he herding her there on purpose? As if spurred by the crack of a whip, the rain picked up, blinding her senses so that she lost the sound of his feet shifting on the tiles behind her. Afraid to look back, she realized she was out of time—the slope of the roof and gravity pushed her forward so that her toes almost hung over the roof's edge. She needed to time her next move perfectly, relying on her own dexterity, which wasn't as reliable now that she knew she was probably going to die. The plan was to get just close enough to the edge so that when he lunged she could duck, sending him toppling off the roof. She imagined him meeting the ground like forked lightning and dispersing across the dirt with a boom.

She worked hard to calm her breathing, willing the rushing in her ears to stop.

She sensed him creeping closer.

Get ready.

"There's nowhere to run," he said, his tone clear. He thought he had won.

"Who's running?" She angled her feet sideways, bending her knees for balance, and pushed herself away from the looming earth as she waited for him to approach.

He stopped beside her, an outline in the darkness, lining up his next move. Except, he was as unsteady in the rain as she was.

"What're you going to do now? Jump?" he said.

"Maybe."

His laughter broke the hum of the rain.

She had been right to think he was crazy.

Blanketed in the dark, she was thankful he couldn't see her face. She needed him to think he'd won, that she was stupid enough to run to the roof and trap herself without a plan just like a girl about to die in a bad horror movie.

She curled her toes, ready to spring into action as she reminded herself why she was up here to begin with. Even with her heart in her throat, she knew she was going to do this. She hadn't come this far for nothing.

"It'd save me the trouble," he said, a smirk in his tone.

She set her jaw. This was the last chance she'd have to find out what he knew about her sister. "Why won't you tell me?" He'd kidnapped her, she was sure of it. She still hadn't figured out why or what he'd done with her. The only thing she knew for sure was that since her sister had been missing she hadn't heard a single word from her, which almost ruined the illusion that no matter how bad it seemed, her sister would be—*had to be*—okay.

"Where's the fun in that?"

"What did you do with her? Did you bury her somewhere?" She had spent hours hypothesizing all the things that might've stopped her sister from coming home, each possibility worse than the last, but she wasn't sure she was ready to have it confirmed.

"You'll never know. You don't deserve to know," he said, anger flaring.

"I'll make you wish you told me." She gritted her teeth and wiped the rain from her face. Hopefully she sounded more convincing than she felt.

He stepped forward, the heat of his skin closing in as the sharpness of his features came into focus in the shadows, ridding him of that clean-cut charm that she'd seen right through, even before she'd spoken to him. She could tell by the way he tried to use it even now that it usually got him what he wanted. "You won't get the chance," he said, closer than ever.

Now.

With a primal scream she dug the balls of her feet into the tiles, using her grip as a spring board to run right at him and knock him off balance, onto the slippery tiles. He rolled toward the edge, trying to grab on to anything to stop himself from sliding. He reached for her, ready to take her down with him.

A light from the street hit his face, catching his irises so that she could see him clearly. He wore a strange look. Stunned and fearful at the same time. Maybe that look was universal, the gaze of someone as they realized they were about to die.

His hand twisted toward her ankle until his fingers were

circling it. The slick roof slowed her, making it impossible to regain her footing. She felt him pulling at her ankle, both of them tumbling toward the ground.

Was this her punishment for trying to end his life? Maybe she'd fall to her death out here with him.

She braced herself and waited for her body to hit the ground as they both went over the edge, almost three stories between them and the earth.

2

Chapter 2

Oscar

Now

Oscar's phone rang insistently, rousing him from sleep. He rolled over and scrabbled around on the side table.

Hayley stirred next to him, and he knew the harsh blare of the phone had awoken her. "What is it?" she asked, her voice heavy with sleep.

"It's Caroline," said Oscar. The name flashed bright in the room's darkness. He sat up, knowing he needed to answer. He hadn't heard from Caroline in a while and she wouldn't bother him on a Sunday morning if it wasn't important.

"Why is she calling so early?" asked Hayley, golden hair falling over her face as she rolled onto her side to look at him.

He checked the time on his phone—6:02 a.m.

The bleariness fell away as he spoke. "I don't know, but I should probably find out." He nuzzled his nose against hers.

"I'd prefer to stay here with you."

She smiled and rubbed his arm. "Me too, but it's probably important, and she has practically been a mother to you."

Two good points—and two good reasons for the sense of dread building in his chest. "Nah. She probably just won the lottery and wants to brag," he said, trying to sound relaxed for Hayley's sake. He kissed the back of her hand and slid out of bed to take the call in the living room. "Caroline?"

"Oscar! I'm sorry to call you at this hour," said Caroline, her voice fraught with worry. "Especially on a Sunday," she added, "but I have a favor to ask."

"Okay," he drawled. He'd known Caroline since he was eleven, and he couldn't once in all that time remember her asking for a favor despite giving him so much. He sat down on the couch, resting a leg on the cushion.

Caroline had stepped in to comfort him when he was just a kid trying to figure out why his mom had left him. She'd taken his older brother, leaving Oscar behind with an abusive, alcoholic father. He'd spent a lot of time at the library to avoid going home. Caroline had found him browsing the psychology and self-help books and struck up a conversation. Oscar wasn't much of a talker, but he'd immediately felt comfortable talking her Caroline—she didn't treat him like she wasn't sure what to say to him like the other adults, and if she wasn't sure about something she asked questions instead of assuming she knew the answer. She'd become his mentor and friend, encouraging him to pursue a career as a psychiatrist like her—something he wouldn't have thought he was capable of.

"There's been an accident," said Caroline softly.

"Is it Jane?" asked Oscar, referring to Caroline's partner.

"No, Jane's fine. It's a patient. I'd like you to speak with her. She's been through a lot, so you'll need to take it easy."

"A patient?" His surprise was clear. "Since when do you need my help with work?"

Caroline was a capable psychiatrist in her own right. She'd taught him much of what he knew, both professionally and personally.

"I don't need your help. I want your expertise. This woman was locked in a house but she managed to escape onto the roof. It looks like her captor followed her up there."

There was a good chance Caroline was trying to keep Oscar busy—he'd left his position as the director of Whitner Psychiatric Hospital almost two months ago and he still hadn't figured out what he wanted to do next. Caroline and Hayley had been trying to help him rediscover his passion for psychiatry since, but he wasn't sure he'd ever look at it with the same passion he once did.

"They fell from the roof of his house. There were two stories and a loft, so it was a big fall. Each is saying the other is responsible."

"So, why do you need me?" asked Oscar.

"Because I want you to find out which one of them is lying."

If Caroline was trying to sell the puzzle to him, she was doing a good job. "What's her name?"

"Verity."

"Truth," said Oscar, not realizing he'd said it out loud at first.

"What?"

"Nothing."

He could tell Caroline was waiting for his inevitable explanation, leaving a gap in the conversation for him to fill like she used to when he was a kid with a new fact he wanted to share.

"Verity. It means *truth*. Claude Buffier, the philosopher, identified the eternal verities—a set of moral principles."

"Oscar, it's a little too early in the morning for a philosophy lesson," Caroline joked.

"Didn't you call me?" he asked incredulously.

"I've always envied your curiosity," Caroline chuckled. "I used to wonder where you stored all that knowledge from those books you constantly read," she said, growing serious again. "I'd really like your input on this. You're good at reading people. The best. The way you can find out what's really going on. It's like you make people feel seen, so much so that they can look at themselves and see what's there."

Caroline spoke like a proud parent. It had made all the difference when Oscar was growing up, even if he didn't always show it.

"Wouldn't Verity feel safer talking to you, given what she's been through?" asked Oscar.

There was feedback and the distinct beeping of hospital equipment in the background from Caroline's end. Oscar shifted the phone, but it didn't help to quiet the noise.

"Are you at the hospital?" he asked. He'd assumed she was home with Jane, probably loading up on coffee and doing the crossword.

Oscar went through to the kitchen, surprised to find Hayley out of bed and balancing ingredients from the fridge to take across to the kitchen island. He smiled. Sunday brunch was usually his deal, and it was *always* at a more palatable hour.

"Yeah, I'm at the hospital," Caroline confirmed. It was outside of visiting hours and she didn't usually work on

9

Sundays, so she probably wasn't there to deliver flowers and a "get well soon" card.

"Is Verity all right?" He considered whether to ask his next question, knowing she'd probably ignore it. Caroline saw a lot in her line of work, but she always seemed to shoulder it. "Are you okay?"

"She's doing much better now than when they brought her in. I'm just outside her kidnapper's room. She did quite a number on him," said Caroline, ignoring his question.

Oscar had a lot more questions and was unsure where to start, but Caroline saved him from figuring it out by launching into a background. "It looks like he locked her inside of his home. At some point she managed to free herself and she made it onto the roof, probably looking for an escape."

It must have been awful—not knowing whether she'd get out alive, or whether anyone was looking for her.

"She climbed out of the window, but he followed her out and somehow they both ended up in the dirt," said Caroline. She stopped, leaving Oscar some time to process.

"Oscar? Are you there?" she asked when he didn't respond.

"Yeah. Sorry." He cleared his throat. "Did he push her off the roof?"

"We're not sure. It looks like he might've jumped and taken her with him. He's not saying much other than that he didn't lock her up and that she attacked him."

He could sense her uncertainty—Caroline wasn't sure she believed either version of events.

"What do you think happened?" he asked.

Caroline hesitated, possibly finding a spot where she wouldn't be overheard. Oscar imagined that if Verity and her kidnapper had just been brought in there would be police roaming the hospital corridors, waiting to speak with both of them. Usually, the psychologists and psychiatrists were brought in after the police and the lawyers were done, unless the people involved in the crime needed to be assessed immediately.

"I'm not convinced she didn't lure him out there. I mean, why would you run to the roof instead of trying to escape out the front door?"

"I don't know. Maybe he kept it locked. If she was there for a couple of days and she'd already tried to escape she might know that."

"Well, I'd like to find out exactly what happened and I think you're the right person for the job. I was hoping you could speak with them both and see what you think?"

She was trying to get him to return to work—this was the kind of case Caroline would usually take care of herself and Oscar wasn't sure he was ready to return yet.

"Aren't the police already trying to figure out what happened?" asked Oscar.

"Yeah. They're deciding whether there's enough evidence to charge him right now. Detective Payneham called me because if this case isn't handled properly it'll be a PR nightmare for them. They've had a run-in with Dale Carmot before."

"Dale Carmot?"

"Yeah."

"The business mogul Dale Carmot?"

"That's the one."

Oscar brewed a pot of coffee. He didn't usually drink caffeine this early in the morning, but the coffee made leaving Hayley alone on a Sunday a little more bearable. He remembered the addiction study he did back in his undergrad course. Caffeine

11

had been one of the drugs they talked about. That was where he learned that it aided concentration in small amounts, and right now he needed a boost.

"So, they want a psych evaluation? I mean, he has resources—he could probably weasel his way out of this. I'd be following the professional witness path too if I were a cop and I wanted something to stick." What better way to counter Dale's lawyers than with a professional whose job it was to assess people's minds and motivations?

Caroline agreed.

Oscar sipped his coffee, thinking about the last time Dale Carmot's name had caught his attention. It came to him in a rush.

"Wasn't Dale Carmot in trouble a couple of months ago? They thought he murdered that nurse who disappeared... what was her name?"

"Ashlee Casmere," said Caroline.

"Yeah, that's it." Obviously someone had decided that Dale was innocent, or he'd still be locked up. Either that or he had great representation. *Or they didn't have enough evidence to convict him.*

"There's more," said Caroline. "Carmot requested the psych eval."

"Usually they ask for a lawyer, not a psychiatrist. He's concerned about his mental health?"

"He didn't request the evaluation for himself. He requested it for Verity."

"That's unusual. Did he say why?"

"It was a bizarre request, but he said we should talk to her. I was hoping you could find out more. Oscar, I wasn't just stroking your ego before. You can read people better

12

than anyone I know. I suspect one of them is lying, and I'm confident you'll know which one it is." She paused. "There's something else you should know before you agree."

"Okay," said Oscar, adding more sweetener to his coffee, creating a vortex in his mug as he stirred. Caroline was usually more of a throw-him-in-the-deep-end-and-watch-with-pride-as-he-tried-to-swim kind of person. If she was warning him it must be bad.

"They cleared Dale Carmot of abducting Ashlee Casmere. They haven't found a body. She's technically still missing, but it doesn't look like she's going to show up alive."

Oscar stopped stirring the sweetener. "And you think he knows where she is?"

"I'm not sure," said Caroline. "But Verity Casmere is her sister."

Verity Casmere. He knew her. Verity was a caseworker. They'd met during a patient admission at Whitner. She waited with a woman she'd referred to the psychiatric hospital for treatment until she was settled in, and had visited her a few times afterwards. Oscar didn't know Verity well, but he knew her.

3

Chapter 3

Verity

Then

I'm sitting in my sister's New Haven apartment without her when the news sinks in. The chemo treatment was months ago, but it hasn't been as successful as we'd expected and the cancer in my breast didn't shrink like we hoped. It's interesting how with cancer the numbers move down the stages as it progresses, like levels in a video game. If life were a platform game I'd be in the arena, facing the boss right now. So far, it's been one hell of a fight.

Almost a year of treatment and the déjà vu of the chemo cycle is still with me. Months of telling myself it's all for a reason, that each time might be the turning point when the mutated cells disappear for good. But the only thing that finished up since the last round of treatment was the hair loss, because eventually there wasn't a hair left to lose.

Now we're trying immunotherapy, hoping my immune system will gear itself up to fight. The treatment has left me nauseated and fatigued, but my hair has grown back over the last months. It's thinner than it used to be, but it's long enough to style into a pixie cut, each inch a victory.

The habit of double flushing the toilet to get rid of any residual chemo meds is still with me. It's a habit I might never break.

I've been thinking about it since my doctor told me. He was hopeful we might shrink the cancer, of course, hopeful that just one more cycle would help. With the right combination of chemo drugs it was always just within reach.

When I asked if this might be as far as my life went, he didn't want to answer. It was only when I pressed him that he acknowledged it could be. "Perhaps it's best to prepare yourself in case that happens. There's a good chance we can buy you more time."

How do you prepare yourself to die? Did he mean I should learn to accept it, or that it was time to figure out what I wanted to do with the time I had left?

I'd asked how much longer I'd have if we went ahead with treatment and received a vague answer that treatment outcomes were different for each patient.

In cancer terms, everyone talks about the five-year survival rate. Despite Dr. Alderton avoiding my question, he'd finally acknowledged that the probability of being alive five years after being diagnosed with metastatic breast cancer was low. Lower without treatment. Some people only survived months, but I'd read the statistics, morbidly poring over the numbers like a person possessed. My chances of surviving beyond five years were less than 3 out of 10.

Treatment had used a good chunk of that time already, and it looked like I might be more of a "months to live" kind of girl. All he could say for sure, his eyes hidden behind reflective glasses, making it impossible to read his expression, was that the cancer wasn't shrinking like we'd hoped.

I look at the photos on Ashlee's refrigerator. Each one captures a different moment in her life. Not just the milestones, but the little moments like a day at the beach. Even though I've been living in her apartment, there is nothing of mine here except for the day-to-day things I'd brought. Clothes, toiletries, a laptop and my medication.

In the photographs Ashlee is smiling, looking happy and carefree. We're together in one picture, arms slung around each other, our cheeks almost touching. Even then, when death hadn't touched us and there was no reason to believe anything but the best, my smile was closed, lips pressed together while Ashlee leaned toward the camera, showing off two rows of straight teeth.

When you're dying, a lot goes through your mind. Who will notice when you're gone? What *really* matters in your life?

I sit for a long time, the questions coming one after another, getting increasingly existential. What does living really mean? Is it merely the state of being alive or is it more than that, like pursuing happiness or finding a purpose?

Overlaying every thought is the panic instilled by Dr. Alderton's words. *Resistant.* The word gives me images of a petulant child refusing their vegetables, just like the cancer refuses the treatment offered. I go to the bathroom mirror and look myself over, trying to find outward signs of what's eating away at me from the inside.

I inspect the color of my eyes to make sure it hasn't leached out, faded by my illness. They're still blue and bright. If eyes really are windows to the soul, maybe they'll be the last to fade. Next, I press gently on the pillows beneath my eyes, which make me look like I haven't had a good night's sleep in a long time. I expect something more obvious, more sinister, something that tells people that my body's out of control, but there is nothing but my thinned out hair and willowy frame to give me away. I inspect my body even closer, scrutinizing myself before I conclude that a stranger might think I'm a pilates addict with a poor diet instead of a cancer patient.

At some point I acknowledge that I need to decide how I want to spend the time I have left.

There are things I used to want to do. A whole life which at thirty-two, I haven't experienced. The regret of putting off overseas travel is strong and harsh. I'd thought finishing college first and saving to go on a trip later was sensible, but saving money on my salary as a social worker was slow, especially in those first years. Later, I had put it off because my mother was uncomfortable with the idea of me traveling alone.

I settled for road trips and weekend getaways down the coast with my ex, Jay. He was great at making it seem like it could be fun, just the two of us on a romantic, impromptu vacation exploring the beaches along Long Island Sound. Except, he was always short on cash and I always ended up spending more than I wanted to, trying to save the romance.

One day I stopped fighting so hard to keep the relationship functioning and the romance fizzled entirely.

He wasn't my great love, and thinking that he might be as good as it gets for me makes me want to cry. We haven't spoken for more than a year—not since it ended. Would he care now if he knew I was sick?

I'll never know.

I consider calling my mother to tell her, but we haven't spoken since my sister, Ashlee, disappeared, and it's not the kind of news you want to call someone out of the blue with.

How do you tell your mother you're dying when you can't admit it to yourself? Saying it out loud feels like acknowledging my mortality.

Mom would ask questions I wasn't ready to answer. With Ashlee missing I was all she had left, and I didn't want to take another daughter from her.

I can't say out loud that I'm dying. I don't want anyone to know, afraid they'll look at me differently, a half smile on their faces as if I'm already dead and gone. A living ghost, casting an imperfect shadow on their lives. The only person I'd told any of this to was Ashlee. Even then I'd downplayed it. All she knew was that I was undergoing treatment and that it should help to stop the cancer from spreading.

As much as she'd tried to treat me the same, I'd noticed she'd become nicer, more considerate of my feelings. Except for the night of the gala.

I don't want other people to treat me like I'm fragile too. If I'm going to die I want the time I have left to be as close to "normal" as possible.

Abandoning the idea of telling my mom, I let my eyes fall to the pantry. I can't see them but I know they're there—a couple of bottles of red hiding in the back. Surely one glass will be okay?

I take a bottle of peppery Shiraz from the shelf and open it, pouring too quickly into a wineglass until it's filled almost to the top. It's more than I intended and I consider emptying some back into the bottle, picture the mess if I miss, and cap it.

I'm about to take a sip when I remember Dr. Mason's warning to avoid alcohol before beginning another round of treatment. I haven't decided whether I want the treatment yet, but I definitely want the glass of wine. There's a chance I'll spend my last days feeling sicker than I would without treatment and then die anyway.

I'm about to take a sip when I think of what Ashlee would say if she were here.

There's no way you're giving up that easily, not for a sip of wine.

Reluctantly, I abandon the glass of wine and pour some kombucha, hoping the bubbly cherry-plum flavor will compensate for the rich, velvety red at least a little.

A strong pang rips through my chest, reminding me how much I miss my sister. She'd drink the kombucha with me and pretend she didn't miss the subtle burn and giddy happiness of a glass or two of wine. We were always close, especially as we transitioned from just being siblings who were thrown together through birth, and became friends. Her absence has made me feel more alone than any other time in my life. Without her, there was no one to push me out of my comfort zone or get me out of the house on a bad day.

For a long time all I thought about was how she had disappeared so suddenly. Like a tripped wire—she was there, living and vibrant, until the lights went out and a hollow emptiness filled the space she had occupied. I prayed I'd see her again. When I did, would she be alive or lying in a casket with everyone saying goodbye?

The police had issued an appeal for information but no one seemed to know where she was. Someone must've seen something. Someone knew where Ashlee was, but for some reason they didn't want to come forward.

I feel sick from the possibilities. Ashlee locked up with a stranger, wondering what they'd do with her. Maybe death had found her suddenly the night she went missing? Knowing Ashlee, she'd fight until her last breath.

I let myself imagine that she'd be the one to beat the odds. I needed to believe she was safe, that maybe she needed time before she reemerged from wherever she was hiding.

Except I know that's not true. She wouldn't scare me like that. She'd tell me if she was going away and needed some space. And if she was being held by someone and escaped, the first thing she'd do is find a way to let me know she was okay.

It had been almost two months and my responsible sister—who was always a nurse, even when we were kids playing doctor with a little plastic kit, putting plaster on my knee to hide a scrape—had contacted no one.

I used to wonder whether she'd wandered off in the wrong direction and some kind of accident had befallen her after the gala, but the police had checked the surrounding hospitals and she hadn't shown at any of them. Then I heard she was seen leaving with *him*. I thought that once the police started questioning him it was only a matter of time before it was all over and we brought her home, but it hadn't gone how I had expected.

Now that Ashlee had entered my thoughts there was little chance of focusing on anything else. Tonight wasn't the night for sobriety. I reclaim the glass of wine and take the bottle with me, settling atop my bed covers. I place the bottle down on the bedside table and drink from the glass in my hand with avidity before pouring another.

"One for you, Ash." I hold up the glass to the empty room, hoping that wherever she is, she knows I haven't given up on finding her.

I fumble for the TV remote and hit the power button, relieved as the screen comes to life and the voices drown out the silence.

I'd stayed in Ashlee's apartment so that someone was there if she came home. The décor reminds me of her—bright and full of energy, like the beginning of spring. Her apartment has the feel of a vacation house beside the ocean. I miss the muted colors of my own apartment, but my smoky gray ottoman and shaggy rug would be out of place here. I look around at Ashlee's stuff, at the pictures on her walls, wondering what will happen to it all if she never comes home.

While I'm navigating the apps on the TV, a flashy banner appears. At first I think it's just an ad, but as his face fills the screen, the voice of the reporter low and serious in that tone that reporters everywhere seem to emulate, I realize it's a news flash about Dale Carmot.

My stomach jolts and I freeze with the glass of wine still in my hand. This could be it. This could be the moment he goes to jail forever for what he did to Ashlee. People mill about behind him, blurred in the background so that viewers aren't distracted.

Of the half-dozen people questioned when she went missing, only one seemed like they might know what had happened to her. And there he was, smiling with the confidence that comes with a charmed life. Everything from the fresh haircut to the pressed suit is perfectly compiled to exude success and power. His features are sharp and perfect but none of it looks natural to me, except for his stormy blue-green eyes.

He waves at the camera as if he's a celebrity. It's not even his arrogance that irritates me. It's the way he moves with the easy gait of someone who is free in a way I will never be while my sister is missing.

He was the same at the gala. So self-assured, believing he was so much better than everyone else. He seemed to think that nothing could touch him, that no one would dare try. Those fundraisers were just as much an excuse for the medical community to network with other hospitals—more of an informal conference than a party. They drew people like Dale, people who thrived on the power and status their jobs provided.

Had anyone else seen the way Dale watched Ashlee at the gala?

I turn up the volume on the TV and listen to his silky voice, carefully controlled to come across as the right mix of friendly but knowledgeable.

"It's important to give back, and our hospitals are a corner-stone."

My eyes rush over the on-screen banner.

Business tycoon and philanthropist Dale Carmot hosts charity event to raise money for Bayswater Hospital after being acquitted of murdering local nurse Ashlee Casmere.

It's the same hospital Ashlee did her training at when she was studying. Why would he be hosting a charity event there so soon after Ashlee's disappearance? It can't be a coincidence. It feels like he's mocking her, and I wonder if I'm the only person to notice.

The reporter is barely in the shot, but I can hear their voice. "Mr. Carmot, how has life been since the murder allegations were dropped?"

His face changes. For a moment he looks hurt, then annoyed—the reporter's question is at odds with his save-the-day hero act, and for a moment his blue-green eyes grow stormier. "I have nothing to say about that, except that it's in the past." He pauses, a heartfelt look on his face. "While I feel for the family of the missing woman, I would very much like to move on."

"Mr. Carmot, did the police find Ashlee Casmere's body?"

Dale blocks the camera from getting a tighter shot of his face. The gesture makes him seem humble, not hostile, as if their question is painful, but the first part of his answer feels like the truth—Ashlee's disappearance is just something that happened and it's in the past, something to forget about. If it hadn't disrupted his life he'd care even less. "I hope so," he says.

There were rumors. A love triangle? Maybe a romance turned sour? But Ashlee had never mentioned anything to me.

The Friday night she went missing, I figured maybe she was still mad about our argument at the gala. I was stupid enough to give her space when all I really wanted to do was go to her apartment and talk. Not checking in with her that night is the biggest mistake of my life.

Ashlee didn't show up for work on Monday and people started speculating about what had happened to her.

Why did she leave with Dale? Maybe they were seeing each other. She was beautiful and bright and funny. It wouldn't be surprising if he was attracted to her, but he didn't seem like her usual type. Maybe she thought there was more to him than his player persona suggested. Or was the only reason she left with him because he'd offered to give her a lift when she was avoiding me?

WHEN YOU'RE DYING

None of the theories so far explained why he'd want to kill her.

Had Ashlee seen something she wasn't supposed to? She was agitated that night, but when I'd asked her what was wrong she'd insisted it was nothing. I'd asked the police what they knew, but they were tight-lipped and I could only guess.

All I knew was that Dale was a suspect, and then somehow he was allowed to go free. Once their only genuine lead fell through it felt like the police gave up. They hadn't uncovered a strong lead since.

The news segment with Saint Dale is over but I'm still seething over the nice-guy act. The donation to the hospital was probably a PR stunt to divert attention away from his previous publicity.

I turn to pour another glass of wine and realize the bottle is almost empty. I pour the last drops and take a sip, my mind hazy. It occurs to me that the police might not realize that Dale's giving money to the hospital Ashlee trained at as an intern. They need to know.

I check the time. It's not even seven and my eyelids are already drooping. I'm tempted to crawl under the covers and sleep, but decide to wait for a respectable hour. Even if I tried to sleep now I probably couldn't—Dale donating to Bayswater has gotten under my skin.

I fumble for my phone and search for the number of the detective working on Ashlee's case. I can only find a general number for the station. It'll have to do. I hit dial and wait. The rhythmic buzz seems musical after the third cycle, until a sharp, impatient voice interrupts with a gruff greeting.

"Is Detective Payneham there, please?" I ask.

"Who's calling?"

"It's Verity Casmere. Detective Payneham worked on the case involving my sister, Ashlee." I wait, hoping he's still at the office. I know he's probably there because he always called early in the evening when Ashlee first disappeared.

"One moment."

The telltale click tells me I'm being transferred. The call is accepted immediately—a small victory at this time of day. "Detective Logan Payneham speaking."

"Hi, it's Verity. Verity Casmere."

"Verity. How are you?" He doesn't wait for a response. "Listen, I'm in the middle of something right now—"

I recall a conversation we had early in Ashlee's case when I'd gone into the station to talk to him, so I know that if he's still at the office he's probably finishing up paperwork. I respect his time but I don't have the patience to be prioritized below paperwork.

"I'm dying, Detective. Cancer." I take a deep breath. The wine has loosened my tongue and I hope he doesn't notice the slur in my voice. Somehow, the words don't feel as difficult as they would sober, and I find myself still talking. "The only thing I care about before I die is finding out if someone killed Ashlee, and who it was."

"I'm sorry," he says, clearing his throat awkwardly. "I didn't know."

"Yeah, I haven't exactly broadcast it," I say. "I'm telling you because I don't want to die not knowing what happened to my sister."

"I'd like to help you get that closure, but there's not much to follow up on right now. Without new information the case is at a standstill. We don't have the funding. And Verity, I really am sorry about your, uh, news."

His response is disappointing but not unexpected.

"What if I told you that Dale donated money to the hospital where Ashlee trained? I just saw him on the news."

"I'd have a rough time proving he knew she trained there, but I can take a look. I wouldn't count on anything coming of it though," he says, sounding as deflated as I feel.

I know he's been giving the investigation his best, that he wants to know what happened to Ashlee as much as I do. "So, that's it then? We just hope that the powers that be decide her life's worth enough to continue looking for answers?"

"I wish I could give you more, but Verity...?"

"Yeah?"

"You need to leave this alone. Dale Carmot's not behind bars, but that doesn't mean he isn't dangerous—" He breaks off awkwardly before sputtering back to life. "Don't put yourself in danger. Please. Especially in your state."

"I know how to handle people like Dale," I say defensively. "I'm a social worker. My clients deal with jerks like him every day." I'm hiding behind my job, trying not to show he's hit a nerve.

"Yeah. That's why I'm asking you not to do anything stupid. If you're thinking about hiring a private detective—"

I cut him off, irritated. "I came to you, didn't I? Listen, I just want to be able to die in peace when the times comes."

"Well, maybe someday we'll know."

He stops, and I wait for him to realize what he said. I remind him, just in case. "Someday might be too late."

"Verity, how long did they say you have?"

Not solving the case feels like a failure to him too. It's probably why he's still talking to me, why he took my call in the first place.

"They don't like to say. Maybe a couple of months. The last course of treatment didn't work like we'd hoped. The cancer metastasized."

"Metastas—"

"It spread. From my breast to my bones."

"Wow. Uh—" I imagine him blushing at the mention of breasts. It's funny that he reacts to the word "breast", but not to "cancer", and I have to stop myself from laughing out loud, the alcohol making it difficult.

We're at the part of the call where it usually ends, but I've got too much riding on this. "I've been thinking about what's important in my life, and what I want to do with whatever time I have left." I wait for a reaction, some hint that he's at least curious, but I've already made clear what I want. "I need to know what happened to Ashlee. But more than that, if someone hurt her I want them caught so they can't hurt anyone else."

He breathes down the phone line. Heavy. Resigned. Has he given up on her? "Verity, I know this has been hard. But without her remains there's not much I can do. People go missing all the time. Sometimes because they want to."

"She hasn't used her bank card or tried to contact anyone. That's not enough to assume that maybe she's dead?" I hear my voice crack, and realize I'm scared his superiors won't take it seriously.

His voice shifts. "If she wanted to disappear she might've already set it up so she didn't need her bank card."

The line is silent and for a moment I think he's hung up on me. What would convince them to put the resources into finding her?

"There's no way," I say. "She knows I have cancer. She

27

wouldn't leave now."

"Stressful situations make people do strange things." I hear the crack of the ring tab on a can. He drinks deeply and I wonder whether he's drinking soda or beer. "Let me see what I can do. I'll get back to you as soon as I can."

There's nothing left to say, so I thank him and end the call.

I contemplate the remaining red liquid in the glass.

I know I'm supposed to feel lucky that I'm still alive. I'm supposed to live each moment to its fullest and look for new experiences, but all I can think about is finding Ashlee before I'm gone too.

I swish the wine around the glass until it twists into a sweeping vortex. I imagine being sucked into the center, and before I know it, the glass is empty and I'm dreaming of Ashlee trapped in a vortex with red swirling around her. From the outside the vortex is a tiny hole, the sound of rushing water audible from within, invisible from the outside. People walk by the hole, oblivious to the chaos inside. If they take one wrong step, they might fall in too and become lost with Ashlee.

I see myself pass by in my dream, watching it play out like a voyeur. My sable boots splash in a puddle, narrowly missing the tiny hole; I'm unaware that it's even there.

4

Chapter 4

Oscar

Now

"I don't know," said Oscar, still unsure how involved he wanted to get. It wasn't like Caroline needed him. She could take care of this case by herself. "Dale Carmot wormed his way out of bad publicity the last time he was accused of something like this. I wouldn't be surprised if the experience helped him find the resources to get away with worse things."

"Are you worried you'll ruin your reputation by dirtying your hands with the case?"

"No, that's not it. I'm not sure I can get the answers you want from him. He might not relate to me enough to get somewhere with this."

Hayley's golden lab, Artemis, came bounding enthusiastically at Oscar. He settled her energy with scratches, working the buttery soft fur behind her floppy ear.

"I doubt it," said Caroline. "He'll at least consider you an intellectual equal."

"There are plenty of excellent psychiatrists who are available to talk to him. I'm talking to one of them right now."

"None of them have your notoriety right now. You had a huge success with Jessica Green, and then you up and left Whitner Psychiatric. It was hot gossip. He'll know your name. I want him to feel like a bit of a celebrity—he's used to being in the limelight, having people like himself around. You can use that to bond with him."

Oscar still felt uncomfortable with compliments. His dad didn't dish them out freely, and Oscar had never really gotten over his mother leaving with Steve. He'd wondered if she liked Steve more. He and his brother had such different temperaments and sometimes it seemed that she preferred Steve's fire to Oscar's quiet contemplation. They even looked different. Despite having the same dark hair and slightly downturned noses, you mightn't pick up on the subtleties that showed they were brothers unless they were side by side. Oscar leaned toward his mother's finer traits, where Steve had their father's robustness. Their eyes were the most similar; the same angles with the same golden-brown hues in the center and long, fringed lashes. It was the best feature they'd inherited from their dad but belied their mother's Japanese heritage.

Oscar and Steve had grown into their own features as they matured, but the similarities were still there.

"Hayley and I were planning to spend the day relaxing. She's had a long week at work."

"Sorry. I wouldn't ask if it wasn't important," said Caroline. "Take a few minutes to think about it and let me know."

The call ended and Oscar slid into a chair, resting his arm on the kitchen island while Hayley finished up cooking breakfast. He unlocked his phone and searched "Ashlee Casmere." There were a few direct hits and two random people named Ashlee on LinkedIn. He found an article detailing the disappearance, but without a body it wasn't the media frenzy it might've been.

A picture of Ashlee in her nursing uniform portrayed her as a caring, hardworking nurse, dedicated to helping others. She had the same smile as Verity, warm and sincere, but it wasn't obvious they were sisters.

Who would Lila look like now? The thought was intrusive, but Oscar followed it through. When his sister Lila was little, she'd resembled their mother, her long, dark hair just as silky and lustrous. Thinking about her brought up another painful memory; the anniversary of her death was fast approaching.

The sound of cutlery broke Oscar's concentration as Hayley handed him an onion and green pepper omelet. "I figured you'd be going in, so I made some breakfast." She smiled.

"Aw, you made me eggs," said Oscar. Hayley mostly ate a vegan diet, so it was a special gesture. He moved around the kitchen island, ignoring the food to scoop her into his arms. "I love you," he said, kissing the side of her neck.

She laughed. "Love you too, but you better eat—Caroline's expecting you."

"I don't care. I'll call and tell her I can't go," he said, kissing her deeply.

She returned the kiss. "I'll be here when you're done. I have some work to catch up on anyway. Go." She smiled, shoving him gently.

Reluctantly, he pulled away, half hoping she would give him an excuse to cancel and spend the day with her.

He kissed her goodbye with a need more intense than he'd felt with anyone before.

Oscar met Caroline on the green hospital grounds. Her face broke into a smile that filled out her cheeks when she saw him. "Morning," she said, holding out a cup. "I thought you could use this since I called you at this ungodly hour."

She handed him a tall cup with tendrils of steam wafting from the hole in the lid.

He took the drink and thanked her. He hadn't had a chance to finish more than a few sips of coffee at home. "Sorry, it took a few minutes longer than expected. Hayley made some breakfast before I left."

Caroline smiled knowingly, and when Oscar questioned the look on her face, her smile deepened. "I like how happy you look when Hayley's name comes up."

Oscar shrugged. "She's great."

"I know."

They walked the grounds, away from the clusters of people near the doorways. "Are you sure you don't want to take this case yourself?" asked Oscar as they strolled. "I can't say I blame you if you don't. Dale's had some bad publicity. If he hurt Ashlee Casmere and got away with it—and I'm not saying he did—then he's probably got friends in high places. If Verity's looking for her sister, I don't want to set her up for disappointment."

"That's exactly why I want you to do it," said Caroline, patting Oscar on the shoulder, a motherly gesture that years ago—when he was just a scared kid in a bad situation—made him feel like he had someone looking out for him. "Because I know you won't disappoint her. You'll give her the truth, but you'll do everything you can to give her closure and help her heal."

Oscar's pace slowed, an old knee injury stirring from a mix of cold weather and walking.

Caroline picked up on the change and slowed down with him.

"Tell me more about what happened."

"They found Verity at one of Dale's properties. It was leased under a different name for business purposes, so no one knew to check for her there. The property's being searched for signs Ashlee was there too."

"Is it possible that Ashlee *wasn't* there? That Dale really doesn't know what happened to her?"

"It is," said Caroline, pausing. "But it's looking less likely. What're the chances Dale would be accused of murdering one Casmere, then kidnap another?"

"Why them? I mean, it's pretty risky, given he almost went to jail for Ashlee's disappearance."

Caroline nodded. "Agreed. That's another thing I wanted you to find out. Perhaps Verity knows something Dale doesn't want anyone to find out. Maybe Ashlee did too."

"Why wouldn't he just kill Verity?" asked Oscar. "I mean, why keep her locked up?"

"I'm not sure yet. Could be a personality thing. He's used to controlling things, people, situations. Maybe he thought he had things under control, so he didn't feel the need."

Oscar scratched his chin, already shadowed with stubble from skipping a shave that morning. "How did the police find Verity? Did someone report her missing?"

Caroline shrugged. "She was only missing for a few days. Apparently she didn't have Friday night plans with anyone she knows, so no one noticed she was missing all night. She hasn't been particularly social since Ashlee disappeared. Her friends and her mother hadn't heard from her for weeks, and her colleagues said she mostly kept to herself when she was at work after her sister disappeared." Caroline cleared her throat. "The neighbors didn't notice what happened during the storm. Mrs. Lane next door said that maybe she heard a fall, but it could've been thunder."

Oscar pushed forward, ignoring the aching protest in his knee. "So no one can verify whether Verity seemed distressed?" he asked.

"No." Caroline clasped her hands together. "Verity wasn't breathing when emergency services arrived. She's very lucky. It looks like there was a struggle on the roof. Dale has a concussion and a shattered leg. He got off lightly considering they fell from the roof, but he'll be going to jail for a long time if he's convicted."

Oscar stared into the distance, putting the information in order, building a picture. "Do you think he'd be better suited to a mental health facility?" he asked, the question unloaded.

"Maybe. I want you to assess him and tell me what you think."

"When did all of this happen? When did they find Verity?"

"Around a week ago."

"A week? But you only called this morning."

"Verity regained consciousness this morning, and that got me thinking that you might be the best person to assess her." Caroline pointed toward a side entrance. "Let's see what she can tell us."

"Are we talking to Verity first?" asked Oscar, the twinge in his knee easing as the rising sun started to warm the morning air.

"Yes. I think you should hear her version first and contrast it against Dale's, in case you want to dig deeper into whatever story he spins." It was clear from Caroline's tone that she wasn't sure they'd get the truth from Dale, but it didn't matter—Oscar had plenty of practice sorting the truth from lies.

Oscar started across the lawn, toward the entrance. Why would Dale risk more trouble so soon after the publicity he got from Ashlee's disappearance? It made no sense to draw that kind of attention to himself unless there was some kind of payoff.

"Has Verity given a statement? Do you think she'll be up for visitors? I imagine she's feeling pretty awful."

The square heels of Caroline's pumps sank into the dirt a little with each step. "She's spoken to the police, but they want her to speak with a psychiatrist because of the distress the ordeal has caused. She also took a blow to the head, so they need to make sure her memory is intact." Caroline gave a warm smile. "And I'd like to make sure she's all right before the police bombard her with more questions if they haven't already. She's been through a lot."

They walked through the hospital doors, the sun blinking against the large glass windows. They signed in as guests before riding the elevator to Verity's floor. The nurse's station was empty, everyone probably busy seeing to patients.

Oscar and Caroline walked through to Verity's room where Oscar knocked on the door and waited for an invitation to enter.

No one answered.

He looked at Caroline—maybe Verity didn't want visitors? "Is she expecting us?" he asked.

"Yes. I told her I'd be bringing you by." Caroline knocked softly again and waited.

They listened, but there was still no response and no sound from inside—not even the beep of a machine.

Turning the door handle gently, Oscar stepped slowly inside until he could see the bed where Verity should be propped up against an arrangement of hospital pillows.

Instead, all he found was an empty room.

5

Chapter 5

Verity

Then

The next morning, I drag myself out of bed and shuffle to the shower, my body fighting fatigue, achiness, and a persistent headache that feels like a wasp has been let loose inside of my head. The sensation is made worse by a hangover.

Then I remember my drunken call to Detective Payneham. *Think, Verity. What did you say to him?* As much as I try to remember, I can only piece together snippets. Something about Ashlee and doing more to find her.

I want to roll over and go back to sleep—not just because of the embarrassing conversation I had with a police officer, but because of the fear that something terrible has happened to her. My head continues to pound, a dull ache in my arms and legs joining the fray. What if the achy body isn't just the wine? What if my best days are behind me and this is the cancer making itself known?

I regulate the shower temperature. The fear lets go a little as warm beads of water fall against my skin. When I'm done, I dry off and dress in work clothes—a plain blue dress with a blazer over the top. Next, I apply some tinted lip gloss and mascara and grab my satchel on the way out.

My little white hatchback blasts tunes on the way to work, and I stop for a cappuccino, grateful to the barista for providing me with the energy to keep going.

My phone has my daily schedule, but I forgot to check it this morning, so just as I realize I'm supposed to be at the community center, I'm already pulling into the office parking lot.

I'll never get there on time.

I down the rest of my coffee and shift the car into reverse. Ironically, I don't remember being this forgetful before cancer.

I pull my surface tablet from my satchel when I arrive at the center and set it up in a hired room shared by the social workers who are employed by the public services administration. There are two rooms and I'm in the one with the small window because the large room with the potted plant is taken.

Once my computer fires up, I open the notes they sent me for my first session with a girl named Clara Hauseur—the third to be added to my caseload in the past two weeks. My eyes skim the words, each one bringing me closer to an understanding of who Clara is. It seems she's processing a relationship that ended in a restraining order, and having a hard time doing so. Like a lot of my clients, it seems like she's having a hard time navigating life.

Clara's a few minutes late and she arrives looking uncertain and fragile, ribbons of hair spilling into her face as if she's trained them to fall that way. She is breathless, her hair frizzy at the ends.

"Have a seat," I say, smiling for her benefit.

She sits in a cantilever chair, hugging the right side. She folds one leg over the other and waits for me to speak first.

I introduce myself and ask how she is.

"Fine." Her eyes dart, birdlike, giving the impression that she's on alert.

I follow her eyes to the window and begin, hoping my small talk is nonthreatening enough to encourage her to speak. "Do you have much planned for today?"

"Not really. Just work this afternoon."

That's a start. When I ask her where she works, she shrugs, scrunching her nose as if she doesn't really like her job. "At the grocery store on my corner."

"What are you hoping to get out of today, Clara?"

She hesitates, as if she's still not sure whether she can talk to me. I sense her discomfort as she confesses that she feels stupid for being here. For messing up. For being human.

"There's nothing you can say that'll sound stupid to me. The bravest people say what needs to be said, even when it feels stupid." I smile, hoping I don't sound like a bad self-help book.

Her lips turn up at the edges. "I guess I'm here to talk about what happened with my boyfriend."

She's already identified what she wants to talk about. Sometimes it takes a long time to get to here. People are reluctant to admit there's a problem, or to say anything bad about people they know, especially to a stranger who doesn't have the context to know that it's not secretly the person who has come seeking counsel, but I can see Clara's curious and wants to test her own assumptions.

"Do you talk to people like me much?" she asks.

"People like you?"

She rolls her eyes self-depreciatively. "Women who fall for the wrong guy."

I almost don't want to tell her I specialize in justice and corrections. It will sound like I'm on the other side counseling the "wrong guys" she mentioned, and I don't want to lose her trust. I tell her anyway.

"You help criminals?" She balks.

"Sometimes criminals, sometimes the people they impact." I almost add that I help out at a women's shelter too, as if that might redeem me.

"Victims?"

"Survivors," I say emphatically, hoping to remind her that she made it through a dangerous situation.

"It doesn't feel like I'm surviving." She places her hands atop her legs, her chest rising and falling in exaggerated bursts.

I pour her a glass of water and slide it across the table.

"Tell me what happened."

She talks fast, sounding like a podcast played at double speed. Her story is familiar.

The first thing I notice is that she won't say his name. I find out that "he" was charming at first. He pursued her with flowers, chocolates, and syrupy words. She fell in love with him, but things changed about a year in. He became suspicious of what she was doing, where she was going, and who she was with. He worked late and would call her dozens of times a day just to 'check in'.

When he got home from work, he would accuse her of things like not wanting him home. Or he'd criticize what she was wearing, always in a way that could be mistaken for concern. *Are you sure you want to wear that...? They're doing some cooking classes down at the community center—didn't you say you wanted to learn something new?*

When they had company, it was like a switch flicked and he returned to the charming, doting person she'd fallen in love with.

She tears up, but finds her voice again to continue.

"He'd pretty much stopped talking to me altogether, unless he wanted something. I thought he must be seeing someone else, so I asked him about it and he got defensive." She collects the tears with a tissue. "He said that maybe I was asking because that's what I was doing."

"He deflected the question," I say.

"He said I was jealous because I was insecure, that I couldn't even handle a little harmless flirting."

"Were you jealous?" I ask.

"No." She thinks about it and tries again. "Maybe."

"Clara, you had a right to tell him if something was bother-ing you."

She sips her water, gripping the glass. "Not long after that, things got violent. The first time he apologized and I believed he was sorry. I forgave him because he swore it'd never happen again." She focuses on the glass as the water inside ripples.

What she's saying isn't uncommon. I've seen smart, edu-cated women who don't even realize they're being manipu-lated. She tells me it's not the first violent relationship she's been in, as if she's ashamed that it happened again.

"Did you report what happened to you?"

41

"You probably think I should've, but no. I didn't want him to end up with a record, and I believed him when he said it was the last time."

Her face crumples, her shoulders turning in. But she doesn't make a sound. She has perfected the silent cry—probably to avoid anyone overhearing and the possibility of being punished for it.

"I don't think anything. You did the right thing for you," I say, wondering if he convinced her not to report it. I rarely got the entire story from clients—it was often worse than they could admit. Sometimes they changed the story to protect their abuser, sometimes to hide their shame at what had happened to them.

I offer the box of tissues and she pulls one free and dabs at the corners of her eyes. I'm not expecting her to say what she says next. "How can I get him to tell me what I'm doing wrong?"

I want to ask her how things might look if she stopped waiting for him to give her the answers, if she gave herself the closure she's looking for, but it doesn't sound like she's ready to hear the truth.

Like me with Ashlee.

"If you could find out why he isn't speaking to you, would it make a difference?"

"Yes," she says, her tone decisive and certain—the tone of someone who hasn't dared to consider any other possibilities.

"What are you trying to figure out? Do you want to know why he hit you? What made him cheat? Or why you ended up in a relationship similar to your previous one?"

She pauses. "I guess I want to know all of it. If I know what I'm doing wrong, maybe I can fix it."

"What if it's nothing you did and there's nothing to fix? Could you accept that?"

"Maybe..." says Clara with the optimism of someone who has all the time in the world to ignore that he might be the problem, and not her.

When you're dying maybe time becomes more pressing, and patience is a luxury more than a virtue. Time eats at me with a ferocious appetite, devouring everything but my need to find Ashlee.

I need to find my sister before it's too late.

6

Chapter 6

Oscar

Now

"Are you sure this is the right room?" asked Oscar.

"Yes," said Caroline, "but I'll ask someone to check, in case she was moved."

Oscar followed Caroline into the lobby where she caught the attention of a passing nurse.

"My name is Doctor Caroline Taylor. My colleague and I were supposed to meet with Verity Casmere this morning but she's not in her room."

"Sorry. I just started my shift but I'll see if I can find out where she is."

The nurse disappeared behind a computer desk, keys clicking gently as she typed. Judging by the look on her face, she didn't have good news. "Verity's in the operating room."

"Is she okay?" asked Caroline.

"It looks like there was a complication. She should be out of surgery soon. I should have more information by then."

"Thank you. You've been very helpful," said Oscar.

The nurse's gaze lingered on Oscar.

"Thanks," said Caroline, handing the nurse a card with her number on it. She turned to Oscar. "It could be a long wait. Why don't you talk to Dale Carmot? He's on the next floor, one up."

"Dale's at the same hospital as Verity? That could be quite distressing for her," said Oscar.

"I thought so too, but apparently there wasn't time to take him to a different hospital. Given the state Verity was in when they found her, it sounds like they loaded him up and brought them both in. Once he was receiving treatment it didn't make sense to send him somewhere else."

Caroline didn't miss much. Of course she'd asked about it. Still, it had been a week since Dale and Verity fell from the roof. He would've expected him to be released by now—or charged with something and taken to the station.

"Why is he still here?"

"He developed an infection. The fall split his ankle apart so they've kept him on obs to make sure the infection's gone."

"I would've thought he would ask to move to a private hospital—somewhere fancier than here." While there was nothing wrong with where they were, Dale had the money to pay for the luxury hospital experience.

Caroline smiled. "That's the price of being visible. I have a feeling it's a political move he can use later."

Oscar sighed. "Of course it is. What's he angling for?"

"Public funding, mostly. To help pay for his private enterprises. The more hospitals he can sell drugs to, the more money he makes. And what better way to upsell than to use his very own hospital stay story?"

"Couldn't he campaign just as easily in a private hospital?"

"He could. But he probably already sells medical supplies to this hospital. It wouldn't go well for him if he was demanding private hospital care, especially after the business with Ashlee Casmere."

Caroline was right. He supposed a public hospital experience was different if you were someone important who was paying for it, but Oscar wondered if Dale's real motivation was trying to find Verity and finish what he'd started.

He added it to his list of things to find out.

He was ready to talk to Dale Carmot.

7

Chapter 7

Verity

Then

It's been days since my conversation with Detective Payneham. I've been putting off calling him again, thinking that maybe if I'm patient he might surprise me with some good news.

It's lunchtime and I'm eating a chicken Caesar wrap at the park, under a tree. It's the kind of park where people walk their dogs, and I compare them to their owners as they pass by. I chew thoughtfully, thinking about my next client.

The phone interrupts my thoughts as it buzzes in my pocket.

I clear my throat, hoping it doesn't sound like I still have a mouthful of food.

It's Detective Payneham, and judging by his tone he doesn't have good news.

I try to remember what I said—hopefully nothing too stupid—but his words take all my attention.

"I did some asking around and I'm sorry, but without a reason to dig we can't do anything more."

Hope slips away. "So, I'm supposed to just be okay with that?"

I know my words are unfair, but nothing about this seems fair, and I have nowhere else to direct my frustration.

"I don't know what to say, Verity. Without a body—" He stops himself but it's too late, the implication is there. Unless they find her body there's no point in looking for a killer that may not exist.

I want to demand that someone go out and find Ashlee, but it won't help anything. "Didn't she leave with Dale? Isn't that enough to keep looking?" I ask, clutching my phone.

"There were conflicting accounts of how she left."

I'm running out of time to convince him. "Well, maybe there's a loophole. Is there someone else I can talk to?"

"You can try, but there's no funding, and we're swamped as it is."

"No budget? Let me guess, there's better things to spend it on?"

"That's not what I said." He sighs, sounding tired. Of me? Of the system? His tone shifts. "I know you're upset, but don't go doing anything silly, okay?"

I resent the reprimand. He doesn't want me to look for her, but we both know he probably won't find her, so am I supposed to just accept that I might never know?

"Sure," I say, and our call ends, putting me in a bad mood. I'm no closer to getting the answers I need and my chances of finding Ashlee feel worse than yesterday, when I still had hope that Detective Payneham could pull some strings.

By the time the call ends, lunch is over and I head back to

the office reluctantly. I know I won't be able to concentrate for the rest of the day, and I'm tempted to take the rest of the afternoon off, but I'll need that time for treatment.

If Ashlee were here she'd tell me I'm being silly, that it's unreasonable to think the police can do anything more than they already are.

Or would she tell me to fight for her?

I close my eyes, trying to imagine what she'd want me to do now. My memory lights up with images of Ashlee laughing, talking, and just being Ashlee.

Things might've been different that night. If we hadn't argued she wouldn't have gotten into Dale Carmot's car—we would've left together and grabbed tacos on the way home.

It's not fair that she's gone and Dale's free. How is he out living his life while the people who knew and loved Ashlee are only half living, waiting for her to come home? If the police had kept the active search going what would they have found? I open my eyes suddenly, before I can picture all the horrible scenarios.

Detective Logan Payneham didn't seem to think Dale was responsible for Ashlee's disappearance, but he must've missed something. It was too much of a coincidence; people saw them together on the night that Ashlee disappeared. They were at least talking that night—what happened next, maybe only Dale knew.

I feel a pang of guilt. I would've stayed at the gala if I'd known I wouldn't see her again. I would've dragged her out of there and driven back to her apartment to watch a movie, something funny.

Had Dale Carmot wormed his way out of trouble by bribing the police to stop investigating Ashlee's disappearance? A police officer who'd been on the job for too many years would be a great bribe target—overworked, underpaid, and disillusioned with what they thought would be the kind of job where you got to help people, only to discover that some people didn't want help.

Dale got away with murder. I doubt any of it will go on his record. What else has he paid his way out of?

I pull up a browser on my phone and search for "Dale Carmot." There's a lot about his charity work, his company, and an article in an architecture magazine about the design of his home. Digging deeper, I find a great view of his house on Google Maps. The homes in his neighborhood all look well tended and expensive—the kind of gated community where you get fined for failing to trim your lawn to the correct height.

The idea comes to me like a revelation. I know where he works and now I know where he lives.

If the police won't keep looking, I will.

8

Chapter 8

Oscar

Now

When Oscar arrived, Dale Carmot was in a private hospital room, leg propped up in a cast, trying to type on a laptop.

The room looked different from other parts of the hospital, the furniture newer, the paint fresher, like the room of a newly added wing. A barely touched food tray sat to the side, the lid askew—perhaps Dale didn't like the hospital cuisine on offer. Oscar assumed he was accustomed to richer foods prepared by restaurant chefs and personal staff.

Dale's door was already ajar, so Oscar didn't knock. "Mind if I come in?"

Dale sat up straighter when he saw Oscar, shifting his leg awkwardly, limited by the cast. He eyed Oscar, as if trying to place him. "I'm sorry. Have we met?"

"I don't think so. I'm Dr. Oscar de la Nuit. I heard you

wanted to talk to a doctor about what's been happening these last few weeks?"

Dale sized him up. "Well, that depends on what you mean. Lots of stuff happened in the last few weeks, but you said you're a doctor, so you either want to talk about the infection in my leg, or you're the other kind of doctor and you want to discuss the woman who has been stalking me."

He was defensive, not remorseful. He thought he was the victim here, but he didn't expect anyone else to see it that way.

"I'm a psychiatrist, but I'm happy to talk about either. Which would you like to begin with?"

"Who sent you?"

"Dr. Caroline Taylor, a colleague of mine. The police said you wanted someone to assess Verity Casmere's mental competence?"

"And yet here you are, talking to me."

Oscar gestured toward a chair across from Dale, asking before sitting. "I thought you could use someone to talk to after everything that's happened.

Dale offered the seat, unperturbed by Oscar's reason for being there. He shifted, grimacing as his leg moved. "It's been a week but the nerves were smashed. It's pinned up pretty good. What do you want to ask me?"

Oscar nodded, slipping off his coat. Dale would probably have seasonal pain long after it healed, the same as Oscar's knee, which still ached some days from a childhood accident.

"I thought it'd be good to get your version of what happened."

"Okay," said Dale cautiously.

"Is it okay if I record our conversation?"

Dale nodded and Oscar started the recording, detailed the

date, and asked Dale to confirm his full name.

"Dale Thomas Carmot," said Dale confidently, as if his name meant something. "Are we done?" he joked.

Oscar smiled. "Not quite. You could start by telling me how you ended up here."

Dale laughed, an airy sound escaping the back of his throat. He'd guessed that Oscar had already heard at least one version of what happened, by the way he began. "Well, obviously it looks bad," he said. "But I swear, I wasn't going to kill her. Do I need to have my lawyer here for this?"

"That's up to you," said Oscar.

"What do you think?"

"If your lawyer would like a copy of our discussion, I can provide one," offered Oscar.

Dale shrugged. "That works for me."

"How do you know Verity Casmere?"

"I don't. Not really. She was at a bar I went to. She was alone, watching me. I assumed she was looking to pick up, so I said hi." Dale shrugged.

"And at some point you locked her inside of your house," said Oscar.

"I—" Dale blew air through his nose, a bull getting ready for the charge. "She was stalking me. I thought that if I scared her enough she'd leave me alone."

"I thought you said she was at the bar?"

"She was. I think she followed me there."

"Okay," said Oscar, trying to piece together Dale's account, which wasn't adding up so far. "And you wanted to scare her so she'd stop following you?"

"Yes," said Dale, as if Oscar was finally getting it.

"And you thought keeping her prisoner would do that?"

Oscar asked, hoping for an explanation.

"She was at my house because she wanted to be there. It's not like I forced her to come home with me. She seemed to enjoy the flirting."

"So, you picked her up at a bar and took her back to your house?"

Dale shrugged again. Too blasé for a guy who had been accused of kidnapping. "She seemed fun." He frowned in a way that suggested he was busy thinking. "Smart, funny, sexy. But when we got to my place, she changed. It was like she was a totally different person."

"And is that when you decided to keep her there against her will?"

9

Chapter 9

Verity

Then

The day drags on, leaving me feeling drained. By the time I return home that evening I can't think of much else except what Detective Payneham said about needing a body in order to investigate Ashlee's disappearance further.

In an inspired moment, I grab my keys and head out the door. I drive toward Dale's office building with no real plan of what to do when I get there. If I think about why I'm going there, I know I'll probably turn around and drive home. *One step at a time.* The feeling of doing something is so much better than just sitting there feeling helpless, and for a moment I feel rejuvenated.

When I arrive at the building I park in the underground lot which charges for parking by the hour. I circle the lot and find Dale's navy BMW in his reserved space. I stop a few spots down before cutting the engine. Despite the warmth inside the car my skin grows cold as I realize how isolated the parking garage is from the main road. No one would notice if Dale tried to kill me here.

I sit for forty minutes, refusing to listen to Detective Payneham's voice ringing in my ears, warning me not to get involved. I peer in my rearview mirror every time I hear a noise, waiting for Dale to come around the corner. There's a good chance he's one of those guys who virtually sleeps at the office. I could be waiting for a long time.

I'm about to get out of the car and enter the building when I see Dale enter the lot and cross to his car, a slim laptop tucked under his arm. I didn't expect him to leave this early, and I've taken too long working up the nerve to go inside. Maybe he's saved me from my own impulsiveness. I'm not sure what I thought I was going to find by entering the building—it's not like I could walk into his office and just look around.

His mouth moves, and for a moment I think he's talking to me. I hold in a breath, releasing it when I see the earbuds; he's on a call.

The sound of his car alarm being disarmed echoes through the garage like a digital insect. He pauses to listen, laughing at something the other person said. Why does he get to laugh when Ashlee can't? Why should he speak with anyone when I can't ever call Ashlee again?

I wind down my window, just a crack, and catch a few words. "It's good to be out. No. No one needs to know that. Because... she was always going to end up exactly where she did."

I freeze at his words. He can't be talking about Ashlee. Maybe he's referring to an employee?

A part of me wants to get out of the car and make him tell me what he means. Where did she end up? But I'm getting ahead of myself. If I get out of the car and start making demands I could end up wherever Ashlee is.

At least I'd know what happened to her.

My phone buzzes, the sound startling me. Why did I think it was a good idea to go looking for Dale? He's unpredictable; there's no telling what he'd do if he saw me watching.

My pulse pounds deep in my throat as I check the message. It's a notification from a dating site I joined months ago. I feel heat rush to my cheeks. I'd almost forgotten about it after my first experiences with the site—men didn't want to date a social worker unless they worked in the industry, or they were looking for free counseling, but the guy who left the message is attractive, all square lines and tanned skin, and my curiosity gets the better of me.

I open his profile. His picture isn't overly showy, just him and his dog—a mixed breed with shaggy ears—posing together for a selfie on the beach. His name is Wes.

The beach is a cliché, but it looks natural and unstaged, and his tanned skin suggests he spends a lot of time outdoors. His hair is almost black and cut short. According to his profile, he lives in Hartford, not forty minutes away.

I read the message.

Hi Verity,

Your name made me think of Claude Buffier's Traité des premières vérités, and I had to say hello.

Your profile says you're a social worker, so maybe you're familiar with his work?

Buffier described aspects of human consciousness as The Eternal Verities.

He talks about how our thoughts are the basis for the first truths.
Right and wrong. Good and evil.

Anyway, if you're still reading, I'll take it as a sign you might
want to message back?

Wes

I'm still not sure I want to reply—there's a chance his profile
picture isn't even him. I scroll, trying to learn more about him,
to figure out if he wants a conversation about philosophy, or if
he's just trying to impress me with the Google search results
from my name.

The sound of an engine roaring to life grabs my attention.
It's Dale's car, but he stays in the parking space—he probably
owns the lot and doesn't have to worry about the cost.

I wait. If I follow him too soon, I risk drawing attention to
myself, so I wait a few beats, distracting myself with Wes's
profile. I study the pic, making judgments about the kind of
person he might be. He has an easy smile and warm eyes,
not the cold, glassy kind from some of the other profiles I've
scrolled.

I remember why I signed up to the site in the first place and
blush.

Wes's profile says he's a teacher, but it doesn't say what he
teaches.

Maybe that's why he knows about Buffier.

I look up, but Dale still hasn't left the garage—probably
scrolling through messages on his phone.

I type a response to Wes while I wait and read it over.

Hi Wes. A teacher, like Buffier. What do you teach?

He responds immediately.

Well, Buffier was more of a writer, really. He didn't teach at

Lycée Louis-le-Grand, but that's enough about Buffier. Why don't you tell me something about yourself?

Maybe he didn't learn everything he knows about Buffier from a Google search.

I can't think of anything to say about myself that doesn't involve confessing to my illness. Not telling him feels like a kind of lie even though I don't know him, but I don't have time to explain now—Dale could start moving at any moment. I type quickly.

Do you want to grab a coffee sometime, or a drink?

My hand hovers over the send button while I consider deleting my message. I look up again and it looks like Dale is about to leave the lot. The tip of my thumb brushes the screen, but not over the button I intended to tap.

My phone shows the message was delivered.

I hang my head in my hands, the beep of another notification catching my attention.

I'm afraid to look, unsure what I'm dreading more—a yes or a no.

Sure.

We decide Friday's a good day and agree to meet at a bar masquerading as a café.

That's when I begin to worry. What if it's one of my bad days and my body dishes out fatigue, nausea, and dizziness? It's why I've avoided dating, why an online hookup seemed like a good alternative—no hard feelings if I didn't have the energy to answer the phone or go out on a second date. Besides, you can't start a relationship by telling someone you have a terminal illness, but it feels equally bad to avoid talking about it only to spring it on someone a month in, just when they're getting used to the idea of keeping you around for a while.

59

Maybe Wes and I could grab a coffee with no expectations and that'd be it. Two people meeting on a dating app and catching up for a chat. And then—

I stop myself. Out for drinks. That's as far forward as I need to plan. Usually, I wouldn't go out with someone I'd just met, but if I wait a month I might not be able to go out at all.

The new drug I've started seems to be helping with the dizziness—for now, at least. I'd just have to accept the fatigue, but the fear that things could get worse makes me aware of each moment like I've never experienced before. A sunset is happening from the moment the sun rises, but it's only when it's about to dip below the horizon that we notice the light disappearing.

Go for coffee on Friday, maybe something a little stronger. Have fun while you still can.

My thoughts are broken by the sound of Dale's car exiting the lot.

He's just ahead and I have no trouble following him. He takes the exit and I move seamlessly with the traffic, blending in as another commuter on their way home.

* * *

I follow Dale to the urban district, where the homes are little more than one bedroom boxes, dressed up to feel like you've made it, but tolerated because it puts you closer to the center of the city and a sense of being part of something more than your own existence.

The coffee shops and trendy wholefood grocery stores give

60

the impression of luxury, and Dale's BMW fits right in as he parks it on the street and climbs the stairs beside a boutique wine bar. I make a turn and park down a side street facing the building, catching a glimpse of Dale at the door as it opens. I can't see who's inside, but Dale speaks to them, waving a hand like he's refusing an offer to go inside. He hands over something and receives something in exchange. I watch as they talk, as Dale's face changes. It looks like they're arguing now.

I see a hand wrap around the door and pull it shut, and Dale walks away, his fingers gripping his chin. He bumps into a man rushing the other way and hesitates. For a second I wonder if he's going to turn back and attack him, but he moves on quickly, the man already lengths ahead.

Dale is walking directly toward me, his eyes straight ahead as if he's seen me and isn't happy about it. My heartbeat echoes in my throat, a steady thrum of blood pushing through my head. I realize it's anger not fear that has overridden the rest of my senses. I've never wanted to hurt someone before, but a vicious rage threatens to overtake me.

Would anyone even miss Dale if he were to disappear?

I could follow him until we were alone, no witnesses to save him. Then, I could torture him until he told me what he'd done with Ashlee. Once I knew for sure where she was and what he'd done, I could take the light slowly from his eyes, until he was left forever in the dark like I had been these past months.

Before I can convince myself that no one would miss him, I put the car into gear and drive away slowly, my hands shaking at the wheel.

It's only on the drive home that I realize how desperate I am to find my sister, that I would've taken it further if it weren't for the risk of getting caught.

I need a better plan, something that'll stop him for good.

10

Chapter 10

Oscar

Now

Dale held his leg, shifting gingerly, trying not to disturb the broken bones.

"Can I help?" Oscar moved closer but Dale held up a hand.

"It's fine. The painkillers are wearing off," said Dale with an edge to his voice, making it clear he was eager to finish up the interview.

Oscar offered to call a nurse, but Dale declined.

"Listen. One minute she was into me and then the next it was like she was a completely different person. Is there anything else you want to know?" asked Dale, his patience wearing thinner with each passing minute.

"How did Verity change?"

Dale shrugged. "She went from flirty and a little tipsy to... " He struggled for the right word before settling decisively.

"Angry. She was angry."

Dale grit his teeth and shifted again, unable to get comfortable. Soon, he'd lose patience for the conversation altogether, but Oscar needed Dale to get to the point where he was uncomfortable enough to talk freely, even if it was just to get rid of Oscar.

Oscar waited it out, timing his question carefully. He sat back in his chair like he planned on staying awhile. "Why was she angry?"

"I didn't know at first. I thought I might've said the wrong thing. I didn't know who she was, that her sister is..."

"You didn't know Verity was Ashlee's sister?"

"It was late. I was kinda drunk, and she was sexy. She told me her name was Eliza. I went out drinking to just let loose and party. And then I saw *her*. She looked familiar, and eventually I realized that I'd seen her before. She was the chick that followed me when I left work, so I thought I'd find out what she wanted."

He says it like she might've been fangirling over him, the kind of attention he would've welcomed—possibly even the reason he'd approached her at first.

"What'd you tell her your name was?" asked Oscar.

Dale's expression grew cold. "I don't know. Dale probably. Like I said, I was already a bit wasted."

"Why do you think she gave you a fake name?"

Dale shrugged. "Lots of girls lie about who they are—usually when they don't want their boyfriends or their husbands to find out what they're doing." He said it like someone who knew from experience. "Maybe she was looking for a hookup. It might've been part of the game for her. That night, maybe she was Eliza." His tone was mocking. "Or maybe she didn't want me to figure out who she really was because she was setting me up."

Oscar didn't believe that Dale could really think Verity—*Eliza*—followed him because she was a fan of his. The way Dale said it suggested it happened regularly, and he supposed he could see people being drawn to Dale's money, his status. Still, Oscar figured that Dale had realized Verity was Ashlee's sister and tried to deter her from looking into Ashlee's disappearance by locking her up just long enough to scare her.

Dale shot Oscar a look. "You should ask her. I *didn't* know who she was at first. I think she came back to my place hoping to find her sister—like she expected me to have her locked up in the loft or something. Maybe she was angry there was nothing to find. I don't know what happened to Ashlee, but I didn't kill her."

What annoyed Dale more? Was it that he was fooled by Verity, or that she didn't seem moved by his charm? Dale's ego seemed misplaced for a guy being questioned about someone he thought was dead. "Kill her?" said Oscar. "What makes you think she's dead?" There were no reports that a body was found. Did Dale know something?

"I didn't. Her sister did. Eliza, or Verity, or whatever her name is."

"Why would she risk going home with you if she thought you murdered her sister?"

Dale didn't hesitate—he either believed what he was saying, or he already had his story planned out. "I already told you. She was hoping to find Ashlee, or find out what happened to her."

Oscar looked skeptical, his brow raised, waiting for the

truth.

"I think she was planning on framing me." The urgency to get rid of Oscar made Dale more direct, but it didn't seem like he was trying to hide anything. Besides the pain causing the occasional grimace, his words came easily. "She needs someone to blame for her sister being missing or whatever." He gritted his teeth, the pain in his leg intensifying.

"You should get something for that—not just drugs, but physio when it starts to heal," said Oscar, standing and stopping the recording. "I'll leave you to it." He tapped the doorframe, limping slightly as he left.

* * *

Oscar was reeling as he walked down the hall to the exit. Dale seemed more concerned about Verity being punished for the inconvenience she'd caused him than getting to the bottom of what happened to Ashlee.

A fully uniformed officer passing by the hallway caught Oscar's eye. He stopped when they said his name, pronouncing it "deey-lah nu-eet." "Caroline said you'd be in today. I didn't expect you to still be here." He offered a hand to shake. "Detective Logan Payneham."

"Oscar's fine, detective," said Oscar, shifting his weight to his good knee. "You know how hospitals are—a lot of waiting around before anything happens. I had to wait a good hour to speak with Dale."

"Did you have time to speak with Verity Casmere?" asked the detective.

"No. She was in surgery when I arrived. I waited to see how she went, but she was still in the operating room when I left."

Oscar stepped to the side as a man in his twenties who was leaning on a crutch to support what looked like a broken leg tried to pass.

"Listen, I think this whole thing might've been partly my fault."

Was he talking about Verity's surgery? Or the case?

"Verity called me to ask what else we could do to find Ashlee. I told her my hands were tied. We're underfunded as it is, and, well..." He lowered his voice. "The chances of finding her alive aren't good unless she's disappeared of her own accord and decides she wants to come home. People go missing because they want a break from their lives all the time. They come back when they're good and ready."

The detective walked with Oscar, the pair moving farther away from Dale's room.

"Did you ask her why she went home with Dale?"

"Yeah," said Detective Payneham. "But she was pretty foggy after the concussion."

Oscar shook his head. "She knew who he was, but she still put herself in danger."

Detective Payneham stopped suddenly and took a deep breath. "I think it's the cancer that made her do it. No one wants to die with a question like that unanswered. I would've helped if I could, but they didn't find a thing in Dale Carmot's house."

Oscar sensed the detective's regret at not being able to help.

"A couple of people say Dale and Ashlee left the hospital together. Others say they left separately. He swears they said goodbye at the gala. Says that was the last time he saw her."

67

Oscar hadn't known Verity had cancer. It explained why she'd risk being alone with Dale. He felt his resolve not to get too involved crumble a little. He'd only agreed to talk to Verity to help Caroline out. He'd planned on passing on his assessment and leaving it with her, but how could he walk away now?

After treating Jess Green at Whitner Psychiatric, he had lost faith in his profession. You couldn't always help—and sometimes wrong and right weren't as clear-cut as it seemed they should be. But what if he could help Verity find some answers?

"Do you believe what Dale said about Ashlee?" asked Oscar.

"I did. And then this happened."

"And now you're wondering?" Oscar noticed people watching the detective as he passed. If the uniform didn't draw attention, the metallic clank of his belt and his heavy-footed stomp did.

"He didn't take Verity to his primary residence. It was a property he bought under another name. We're searching the place now. Maybe we were looking for Ashlee in the wrong places—that guy owns a lot of real estate. Either way, he didn't tell us about the other properties, which makes me wonder."

"Tax evasion?" asked Oscar.

"Maybe." The way the detective said it suggested he was thinking something much worse.

Oscar's skin prickled at the possibilities.

"Did you ask if Ashlee was ever there?"

"Of course, but why would he tell us the truth now if he never mentioned it before?" Detective Payneham had a point, but Dale had more to lose now that they knew he had hidden things from them.

Damn. Oscar's jacket was still in Dale's hospital room. He excused himself and went back to retrieve it. He looked at the time. Sunday was disappearing fast, and he'd promised Hayley he'd be back in time to make it to the park with her and Artemis.

Dale startled when he saw Oscar in the doorway, dropping a bottle into a drawer. It missed, sending the container careening to the floor.

Oscar didn't have to see it to know what it was. If Dale was hiding them, they probably weren't prescription pills. "Forgot my coat," he said, plucking it from the chair and holding it up as proof.

Dale raised an eyebrow.

"You know, they're searching your house," said Oscar collusively.

"Yeah?" said Dale, his nonchalance gone.

Oscar threw the coat over his arm. "What're they gonna find?"

"Who can say?" said Dale cryptically, his eyes searching for the dropped pills.

"Ashlee?"

"Not at my house. I didn't hurt her."

Oscar recognized the sweaty sheen on Dale's skin despite the tepidness of the room. The dilated pupils. Did Dale have an oxy problem?

Oscar walked over slowly and retrieved the bottle, his knee clicking as he bent. The label had been peeled away to show blue pills through the plastic. "You know, you should probably tell the nurses about these, so you don't overdose."

Dale's eyes wandered lazily to his leg. "The problem isn't what they're giving me, it's that they don't give me enough to stop the pain. It's like I can feel it trying to fix itself back together and doing an awful job of it."

Oscar knew the feeling from his own leg. It felt like poorly mixed concrete ready to reopen as soon as it dried. He set the pills down on the hospital table next to the laptop and limped out of there.

If Dale killed Ashlee, an oxy problem would be the least of his problems.

11

Chapter 11

Verity

Then

When I arrive at the office with two cups of coffee in hand, my work wife, Amy, is already there. I walk to her desk and set a cappuccino down next to her before moving to my desk to search for a client file.

"Hey," I say when she looks up from her screen. "Thought you might need that."

She beams at me. "You," she says, pointing toward me with her eyes on the coffee, "are a lifesaver." She takes a sip and returns to her screen.

I glance over at what has her attention and see a screen filled with brightly colored boots.

"Is Matt in yet?" I ask.

Amy looks over her shoulder, as if our boss, Matt, might be standing behind her. She brings a hand to her heart, relieved to find he isn't there.

"You're not scared of the boss are you?" I ask, smiling.

"Not usually. It's just, there's a sale, and I need boots for winter." She gestures at the slashed prices.

"Amy, winter's not for months."

"I know, but it's a sale."

"That's fair," I say, realizing I've avoided planning even a few months ahead. "I'm heading out again. If you see Matt, could you let him know that I'll be in this afternoon?"

"Sure." She returns to her shopping. "And thanks again," she says, taking another sip of coffee.

I grab the notes from my desk. I know I should store them digitally, but something about putting pen to paper helps my brain assess the situation better when I'm building a profile.

My appointment this morning is at Baker's Community Center. I've gotten good at finding comfortable, anonymous places to meet with people who don't want anyone to know they're seeing a social worker.

The drive takes forty-five minutes, and I arrive a few minutes early, my coffee cup drained, and a mind so foggy it rivals the hangover I had a few nights ago. If only I hadn't called Detective Payneham when I was drunk, maybe I could've sold my case better.

My client is waiting when I get there. She's a tiny girl sitting in a green chair, seeming to disappear into the cushions as I approach. She looks too young to be burdened with a woman's problems at just seventeen.

"Hi," I say with a smile. "Emma?"

She nods.

"I'm Verity. Come, follow me."

She slides her purse and a worn jacket with a hood from the

chair beside her and follows quietly.

The blue carpet is thin, almost bare in some places, but tidy. It's not one of my usual spots. I walk down a corridor, scouting for room 5L, which I've booked out for the afternoon.

I test whether the door is locked and invite Emma inside when it swings open.

She sees me eyeing her things and pulls them in closer. We're safe inside the room before she talks. "It's warm out," she says. "I probably didn't need this." She holds up the jacket, and I notice blood on the sleeve. It could be nothing and I don't want her to feel like she needs to explain herself to me, so I don't ask about it.

"It can get cold in the afternoon," I say, my own jacket thrown across the back seat of my car. "Please, take a seat."

She flops down into the chair and dumps her things on the table. When she looks up her eyes remind me of Ashlee's, a sparkling blue, drinking in the world as if she's trying to understand what it all means.

"I didn't want to come here," she confesses shyly. "But I don't know what else to do..."

I nod. "It's hard to talk about personal things with a complete stranger. But sometimes talking to someone who isn't part of the situation helps. Just focus on why you came here today and talk about that."

"Okay." She wipes her hands on her navy jeans and exhales. "I'm kind of a mess. My boyfriend's a good guy. Really, he is. But he has a problem with substances."

She chooses her words carefully to protect him.

"Drugs or alcohol?" I ask evenly.

"Not alcohol." She clears her throat, building herself up to continue.

73

"Has he hurt you?"

"No. It's nothing like that," she says, the timbre of her voice rising. She pauses, and I hope I haven't offended her. "I'm pregnant."

She waits for the judgment that follows, confirming what she already thinks.

"Are you sure?" I ask. She's so skinny, it's hard to imagine anything growing inside her inverted stomach.

"I took a test, and then another to make sure. It was positive both times."

"How do you feel about being pregnant?" I ask, pretty sure it's the real reason she's here.

"You must think I'm pretty stupid. Pregnant when the father's addicted to drugs." She holds her breath and I shake my head.

She releases her breath and her whole body seems to deflate. "I guess I'm scared," she says softly. "What if the baby's sick? I don't know if it's fair to keep it."

There's a sharp intake of air and Emma waits for reassurance.

"Does your boyfriend know?"

"I haven't told him yet," she confesses.

"Why not?"

"I don't know what to say. If I tell him and there's a problem with the baby, he'd blame himself. I don't know if I should get a termination and say nothing. We could try again when he's clean."

Except I can see that she's not sure that'll happen. Emma looks at me expectantly, waiting for me to tell her what she should do, but I don't know her boyfriend and I don't know whether her baby will be okay.

"That could be one option to explore. Have you thought about whether you want to be a mother?"

"I mean, I always thought someday—"

So did I. I imagined doing a lot of things in the future. I'd travel on a great adventure and wind up living somewhere unexpected until I grew homesick and returned with a new appreciation for where I came from. Maybe I'd meet someone and we'd move in together and cook food that was too boring to serve in restaurants, but was comforting to eat and filled the house with a warm aroma. Maybe one day I'd be a mother and watch my baby bloom into whatever kind of person they chose to be.

Despite her predicament, a part of me is envious of this girl. She has her whole life to plan and to experience things. The fuse is long and unlit—she could do anything she can imagine. I immediately feel awful for thinking it—she's here for my help because she needs it.

"Have you been to visit your doctor? They may be able to explain the risks."

"No. I haven't told anyone yet. I only found out two days ago and it's a lot to process."

Her appointment was booked a week ago, but she only found out about the pregnancy two days ago? The baby isn't the reason she came to see me. She must have something else she wants to talk about. Maybe she was struggling with something else until she found herself faced with bigger problems.

"If I go to a doctor and ask all these questions about drugs and then I have the baby, will they know that Todd's a user? I mean, it might be in the baby's system or something. I don't want to look after a baby on my own when their dad's in jail. My parents would kill me. They already hate Todd. They blame him for my grades slipping. They think I waste too much time on him—their words, not mine."

"Have your grades dropped since you've been dating Todd?"

"They were already lower, I guess, before I met him. It wasn't his fault. I just started wondering what it was all for anyway. I mean, you go to school to get good grades, bust your ass for a good job."

It sounds like Emma was cynical long before Todd ever showed up.

She looks almost bored now, resting a fist against her face, looking only half-awake. "Then you bust your ass for a better one before the stress finally gets to you and you have a heart attack."

"What do you want to be when you finish school?"

"I don't know. Maybe a reporter. Or a counselor. My parents want me to be a dentist like my dad, but I don't think I could stand looking in people's mouths all day."

"How would being a parent change your plans? How would it change Todd's plans?"

"I don't know. I haven't really thought about what will happen after the baby's born, I guess. My parents are going to freak out and lecture me about ruining my life." She looks at me like I might take this as an invitation to lecture her too.

"Nothing has to ruin your life. Especially if you have the right support. You need to think about what you want, and then we can look into your options."

Her chin wobbles. I've seen it enough times to know what comes next. I pluck the box of tissues from the table and offer one.

She takes the whole box and pulls out two. "There's a chance Todd isn't the— We broke up for a while and I was a mess.

There was another guy. He was…older. I doubt he'd want to know about this, but what if it's his kid?

"I don't know what happened. I was smart—I was supposed to be the kid that didn't mess things up."

Emma sounds surprised that her life could take such a drastic turn. It's confronting to realize your destiny isn't always your own.

"You're still smart. Unexpected things happen to smart people every day," I soothe. "This doesn't change that."

I was smart, but it didn't stop my body from fighting against itself, the cells proliferating too quickly.

Ashlee was smart, but she was still gone.

"Why did you make this appointment? I mean before you found out you were pregnant?"

She hesitates. Maybe whatever it was doesn't seem like such a big deal now.

"My mom's sick. I wanted to know what I'm supposed to do when she dies."

The way she looks at me is heartbreaking. She's just a girl who needs her mom, and instead of being able to reach out to her, she was carrying a secret that could create a rift between them.

"You do the one thing you can," I say, thinking about what I would've done differently with Ashlee. "You make the most of every day you get to spend with her. It's those moments that make everything else matter. You'll carry them with you after, as a reminder to keep living every day to it's fullest."

She clutches one hand over the other and looks at me, hopeful that I might have something more. "I don't think I can do this pregnancy and lose my mom."

"Tell her, Emma. She might surprise you with her response.

77

A lot of things change when you're dying."

    I go home that night feeling glad I agreed to meet with Wes. I could use a moment that matters, and hopefully I'll find one.

12

Chapter 12

Oscar

Now

The vegetable paella was almost gone from Oscar's plate when Caroline called.

Artemis looked hopeful, following Oscar's every move as he talked on the phone. He scratched behind her ear, but she looked disappointed as his attention moved back to the phone call. She tried appealing to Hayley instead, big brown puppy-dog eyes pleading until Hayley took pity and poured kibble into her bowl.

Caroline's familiar voice was quiet in Oscar's ear as she whispered that Verity was awake. "The surgery went well," she added.

"That's fantastic news. When will she be up for visitors?" asked Oscar.

Oscar watched Hayley as she walked back to the table,

unable to stop himself from smiling. He still didn't know what she was doing with him when she could have anyone she wanted. She looked so effortless and unburdened, even the way she walked, her hips swinging, her body loose and carefree. Sometimes he felt as if he was all wrong for her, like eventually he'd weigh her down.

"Visiting hours are almost over, and she probably needs to rest. Head over in the morning—she might be up for visitors by then."

Oscar took Hayley's hand from across the table and squeezed it. It felt like they were always interrupted whenever they tried to spend time together. *Verity's awake,* he mouthed.

Hayley closed her eyes, her shoulders relaxing with relief.

Oscar's call ended, and he returned to his paella. He mopped his plate with a thick baguette slice.

"That's a lot of carbs," said Hayley, her concern genuine. Since he'd stopped working at Whitner Psychiatric she'd been keeping a close eye on his health.

"What, this?" He pointed at the bread. "I'm just stocking up in case I don't get any carbs with my next meal. This is carbs in the bank."

Hayley laughed as he sidled up to her, tracing his fingers against her leg. "If you're really worried you could help me work them off."

"Don't you have to go to the hospital?" she asked, reluctantly pulling away.

"Not until tomorrow," he said, his other hand making its way under the shirt she'd thrown on, feeling for the clasp at the back of her bra. He still wanted her with the same passion as when they first met. He'd heard that the hot urgency of the first months gave way to a need that wasn't so fierce, but he still felt it the same as when they'd started dating.

After, he held her against his bare skin as their heartbeats slowed together, her hair tickling his chest.

Hayley lifted her gaze to look at him and smiled. "It's good to see you passionate about work again, but I'm glad I have you to myself tonight," she said.

He'd left Whitner Psychiatric without much of a plan. After the first month she'd given up on pushing him to find a new passion, accepting that his resistance might be part of the process he needed to go through before he could come out the other end.

"It doesn't mean I'm practicing again," he warned, brushing her hair back from her face.

"I know. It's just, you weren't sure whether you wanted to get involved at all." She hesitated and cleared her throat. Oscar shifted. Whatever Hayley was about to ask, it felt like it could change the mood of the evening.

"What made you change your mind?"

Oscar swallowed, his throat bobbing. "Verity wants to know what happened to her sister," he said. "And she might not have long to find out. She has cancer."

Hayley rolled over and propped herself up on an elbow, wrapping the sheet around her nakedness. "What? Can they... Is she—"

"I didn't ask. But if there's a chance I can help, I think I should."

A knock at the door sent Artemis running to investigate—she'd adopted Oscar's house as her own and she took her job as protector seriously.

Oscar pulled on some clothes and went to the door. "Who is it?" he called.

A voice answered from the other side. "It's Steve."

He could only think of one Steve he knew, but it couldn't be his brother—they hadn't spoken for at least ten years. Except, the voice behind the door sounded like Steve.

He threw the door open, and his big brother stared back at him, older and a little thinner, but still the same Steve.

"Come in." He moved to the side, trying to figure out what would be important enough to bring his brother to his door. He hadn't realized Steve knew his address—he'd never bothered to visit before.

"No, that's okay. Listen, Oz, something's happened." Steve looked flurried, not even bothering to try and take a peek inside at how his little brother was living. Whatever had brought him to Oscar's door unannounced wasn't good.

Something's happened.

He'd used those exact words to explain to his parents what happened to Lila, and hearing them coming from Steve still made him squirm.

Who had died this time?

"Steve, what's wrong?" asked Oscar, wishing there was something better to say.

Steve took a deep breath. "It's Dad. They've taken him to the hospital. He had a heart attack."

"What? Is he..." Oscar let the words trail off. He'd been waiting for this day since he was eleven. As a kid, he'd tried warning his father, Bill, that if he didn't start taking better care of himself he'd end up in an early grave. It might've been anything. Smoking. Drinking. The greasy food he ate too much of. Back when he was a kid, Oscar had assumed it'd be a police officer standing at his door telling him Bill didn't wake up after a drunken blackout.

"He's alive," said Steve, "but they haven't been able to stabilize him yet. I'm heading there now if you want a ride."

Something bothered Oscar. Why had the hospital called Steve first when Oscar stayed with Bill when Kiko and Steve left? He had made sure Bill ate more than the liquid diet he would've otherwise consumed. He'd figured out how to fry potatoes and beans on his own and learned that if he didn't get it done early enough, his dad would be too far gone to eat. That was the worst kind of vomit to clean up. The stench of beer and bile lingering in the carpet no matter how much he scrubbed at it.

Oscar checked his phone. The hospital hadn't tried to call him.

"What's going on?" asked Hayley, drawn by Oscar's tone. She'd thrown on some clothes and ran a hand through her hair. In just five minutes, she somehow looked like she'd spent an hour getting ready.

Oscar told her what happened, briefly introducing her to Steve.

"Go," she said. "I'll finish up the dishes." She hugged him, squeezing a little tighter than usual. "Let me know how Bill is when you can."

"I'll call you," he whispered in her ear. "When I know more."

Oscar wanted to take his own car, but it felt rude when Steve had come to collect him, rallying together like a real family did during a crisis.

A silence fell between them as they drove, years of not seeing each other and a tense situation creating an unfamiliarity neither of them knew how to break. Oscar knew the boy Steve had been in his childhood, but he knew nothing of the man sitting beside him, driving too fast.

Steve watched the road ahead, navigating the traffic with a heavy foot.

"When did the hospital call?" asked Oscar.

Steve half smiled, as if Oscar's naivety was endearing. "They didn't. I was there when it happened. I called Mom before heading over to tell you."

If Steve was visiting Bill it made sense that he would be the first to know, but as far as Oscar knew, his brother and father didn't have the kind of relationship that meant getting together for roast chicken on Sunday.

He looked at Steve's profile, cut in clean lines and as unreadable as stone. Why did Bill have a sudden heart attack when Steve was there? Could it have been the shock of seeing him? "Jesus. What did you say to him?"

Steve turned slightly, watching Oscar through his peripheral vision. "Nothing."

Bill looked fine the last time Oscar saw him. He did a quick calculation—that was about two weeks ago, but a lot could happen in a couple of weeks. "He gets pretty down this time of year."

Oscar stopped, wondering if Steve remembered.

"Yeah. So does Mom. Doesn't matter that Lila's been gone longer than she was alive," said Steve, as if losing a child might've somehow gotten easier for them. Maybe Steve didn't have kids and couldn't understand what even the possibility of that kind of pain was like.

When he was a kid Oscar thought Steve was the coolest person he knew. Back then Steve didn't have the sports car and expensive clothes, but he had an easy way of talking to people that made it seem like he cared.

"I go every year and leave flowers. Sometimes more often if I'm visiting Riley," said Oscar. The truth was, he felt guilty if he didn't make a quick stop at Lila's to tidy the old flower stems and replace them with vibrant pink and yellow ones. He wasn't sure if Kiko still went but Bill had stopped going a long time ago.

"Yeah, I heard about your son," said Steve. "SIDS, right? I'm sorry, man."

"Thanks."

Steve didn't ask for details, which Oscar was silently grateful for. He couldn't talk about his son's death now. He needed to think about Bill and how he could help.

Steve parked the car in the hospital lot and they hurried inside. So much for coming back in the morning. He went through the sterile doors, the smell of Lysol filling his nose. Being there as a visitor felt different to working there. With it came a kind of vulnerability he didn't have when he wasn't waiting for answers.

They walked together, Steve slightly ahead of Oscar, just like when they were kids.

Oscar struggled to keep up, willing his bad leg to move faster. He waited while Steve made enquiries. Listening to his brother ask questions, Oscar was reminded of the time Steve scored them free snow cones at a fair by laying on the charm and convincing the stall holder how good it would be for publicity when people saw them enjoying the snow cones.

A pretty nurse smiled from across the desk, leaning in to speak to Steve, pointing him in the right direction.

"Thanks, Sarah. You're the best," he said.

Sarah beamed. "Anytime, Steve. The doctor should be with you soon."

"You know her?" asked Oscar, picking up on a familiarity that went beyond name tags.

"Yeah, I have a thing for nurses," said Steve. "Must be great being a doctor." He arched an eyebrow.

Oscar couldn't tell whether Steve was serious until he broke into a dimpled smile. "Just kidding. I sold some supplies to this hospital recently. Sarah was a big help—she got me a slot to pitch to some surgeons."

That explained it. "You're still in sales?"

"It's what I know," said Steve, their conversation cut short as a doctor in scrubs rushed through the doors.

"Mr. de la Nuit?" said the doctor—obviously not one of the surgeons Steve had pitched to.

"Yeah?" said Steve before Oscar could answer. "I'm Steve." He gestured toward Oscar. "This is my brother, Oscar."

"Dr. Newton," said the forty-something surgeon who was still in his scrub cap with a pair of round glasses sitting atop his head. "The surgery went well. He's not fully awake yet but he's been moved to recovery. His eyes are open, but he's still pretty sleepy. He suffered a myocardial infarction; a heart attack. We'll be keeping a close eye on him over the next couple of days."

"When can we see him?" asked Steve.

"He'll be in recovery for a while longer. You can go in for a few minutes, but be aware that he may not recognize you. He probably won't be able to hold a conversation—he's had some pain medication and it'll be a while before the effects of the anesthetic start to wear off. Right now, we want to keep him comfortable and monitor him."

"We can come back tomorrow if that's easier?" said Oscar.

"No, that's okay. Sarah will show you through. It might

help if he knows you're here." The doctor smiled and walked away. He'd probably been in surgery for a few hours and it looked like he could use a rest.

They waited for Sarah to finish up some notes before she led them to a room with machines that sounded like they were speaking a digital language among themselves.

"Hey, Dad," said Steve, going straight to Bill's bedside.

Oscar balked when he saw his dad lying there, hooked up to the beeping machines. He wasn't used to seeing him so vulnerable and frail. Even when he was passed out from drunkenness Bill looked like a sleeping giant, but here he seemed like a shadow of himself.

Bill turned his head at the sound of Steve's voice. "Oscar?"

"Yeah, Dad. I'm here," called Oscar from behind his brother.

Steve took a step back, raising an eyebrow at his little brother as if to say, *That's the thanks I get for being here?*

"I just... I wanted to say—" started Bill, his voice rough and raw from the intubation he'd had during surgery. He coughed, wincing with pain.

"It's okay, you can tell me about it later. Just get some rest," said Oscar.

"Rest?" scoffed Bill. "I need a drink, is what I need."

"Yeah, but you really do need to rest. You just had heart surgery."

Bill tried to sit up, but soon gave up when he couldn't figure out how to maneuver himself.

"Here," said Oscar, racing to his side to shift Bill's pillow so that it supported his back. "Just lie there for a bit. Unless you want to add a few weeks to your recovery."

Sarah stepped forward. "How is your pain level?" she asked.

"Sore," said Bill, but apparently not sore enough that he

couldn't look Sarah over.

Sarah thumbed a drip going into Bill's arm, presumably changing the dosage of painkillers.

"That's probably enough of a visit for today," Sarah said. "But maybe they can come back tomorrow?" She smiled at Steve hopefully. Whatever had happened between them, she didn't look done with him.

"Maybe," said Steve, returning the smile.

She sauntered across to Steve and leaned in to whisper something Oscar could only just make out. "You know, you're lucky I didn't meet your brother first."

Oscar cleared his throat uncomfortably. "We're gonna go so you can get some sleep, Dad. But we'll be back tomorrow, when you're feeling a little better."

Bill grabbed Oscar's arm, pulling him closer. "There's something I have to tell you, Oz. In case I don't make it," said Bill firmly, struggling over the words.

"Don't talk like that," Oscar lectured. "You'll be fine. You survived the worst of it and they've patched you up."

Now finished talking to Sarah, Steve clapped his brother on the back. "I'll bring him back tomorrow," said Steve. "Don't worry."

"What?" said Bill, blinking slowly, fighting the effects of the medication. Oscar watched Bill's breathing slow down. Soon he was snoring, his brow creased like he was trapped inside a restless sleep.

Bill de la Nuit was a man of few words. If he was making a fuss about telling Oscar something it must be important.

What did he want to say?

13

Chapter 13

Verity

Then

In person Wes looks exactly the same as his picture. He sees me and smiles, but doesn't approach, making me wonder if I've oversold myself. For a horrifying moment I think he's going to turn around and walk out. My profile picture was taken barely a month ago, but my face is thinner now, my hair duller after taking months to grow back from the chemo. Worrying about the dullness of my hair seems trivial, but tonight I want to feel beautiful.

I'm wearing a chiffon summer dress and strappy sandals and my hair falls loose around my face, a sensation I missed in the months following treatment. I spent longer than I usually would accentuating my eyes and lips with makeup. Maybe I overdid it—I haven't been out in a while, so I don't know what's trending this season, but as I look around, I notice my outfit is similar to most of the women at the bar.

The bottom of my dress slides across my leg, revealing my calf muscle and a good portion of my thigh. I cover it up, pulling the skirt across like a curtain. It's a battle I've had the whole way here, but the soft fabric falls away again. When I look up, Wes is standing in front of me with the same half smile he has in his profile picture.

"Hi," he says. "Verity?" I smile and gesture for him to sit at the stool next to mine, clutching the edge of my dress stubbornly when it won't settle.

"Wow. You look great. I feel underdressed," he laughs, hands in the pockets of his jeans. He's wearing a gray, casual blazer that brings out the warmer tones in his brown eyes. He is just as attractive as his photo and I try not to stare.

"I haven't ordered drinks. I was trying to fix my dress," I say lamely, but now that I've started speaking, I keep going. "I haven't worn it in a while." I will myself to stop. He probably doesn't care about my wardrobe complications.

His eyes haven't left mine, making me wonder what kind of opinion he's forming. "Well, it looks beautiful."

I'm sure he's exaggerating but I smile anyway and bite back a quip. "Thanks."

It's busy, and the bartender looks overworked, sweat making his black T-shirt cling tighter to his chest. He rushes to our end of the bar, moving as if he's been slightly sped up. He asks if he can get us something, and Wes orders the golden ale on tap before asking what I'd like.

"Just a lemonade for me," I say.

"Oh, I'll have the same then," he says.

"No, order the beer," I insist.

"Lemonade's fine," he says.

I haven't had a drink since downing the bottle of wine that left me with a hangover, but I'm sure I can handle just one glass. "You know what? Maybe I'll have a glass of white."

We've already taken up enough time and there's a group of guys at the other end of the bar gesturing impatiently that they'd like to order. The bartender holds up a hand, a finger raised to indicate he'll be with them in a minute. "Pinot Gris, if you have it," I say.

The bartender moves on and Wes turns to me, looking me up and down, his eyes lingering on my lips. I feel my pulse quicken, excited by the possibilities, but our drinks arrive, interrupting the moment.

Wes pays, and I take my glass and thank him. "I'll get the next one."

"Lemonade?" he asks.

"Maybe. We'll see how the wine goes." We clink our glasses together so that they kiss gently before taking a sip.

"So, white wine, not red, huh? Is that something I need to remember?" asks Wes.

I smile. "That depends."

"On what?" he asks, leaning in close enough that his cologne wafts past. It's my turn to continue the flirting game, but I respond with the real answer.

"It's a warm night, and it's hot in here. I usually prefer red."

"Spontaneous," he says.

"Not usually," I admit, shrugging. The strap of my dress falls off my shoulder and I fix it back into place. "To be honest, I'm not really sure why I asked you out. It's not something I'd usually do."

"Well, lucky me then."

My cheeks flame and I hope I'm wearing enough makeup

to hide it. "I haven't dated much this year," I say, like that explains why I asked him out for a drink. I bite my lip—it already feels like I'm messing things up.

"Really? Why not?"

I sip my drink. "It's hard to find the time to date with my job." Silently I add, *It's hard to know if I'll feel well enough to actually go.*

"So, why me?" he asks.

I wanted to forget my conversation with Detective Payneham. I wanted a distraction from knowing I'd probably never find out what happened to Ashlee, but I don't think that's the answer he's looking for.

I clear my throat. I've been quiet for too long and Wes is waiting for my response.

If only I could tell him that for one night I want to live like I have all the time in the world to flirt with him. Maybe I can show him instead.

I move closer and breathe in his cologne. My head spins. Perhaps the wine has gone to my head—or maybe my body's reminding me that I'm still alive.

Wes puts a hand on my arm to steady me. "Are you all right?" he asks.

"Yeah, just a dizzy spell. I think I drank the wine too fast." I smile and take a deep breath while I wait for the dizziness to pass.

His question hangs between us, unanswered. He's still smiling, and I realize it's the reason I asked him out in the first place. He looks so at ease. I want to feel that kind of peace too.

"I didn't mean to send that message. I was going to delete it, but I accidentally pressed send."

"Living up to your name," he says good-naturedly. "Most people would be too embarrassed to admit that."

"People tell me embarrassing things every day. Maybe I've become desensitized to embarrassment," I say.

He places a hand over mine unconsciously. "Maybe you feel like you owe them the same honesty."

"Maybe. Things have been a little stressful lately."

Even as I say it, I know Wes is right.

"Work stress?" he asks sympathetically.

"Not really," I say. "My sister went missing a couple of months ago. I'm still trying to figure out what happened..."

He frowns and tilts his head to the side as if he's genuinely sorry to hear it. "That's awful. No wonder you needed a night out." His expression changes as he runs his fingers across my hand.

The conversation is taking a wrong turn. I don't want to talk about Ashlee or cancer tonight. I don't want Wes to treat me like I'm fragile. Tonight, I'm the girl I was before I got sick—carefree and looking for a laugh.

The bar is busier now than when we arrived, but I ignore the other patrons. "Let's make it a good night." I edge closer until my knee is pressed against his and lean in to kiss him.

He meets me half way. He's a good kisser and we stay like that for a long time, until I pull away, breathless.

"See, it's good to take a chance," he says. "You never know what might happen."

For the first time in a while, I don't feel like the sick person watching life happen around me. I'm in the middle of the action. I'm alive.

After the kiss he weaves his fingers through mine. I watch his lips move as he talks, struggling to focus on his words until we're kissing again. I giggle girlishly. The wine, the music, and Wes's company are intoxicating.

"What?" he says playfully.

The slight taste of beer stays on my lips. "I don't know why I did that."

"You didn't accidentally hit send on your lips, did you? Because I definitely got that message."

I laugh, realizing I want to kiss him again, but the moment has passed and I'm back in my own head, feeling guilty for having so much fun. A distance builds between us until we could be two friends enjoying after-work drinks. Except, I'm sure the way I'm looking at him suggests something more. I flush. The heat rises to my face and grows hotter.

"Excuse me for a moment," I say, and head to the bathroom. I splash water on my face and my alcohol-hazed eyes look back at me from the mirror. I've crossed over from being a little tipsy to feeling drunk.

I'm not supposed to drink with my upcoming treatment. *To hell with my condition*, I think defiantly. *I've followed the rules and done everything I'm supposed to do, and I'm no better for it.*

Even as I think it, I know it's unfair. I'm probably still here because of how seriously I've taken my health, how seriously I've taken being here to try and find Ashlee. Sitting here with Wes has made me realize how much I've needed some reckless fun.

I hold on to the marble sink, relishing the cool stone under my hands. I splash water across the back of my neck and take a deep breath. I need this. I need to remember that I'm still here.

Ashlee creeps into my thoughts. I'm still here, but what if she's not? What right do I have to be out having fun when I don't even know if she's okay?

I hear her voice clearly in my mind telling me to have fun, daring me to let loose with a mischievous tone.

I step back into the noisy bar, ready for the rest of the night, but our seats have been taken, our drinks swept off the counter, replaced by shiny cocktails and two new faces that look like a late-night, drunker version of Wes and me. How long was I in there? It couldn't have been more than fifteen minutes.

For a moment it's as if I imagined the whole thing. Where did he go? Maybe he changed his mind and went home. Was he waiting for me to take a bathroom break so he could slip out without making a scene?

The heat creeps through me again. This time it's tinged with spice and fueled by my embarrassment. I'd allowed myself to believe that things were going well, that Wes was having fun too, but if that were true, why would he leave without saying something? Maybe I'm drunker than I think. Was I slurring my words and stumbling over my own feet? I've only had two and a half glasses of wine, maybe three—I can't be that drunk.

I spin around, searching for Wes. I catch sight of him leaning across the bar to order another drink. That couple must've stolen our table when he left it. I sigh with relief and walk over to join him, ready to make a joke. When he turns around to reveal impatient blue eyes I realize it isn't him.

"Sorry," I say, pretending I was trying to step past to order a drink of my own.

A bartender asks what I want. I consider leaving, but now that I've caught their attention I run with it. "Just a spritzer, please," I say, and tap my phone to pay, ignoring the exorbitant amount on the interface. *Just one night*, I remind myself.

I sit on a stool and check my cell. There are no messages from Wes. No apologies for leaving early. What a jerk.

Except Wes didn't seem like a jerk. Maybe he was called away to an emergency?

A man with wavy brown hair catches my eye and smiles. He walks toward me, but I look away. I'm not in the mood to make small talk. Instead I watch the string of people entering and exiting, like I'm waiting for Wes to change his mind and walk back through the door.

And then *he* enters as if he owns the bar. Maybe he does. He's the last person I expected to see tonight and my heart races with the shock of being this close to him, of knowing what he's done. He's smiling, as if his freedom was always going to be won back. *How did he get away with it?*

The music is louder now, signaling the night has reached its peak. I wait for a trail of friends or a date to enter with him, but the door closes behind him. He's alone. Maybe he timed his entrance for this part of the night, when the conversations die down and people leave in pairs.

Of course he would think he can walk in now and still have his pick of whoever he chooses. I feel sorry for the woman who leaves with him.

14

Chapter 14

Verity

Then

He's a gamble. Dale Carmot. The horse you bet on when you need a big payout. I should talk to him.

I glance at my face in the mirror behind the bar and wonder if the sallow glow is the hue of my skin or an effect of the dim lighting, which is designed to create calm, warm lines and encourage people to keep drinking.

The light doesn't have the intended effect, making me feel panicked. What if this is where my life plateau's? *Stood up in a bar on a Friday night.*

He walks straight through the middle of the room. People shift to let him pass as he moves toward the back without ordering a drink.

I grab my own drink and follow him, expecting him to stop at a nearby table laden with people.

I sink low, worried he'll notice me staring and realize that I followed him from his office and saw his angry exchange above the wine bar.

He looks around the bar, his eyes searching for something. *For someone.* What are the chances of him turning up here tonight when I'm trying to forget about him, about Ashlee?

Is he looking for another Ashlee to take home, someone he can remove from the world without anyone noticing?

He sits alone at a little round table designed to hold a couple of drinks and not much more. I can see his profile, his straight nose and lips making a taut line, accentuating the angles of his face. Already there are two women talking behind their hands and casting glances his way. He acknowledges them with a nod as I lower my eyes, careful not to catch his attention.

Worrying about his intentions seems silly as I look around the busy bar. Too many people could report seeing him here. He couldn't be stupid enough to think he'd get away with killing someone else.

A server walks by, collecting glasses with foamy residue clinging to the insides. Dale reaches for her arm and brushes it lightly. My breath stalls in my lungs as she turns. When she sees his face she smiles.

They exchange words I can't hear over the drone of music, but it looks like he's ordering a drink. She nods and stuffs a twenty in her apron before disappearing behind the bar.

Dale's eyes scout the room as if he's waiting for more than the server to return with his drink.

The right target?

The giggling women are still watching him with interest until the gigglier of the two seems to arrive at a decision and slides off her stool, beelining straight for Dale's table.

I can't hear her words, but she stands closer than she might if she wasn't in a bar, plied with some false courage and a few drinks.

Dale sits back in his chair, sizing her up while she talks. She flips her hair so that it cascades across her shoulders, falling against a golden tan.

The server from before sets a beer on Dale's table and excuses himself, moving away from the stool and leaving the giggly woman looking incredulous.

Dale makes his way toward me, giving me no time to decide how to react. If I take off now it may look like I have something to hide.

My only option is to feign ignorance. I move to a table that looks like a tall, flat mushroom; the kind you place your drinks on once you're done with them or when your friend drags you onto the dance floor. I turn my head away from him and try to disappear in a small patch of shadow the lights don't quite reach.

I sneak a peek to see if he's still there and we collide, a trickle of beer spilling down his arm.

He stops and holds his drink up high, presumably protecting it from further contact with me. He grips my arm to steady my balance. "Sorry. Did I get you?" he asks, wiping at the spilled beer.

I return the sorry, my senses prickling like an animal snared in a trap. I look at his arm and he releases his hold. He smells like freshly applied cologne. The heady sandalwood tones might be the last thing Ashlee smelled as he killed her.

I search his face, expecting to see signs that Ashlee's death affected him too—puffy eyes, maybe a crease in his brow, but his eyes are bright and his skin is smooth and clear. He looks the same as he did on the news. Untouchable.

The two giggly women from before have moved on, probably to try their luck closer to the front bar where there's always someone willing to buy you a drink.

"I didn't see you standing there," Dale says. It comes across as insincere. He watches me curiously—no hint of recognition. He has no idea what I know about him.

"I'm Jack," he says effortlessly, offering a hand.

Jack?

I look deeper, trying to figure out if he could be who he claims and not the person I think he is.

I'm convinced it's him despite the fake name—maybe it's his pick up name?

Perhaps I'd lie too, if my name was plastered across the news for murder.

He lets his hand linger, waiting for me to take it. If I show I'm repulsed by the thought of touching him he'll walk away and I might never know what happened to Ashlee.

I cover my hesitation by acting shy, taking his hand lightly in mine. I keep it there long enough for him to think I'm flirting.

I can't use my real name. It's too unique—he might figure out who I am. If he's making up an identity, so can I.

"And you are?" he says, making a show of sounding interested.

"Eliza," I say, forcing a smile with the help of the wine.

"So, why are you here alone, Eliza?" he asks, standing close enough that it feels intimate.

"Date gone wrong," I say. "I thought I'd hang around and have a drink."

He nods knowingly. "He wasn't who he said he was, huh?"

He's assuming I ditched my date after seeing him, so I play

along. Being a caseworker has taught me that what people choose not to say can tell you just as much as the things they do.

I smile salaciously. "You can usually tell if it's going to be a fun night in the first five minutes," I say, "and if it's not going to be any fun for me..."

I let my sentence trail off, my tone inviting him to guess.

"Then why waste your time?"

I nod. "Exactly."

"Well, I agree."

"Better not to waste their time either," I add, finishing my drink.

He studies me like a bug under a microscope with its wings pinned. I study him back, casting subtle glances, trying to see deeper.

"You're very honest. I like that, Eliza. So, in the interest of honesty, I'm going to ask you something. I hope you don't think it's too forward."

He waits for my permission before continuing.

I remind myself that he's the only link I have to Ashlee, the only possible way of finding out why she didn't come home the night of the gala, and nod slightly.

He finishes his drink and removes my glass from my hand, setting it down next to his. The glasses clink together and he moves close enough for his arm to circle my waist. "Am I wasting my time?"

The way he presses his lips together tells me he wants to kiss me. If I don't kiss him back, it'll be sending a clear message. *Yes, you're wasting your time*, and he'll leave. If I tell him he's not, we both know what comes next.

Maybe I want him to invite me home, to see where he

might've taken Ashlee, but there's a lot to consider. It could be dangerous. It's too soon to make a decision. I can't tell how the night will go. Right now, he could be deciding what to do with me. How I play my role could determine my fate.

"I haven't decided yet."

He moves slightly closer, and I hold his gaze, wondering whether he'll kiss me. He draws even closer, warming the air between us. Just as our lips are about to meet, he says, "If you're not convinced, maybe I should buy you another drink?"

"That would be nice," I say, pulling away slowly.

He heads to the bar and I follow, looking around for Wes in case he changed his mind, but he's not here and I'm left wondering what went wrong.

The music is still loud, the bar still busy, but on the dance floor there are more couples swaying to the beat in each other's arms with hungry mouths and busy hands.

Dale and I probably look just like them—another hookup waiting to leave for the night.

The way to the bar is obstructed by a group of people standing around talking, taking up too much space with their gestures. We could move around them, but Dale takes my hand and we squeeze through the crowd. "Excuse me," he says as we thread out way through to the bar.

Now we're holding hands, and he doesn't let go. My hand is frozen in his, but I think better of sliding it away. He's smart enough to sense my reluctance if I show it, and I need him to think that I want him, that he has the upper hand.

The bar reeks of stale beer spilled throughout the night. I try to ignore the smell as Dale says something I can't quite hear. I ask him to repeat it, cupping my ear to hear.

He smiles at me, teeth flashing, his breath warm as he moves in to ask what I'm drinking. I almost ask for lemonade, but if I'm drinking lemonade he might do the same, and he needs to be drunk enough to talk freely.

"A wine spritzer," I say. It's alcoholic, but not enough to get me drunk too quickly. Enough time has passed that the effect of the wine I drank earlier is wearing off.

"A wine spritzer and one of those," he says, pointing to a craft beer I haven't heard of.

"Sure."

The drinks are promptly set in front of us on the bar. Dale hands me my drink and takes his beer from the bar before sliding his hand back in mine, squeezing it before we're plunged back into the crowd. It looks like we're heading toward the spot we were standing in before.

It's safe to drink. You saw the bartender make it, I assure myself, knowing that what I'm about to do is riskier than anything I've done before. Adrenaline pumps through me as we navigate the crowd hand in hand.

This could be the day that I find out what happened to Ashlee. Maybe after I know I'll be able to sleep through the night again.

I squeeze his hand back and he interprets my response as a sign that I'm into him as we scoot around a couple who are dancing, their eyes closed, noses bumping against each other, oblivious to everyone around them.

We're back to where we started talking. It's quieter than the middle of the room, farther from the speakers, but my ears still buzz, trying to normalize the amplified sounds around me.

"Well, you said you'd have a drink with me. That's something, right?"

I shrug, noncommittal, which he takes for flirting. "Okay,

you still need convincing."

I know the type. I'm a game to him, someone to win over so he can prove to himself he's everything he wants to believe he is. Charismatic. Desired. Powerful.

Right now he thinks I'm interested, maybe even playing hard to get. He likes the game.

He leans in and talks. "You already know my name. I'm forty-two, and I work in pharmaceuticals."

"Medicine, huh? Why pharmaceuticals?"

"Well, I started out as a doctor, but I stopped practicing."

I hesitate before asking why he stopped practicing—if he was fired it's not something I want to remind him of, and there's a good chance he's lying about starting out as a doctor. Asking questions could go two ways—he could like that I'm taking an interest, or he could think I'm questioning him.

I ask anyway. I want him to know I'm interested and I can't think of something better to say.

He finishes a mouthful of beer before answering. "The hours are too long for a life outside work. It was a lot of effort to become a doctor and I didn't want to give it up completely, but I prefer selling medicine and talking to customers. I already had the right contacts, so I started a pharmaceutical company."

"Do you miss it?" I ask, taking a small sip of the spritzer, afraid of accidentally having too much and losing control.

"The long hours, or the sick patients?" He stops, considering the question a little deeper. "I guess I do miss it, but I prefer pharmaceuticals. Instead of giving patients bad news, I get to be the guy who gives them the solution to their problems."

Pharmaceuticals made sense. Despite the PR attempts to

show him as a caring person dedicated to fundraising and charities, they were obviously just an in to sell more products and network with potential associates. I knew from Ashlee's job that some of the drugs purchased could generate millions of dollars for a company like Dale's.

"What do you do?" he asks, catching me off guard. I wasn't expecting him to take an interest. I don't want him to know anything about me, but I need to be believable, so I keep my answer vague but honest.

"I'm a caseworker," I say, almost as if it's too boring to talk about. "Mostly, I just find channels for people to get the assistance they need."

"Sounds interesting," says Dale. "You must come across some pretty strange people. I bet you have all kinds of stories."

"It's mostly just referrals for things like alcohol addiction, or gambling," I say, hoping it's enough for him to lose interest. "How about you? Do you really test the drugs as vigorously as the bottles promise?"

He laughs, as if that's truly funny. "Of course we do. It would be unethical to sell to consumers otherwise."

I make small talk about his work, watching his beer sink below the label line of the bottle.

He scratches the tip of his nose and leans against the wall when I ask how long he's been in pharmaceuticals. I've hit a sore spot, and I guess that maybe he's lying when he tells me it's been a few years.

"Sorry, I didn't mean to be nosy," I say, turning to something lighter. "What do you do for fun when you're not working?"

I sip my drink slowly. The table to our left has opened up, two crooked bar stools hastily abandoned. My feet are getting tired and I suggest we sit.

I pull him toward the chairs before he can protest, sliding one leg across the other, exposing my calves.

"Let's see," he says, continuing our conversation, watching me as he takes a seat of his own. "I like to collect things."

A lump forms in my throat, but I clear it, trying not to imagine the kinds of things someone like him collects.

"Especially movie memorabilia," he says.

I nod enthusiastically, trying not to think about what else he collects.

"What's your favorite movie?" I ask.

"Does my answer change whether you're going to come home with me?"

I pretend to consider his question. "Probably," I joke.

"Then I probably shouldn't tell you."

"Really?" I ask, trying to keep my tone light. "You could've just made something up that sounds better than the truth. I wouldn't have known," I say, as if we're conspirators sharing a secret.

He smiles approvingly. "I could've. But all I could think of was *Anna Karenina*, and something tells me you would know I was lying."

He's trying to build trust, so that I feel safe to go home with him, letting me in on the line he usually uses. I wonder how many of them believe him when he says his favorite movie is Anna Karenina.

"You're right," I laugh. "I definitely would've known that was a lie."

Did Ashlee know?

"So, what is your favorite?" I ask. I can think of a few possibilities. The ones that stand out that I'd bet on, though

I know he would never tell me, are *Batman*, and probably *Terminator*. Each has a hero that is superior to the other characters in the movie, and a dark side they're concealing. Each has an antihero.

"*Terminator*," he says. "That first time you see them, you kinda wonder if the Terminator has a bigger plan that the humans can't see."

I nod—both an acknowledgment and a silent affirmation to myself for guessing correctly. I didn't empathize with the robots when I watched *Terminator*, but it doesn't surprise me that Dale does.

"Would you like to see my collection?" he asks.

15

Chapter 15

Oscar

Now

"Let's grab a drink," said Steve, standing in the corridor outside Bill's room with Oscar.

"I should get back," said Oscar.

"Have to be home by curfew, huh?"

Oscar smiled. "No. I just promised I'd be there."

Steve nodded knowingly. "You really like her. What's she like?"

Oscar shrugged. He could think of twenty words to describe Hayley, but none he wanted to share. "Smart. Funny. We met at work."

"She's a shrink too?"

"Yeah. She's better than I deserve, really. Hayley, by the way," he said, so Steve didn't have to keep referring to Hayley as she.

"So, what does Hayley see in you, little brother?"

"Honestly? I don't know," said Oscar, eliciting a laugh.

"Is it serious?"

"Yeah. I mean, I love her."

Surely Hayley would understand if he bailed. Oscar hadn't spoken to Steve in years, always meaning to reconnect, but never quite finding the time or a reason to call. He messaged her to say Bill was okay, that he'd talked to him, and that he was going out for a drink with Steve.

She responded immediately. *Have fun xx*

Stay the night at my place. I shouldn't be too long. Artemis is still working on that new hole she's digging in the yard. She could probably do with the extra time before I need to fill it in again.

"Sure. I've got time for a drink," amended Oscar. It couldn't hurt to get reacquainted with his brother.

His phone beeped—another message from Hayley. *I'm outta clothes and have an early start tomorrow :(*

K. I love you. See you tomorrow. He added kisses, but they looked cheesy. He removed them and added them again, sending the message before he could change his mind.

"I know a place," said Steve, leading Oscar to his car. He pumped music through the speakers and Oscar laughed as Steve sang along to "Crazy Train," slapping Oscar on the shoulder, encouraging him to join in. It was his favorite when they were kids, and Oscar had claimed the same, mostly to please his brother. Listening to it again, Oscar remembered Steve blasting it through his beat up old boom box. He joined in tentatively, not sure he could reach the notes. Sometimes Steve let him play air guitar in a kind of virtual band they started, while Steve wailed away on vocals.

"Whoa, where's the guitar?" asked Steve. "You used to

shred."

"I'm not playing air guitar," said Oscar. "I'm out of practice. Haven't played since I was ten."

"Then sing along," said Steve. When they were kids, Steve was always the main singer, and he never let Oscar have a turn on vocals.

By the time they were killing the engine in the parking lot, they were a few songs in at an out-of-the-way bar down the coast. They went inside, surprised to find the interior dimly lit. Oscar had been expecting something a little more holiday-by-the-ocean and less midnight-ocean-cave. An amicable silence settled between them while their vocal cords recovered from belting out lyrics.

They ordered drinks from a woman at the bar, who greeted them as if they were regulars.

"Two of those, thanks," said Steve, pointing to a beer, not bothering to ask what Oscar wanted.

He handed Oscar a bottle and found a couple of stools and a bar table that still had beer from the last customers sloshed over the surface.

"The first drink is for Dad," said Steve, making a show of proposing a toast. "Because if it wasn't for his heart almost giving out, we probably wouldn't be here drinking beer."

Oscar's mouth twitched, but he didn't protest or point out that Steve was being too blasé, given that Bill was lucky to be alive. He raised his bottle before they each took a customary first gulp.

"So, you became a shrink, huh?" said Steve. "They say people become shrinks to understand themselves."

Oscar shrugged. "Yeah, well, it's probably true." Oscar's brow furrowed—he'd never heard that quote. "Who says that again?"

Steve downed his beer, emptying a quarter of the bottle. "I don't know. I think I read it somewhere."

Steve looked more natural than Oscar felt sitting in the noisy bar. He was already eyeing the drinks, deciding what to try next.

"What do they say about salespeople?" teased Oscar.

Steve smiled and held up his beer in a toast. "That we enjoy talking and get the job done."

"Okay, I've heard different," scoffed Oscar.

Steve laughed. "Give me your best cliché, little brother, and I'll tell you why you're wrong."

Oscar pretended to think, drumming a finger on the table. "Let's see. There's the one about being pretty good at bending the truth, and something else about being pushy."

"Well, you've seen me try to get out of trouble when we were kids. I'm not a good liar."

Oscar remembered. One thing in particular stood out. "Remember the time we were playing baseball and we took out Mom's favorite potted plant, the one she kept on the porch?"

Steve gritted his teeth. "Yeah. She didn't buy it when we told her the neighbors did it."

"*You* told her the neighbors did it. What was she supposed to believe—that it was old Mrs. Paulson next door, or the empty house on the other side?"

"Look, if you hadn't looked so guilty, we might've had a chance at convincing her it was some kids on our block."

Oscar feigned indignation. "You could've at least dropped the bat. The ball was sitting right in the middle of the cracked pot. I think she put two and two together, Steve."

"See, I told you I was a terrible liar. And that proves the sales stereotype is wrong." Steve leaned over and clinked bottles with Oscar, the effect creating a low ring.

"Do you like *your* job?" asked Oscar. Needing to earn a commission would make him anxious, but taking risks had always seemed to excite Steve. He loved a good challenge.

Setting the bottle down with a thud, Steve checked how much was left through the glass. "It's okay. It pays well, and I'm not planning on switching careers anytime soon. What about you? Do you like your job? It must be exhausting, living inside other people's heads all day."

Oscar shrugged. "No. It's good. Mostly. I enjoy working through things with my clients. You get to see how other people live, what drives them, what inspires them. You can learn how they come to their beliefs."

"Mostly?"

"Yeah," said Oscar offhandedly. "My last couple of cases have been intense."

"I'll get us a couple more beers, my treat, and then you have to spill."

"It's not that interesting, really," said Oscar, but Steve was already out of his seat and heading for the bar.

He returned with two fresh beers and set one in front of Oscar. "You were saying?"

"Nothing," insisted Oscar. Steve wouldn't want to hear about psychiatry, and even if he did, Oscar couldn't talk about his clients.

"I'm your big brother, and I haven't gotten to do much brothering these past years. I feel bad about it, so please indulge me."

Oscar laughed at Steve's attempt at an earnest expression. It couldn't hurt to give him some vague details without using names. He wasn't saying anything Steve couldn't read about. "It's a case where a woman went home with a guy who she thought might've killed her sister. The guy basically kidnapped her."

"Holy shit," said Steve. "This chick must be brave. Wasn't she worried the guy would kill her?"

"Yeah, I think she was," said Oscar thoughtfully. "But she wanted to find out what happened to her sister badly enough to do it anyway."

"What she was thinking? Wait, do people actually tell you what they're thinking when you ask them that?"

Oscar shrugged. "Sometimes, yeah. And no, I haven't asked her because she's in the hospital. It ended with both of them falling off of a roof."

"Wow," said Steve. "She's okay now though, right?"

"Yeah, mostly."

"Why do they need you if she's in the hospital? Unless her feelings got injured by the fall?"

Oscar ignored his brother's mocking. "I'm talking to both of them, trying to figure out what happened."

Steve nodded thoughtfully. "Well, good luck," he said, upending the bottle.

"Thanks. I might need it."

Steve smiled and inspected Oscar's clothes, and then his face. They sat in silence, drinking beer. "You're quieter than I remember," he said. "You used to bug me, always wanting to use my stuff."

Oscar smiled at the memory. When they were kids, Steve complained about Oscar borrowing his stuff. And then overnight, Steve was gone and Oscar's world changed.

"Where did you go?" asked Oscar.

"What?"

"You and Mom. Where did you go when you left?"

Steve drew a long breath, unprepared for Oscar's question. "We moved around a lot. We didn't really go anywhere. It's like, once Lila was gone, Mom couldn't settle down or relax. She didn't sleep for more than a few hours at a time, and when she did, sometimes I'd hear her talking to Lila in her sleep."

"That must've been tough. Did she see a therapist to talk about what happened?"

"Nah, you know Mom. She just kept going. I think we all did. We had to."

"Did she say why she left?" asked Oscar, trying to make it sound offhanded. He'd hate if Steve knew he'd cried himself to sleep after; he was eleven—too old for tears and without a friend in the world to talk to.

"She just had her own way of dealing with things. I don't know. Maybe being in that house was too much for her, you know? Too many memories of Lila." He said it as if he was bored with the whole thing, shrugging. "It might've been nice if she'd realized we were still alive. When Lila died, I think we all died with her. Mom never appreciates what she has right in front of her. She's always chasing the impossible."

Oscar looked into the distance, uncomfortable with the bitterness in Steve's tone. The way he remembered it, Steve took all of Kiko's attention. It was only a matter of time before one of Steve's angry outburst exploded into action, and Kiko was forever cleaning up Steve's messes, trying to keep the house running smoothly. When Lila died, they doubled down on their efforts to keep Steve from acting out, watching him more closely than before.

Oscar suspected his parents blamed him—he was supposed

to be watching his sister when it happened. He remembered Bill's open hand striking his face, not in a drunken rage this time, but out of disappointment. It'd hurt more than the beatings he'd received at his father's fists, and there'd been plenty of times to count. Whenever Bill thought Oscar might go off the rails and needed to be kept in line, Bill made a point of showing him what would happen if he messed up.

"What are you looking at?"

It took Oscar a moment to realize the person talking was looking in their direction.

A man in his late twenties sat at a table with two drinking buddies. Each held a beer in hand. The one that spoke slammed his glass down on the table, turned to his friends and said, "This guy can't stop staring at me. Must be in love with me or something."

His friends laughed and Oscar made the mistake of looking at them, drawn by the commotion. The one talking was weedy, with a mottled beard. He looked like he could use more nutrients than the trace amounts from the beer hops.

Oscar looked away quickly. He just wanted a quiet beer with his brother, but the weedy one with the big mouth was coming over to their table. He set his fists down in front of Oscar. "Why don't you buy me a drink, and I might give you my phone number."

Oscar sat back, creating as much distance as possible. "That's all right. Sorry if I offended you. I didn't mean to look at you."

"Well, that's all right then. Maybe you could make up for it by buying the boys a round of beer?"

The two friends were watching now, waiting to see if their friend could score them free drinks.

For a moment, Oscar considered buying them the beer to shut them up—they probably ran out of drinking money—but Steve was already shifting in his seat. "No one's buying you anything. Now run back to your table and tell your friends that this round's on you for acting like a bag of pig shit and disrupting our reunion."

"Ahh, I see. He's already got a boyfriend."

There were more snickers from the other table, but this time, a hint of uncertainty had crept back, like maybe they thought their friend should give up and come back.

"My brother's more of an intellectual. Probably doesn't want to dirty his hands on pig shit like you, but me—I'm happy to wash my hands twice after."

"Who you calling pig shit, immigrant?" His tone belied the gamble he was taking—he couldn't tell for certain if Steve was from anywhere specific, which Oscar was used to, being biracial. As a kid it had made Oscar wonder if he really belonged anywhere.

Steve was out of his seat before Oscar could advise against it, his hand wrapped around weedy's throat.

"Let him go," said Oscar, standing. The men from the other table stood, both of them broader and taller than their friend.

Before Oscar could stop him, Steve's elbow slammed into weedy's nose with a sickening crack.

Oscar wrapped an arm across his brother's chest, trying to pull him away as weedy's friends rushed over.

"Your friend's got a mouth," said Steve, holding his ground, as if he hadn't realized there were now three of them against him and Oscar.

The bar tender called from the bar. "Hey, not in here. You wanna drink beer, fine, but you can do it somewhere else. Now get out or I'm calling the cops."

Weedy's friend on the left wrapped a burley arm around him, guiding him out. "Come on, it's not worth it. Guy's gonna call the cops." To the bartender he said, "Is that anyway to treat your best customers?"

"My best customers would know not to start a fight in my bar," he shot back.

Oscar watched them leave, weedy spitting homophobic slurs at him as he went. There was a time when the Diagnostic and Statistical Manual of Mental Disorders had listed homosexuality as a disorder. It had made Oscar wonder what else it had gotten wrong.

"You all right?" asked Steve as they left the bar.

"Yeah. You?"

Steve shrugged. "That was just a warm up. If he hadn't been so precious about his nose, he might've gotten a hit in of his own."

There was something about a fight that seemed to bring Steve to life. Always had. It was maybe the one thing Bill had been proud of—that his son could fight. Oscar could remember his mother going down to Steve's school, trying to get him out of trouble almost weekly, until she couldn't talk them into keeping him there any longer and they spent the next six weeks looking for a school that would take a kid with a history of violence and delinquent behavior.

Oscar had thought Steve's love of a fight would disappear as he grew up, but when he became a psychiatrist, he realized Steve probably had a conduct disorder and needed treatment before his behavior would improve. From what he could see now, it didn't seem like Steve had gotten the treatment he needed.

"You need to start sticking up for yourself little brother. How have you managed to stay in one piece without me all these years?" asked Steve, ruffling Oscar's hair.

Without Steve there, Oscar hadn't needed to stay out of trouble. It wasn't even that Steve looked for trouble, but somehow, trouble found him.

16

Chapter 16

Verity

Then

"Did I pass your movie test? Or should I buy you another drink?"

It's time to decide whether I'm going home with Dale.

"I don't think I could handle another," I say, forcing a giggle and leaning against his arm to steady myself. "But thanks."

He takes the physical contact as flirting, and lightly strokes my cheek with the back of his hand. I force myself to look at him and he presses his lips against mine—a taste of what's to come if I let him continue.

I keep my lips pressed to his and close my eyes to escape the horror of being there with my sister's killer, knowing I've decided to go home with him. I've come this far. I need evidence that Ashlee was at his house.

When he doesn't have cameras or an office full of people to

deal with, what does life look like for Dale Carmot? Does he live like a regular guy?

"You know, I have wine at home. Better than the stuff you just finished." His voice is muffled by the speakers, which pump music so loud that it reverberates off the walls and bounces back, hitting me in the face.

"What?" I call over the noise, catching pieces of what he's saying, enough to know he wants to go back to his house.

"Exactly. Let's go somewhere we can talk without ruining our vocal cords or our ears."

I swallow, my throat coarse from talking over the music. I allow him to take my hand and lead me outside. As I step through the door, it's like a vacuum seal releasing me from the heat inside the bar.

He slides an arm around my waist, which evokes an image of a python coiling around its victim. My limbic system is trying to warn me, but I'm going home with him anyway.

What if I asked him about Ashlee right here on the street? If I begged him to tell me, would he? In the open air he could keep walking without me, never needing to answer my questions. It'll be easier to force him to answer at his own house. He can't leave to avoid the question, and he won't be worried about someone overhearing us.

The need to know what happened to her is strong. I bite my lip hard, reminding myself to wait as we head down the sidewalk. Dale walks in a surprisingly straight line—he isn't nearly intoxicated enough to confess to murder yet. I hope he's not the kind of drunk that guards his secrets protectively, never quite drunk enough to tell the truth. He calls an Uber and opens the door, gesturing chivalrously for me to get in first. I slide across the seat. The smell of over applied car freshener—probably meant to hide nastier smells—assaults my nose. The Uber driver nods once and confirms that he has the right passengers.

I adjust the straps on my dress and pull the skirt across my legs while Dale talks to our driver. I repeat the address in my head to memorize it.

The car is in motion, pulling away from the curb, and I give up on my exposed thigh again. Dale runs a finger from the hem of my skirt to the waist band and resumes our kiss from earlier, moving across my lips slowly. He doesn't want to talk, but I was hoping to learn more about him before we arrive. I don't want him to feel like he's being interviewed, so I abandon the questions I'm dying to ask. I need him to believe I want what he wants, that it's the reason I'm going back to his place.

I match my mouth to his, leaning as far forward as I can, straining against the seat belt. He unclips and switches from the window seat to the middle and our Uber driver pretends to ignore us, stealing quick glances through the rearview mirror. How often do they get rides like us—drunken bar-hoppers fumbling all over each other? It's probably a typical night for a driver, but I wouldn't know because I'm not usually the girl in the back of the cab with a stranger.

We drive for longer than I expected, turning down a street I'm not familiar with. It's out of the way with beautiful greenery, not the urban luxury home I was imagining.

If Wes had've stayed, would I be in a cab with him right now instead?

The car twists and turns, navigating the streets until the driver slows and we arrive at Dale's house. I want to check my phone to confirm how much time has passed, but I resist—Dale can't suspect I'm thinking about anything but him tonight.

His home is a modern multilevel house, but it's not the home that featured in Architect Magazine, and it's not the property he has listed as his home address. He probably has multiple residences across the country, maybe around the world. He opens the front door, and the inside is luxurious, the carpet thick and eggshell white—not the color I'd expect if you wanted to hide bloodstains. The shutters are drawn and I can't see outside.

Fear builds in my chest, heavy and helpless. I won't give in to it, but I can't stop it from making me worry why he's brought me here, to what looks like a very luxurious holiday home.

All the things that might've happened to Ashlee here play through my mind.

I imagine Dale following her. In the image, she doesn't realize he's there, which means he has the upper hand. He takes his time approaching her, going over what he'll do to her once the game begins. He gets up close before saying hello. She hasn't seen him, didn't even know he was there until he speaks. His voice startles her.

Ashlee laughs at her own skittishness and says hello, un-aware that anything is out of the ordinary—she has no reason to think he has bad intentions. She's seen him around at work, maybe even said hello.

He wiggles the key in the lock, my reverie breaking as the door opens. Suddenly, I'm not sure whether I want to go in. What if I didn't run into Dale at the bar by chance? What if he lured me here knowing I was desperate enough to do anything to find Ashlee? The need to know what happened to her has made me careless.

If I excuse myself now and try to leave will he let me walk away?

Inside, everything looks brand-new and untouched, like he's continuously upgrading with no concern for comfort. I look at the shaggy rug, the pristine window shades, the cabinet with drawers at the top that looks as if it belongs in a creative office, and the sofa. His place looks like a glimpse into the future—things that haven't reached the mainstream yet, but might. Things I won't ever have.

"Your place is amazing," I say, stepping inside. It's an easy compliment, one he probably expects.

I could be a few paces away from knowing what happened to Ashlee, but this place looks unlived in, nothing at all like the chaos I expected from someone who thought nothing of taking a life. My hopes of finding Ashlee dwindles a little. I walk around the house as Dale gives me a quick tour, trying to imagine myself in her shoes. Where would I sit? On the bold sofa with the cushion, or in the kitchen, with a table to lean on? I close my eyes and breathe in the space, trying to sense her energy, unsure how I'm supposed to do that. I fall onto the sofa and let it catch me in the soft cushions.

There's no sign that Ashlee was ever here. I have to go deeper, think like her. What might've brought her here in the first place? Would she be lured by some attention from Dale? I can't imagine my pragmatic sister being wooed by someone like him.

"Drink?"

His words bring me back to the sofa. "Maybe a mineral water," I say, forcing a smile.

So far nothing sinister has happened, but going to Dale's house is exactly the kind of thing I'd advise my clients against.

I feel like a hypocrite—hadn't I asked Clara how things would be if she gave herself the closure she needed? And yet here I am, still searching.

"I have champagne?"

"Soon." I smile, trying to keep the mood light despite my heavy thoughts. "I need to slow down," I say, trying to ignore the sensation of the room moving slightly when I shift my eyes.

"I'm just gonna grab a beer. Be right back," says Dale, leaving me alone in the living room.

Once he leaves, a slight panic sets in. I've walked right into the spider's nest without an escape route. My best bet is probably to find what I need and get out. Except, I have no idea what I'm looking for or where to find it.

I stand, rocking slightly on my feet. I wait for the room to steady itself before I approach the cabinet with the drawer. It is the only thing in here that could conceal something—a purse, an earring, maybe a piece of clothing left behind. Everything else in the room is open and crisp, like unused pieces in a showroom.

The cabinet is suddenly close, too close. I stop when I crash into it, reaching out to open the drawer before Dale returns with our drinks. There's nothing in the first drawer except for some pens and a couple of sheets of paper.

I lift them as quietly as I can and check both sides, berating myself for thinking they might tell me something I don't already know. They're blank and I'm caught off-guard as Dale walks silently back into the room. The sharp edge to his voice startles me. "What are you doing?"

I let the pages fall from my fingers and keep the drawer open. "This cabinet is so beautiful. Sorry, I was just looking at the finish. I hope you don't mind." I slur my words a little for effect.

He looks at me, puzzled. I close the drawer and reopen it, as if examining the functionality.

"It's an original," he says.

"Really?"

"A friend of mine is an artist," he says. "He made me this piece."

"He did an amazing job. Pity though. I was hoping I could pick one up at Pottery Barn."

I wrap my hand around the glass of mineral water, brushing his fingers with mine and smiling salaciously. The urge to step away from Dale is strong, but I fight it.

He slips an arm around my waist and pulls me close enough to whisper in my ear. His nose brushes past my earring, and I realize I'm afraid of what he could do to me, of what he's expecting me to do with him.

I place a hand on his shoulder, letting my fingers brush his neck, lingering close to the soft, vulnerable bits. His pulse quickens, but I'm sure mine would win if this were a race.

I've played the game well until now, but despite my best efforts, I recoil. The ruse is up.

"What's wrong?" he asks, but there is no concern in his voice. He is daring me to admit why I'm really here. With a sinking feeling, I realize something I should've picked up on before I walked through the front door to his home—maybe even before I got into the Uber.

Dale planned to lure me here all along.

He knows.

17

Chapter 17

Oscar

Now

The sky threatened rain, storm clouds low and heavy, holding on to the water like an unfulfilled promise. Oscar didn't care if he was caught in it when the sky finally let go.

It began raining as soon as he got out of the car. Part of him had thought Steve's offhanded promise to go in together to see Bill was real, but he didn't show on Oscar's doorstep the next morning, and he didn't answer his phone when Oscar called. He must've gone in without him. Classic Steve.

Oscar's head throbbed despite the aspirin he'd taken earlier. After the bar, Steve hadn't wanted the night to end on a fight, so they'd picked up some beer to drink in Steve's car, and now Oscar was suffering a hangover. It was lucky Hayley hadn't waited for him to get home, or she would've been waiting in a cold bed most of the night.

Oscar checked in on Bill, but the nurse on shift told him Bill was still sleeping. There was no sense waiting around, he could be out for a while. Next he went to Verity's room to see how she was doing. He'd dressed in chinos and a light blazer for the occasion—work clothes he hadn't worn since he was a practicing psychiatrist at Whitner Psychiatric Hospital.

When he reached Verity's hospital room, Oscar knocked. He waited a beat, and for a second it seemed like it might be a repeat of last time, with only an empty room to greet him.

"Who is it?" called a tired voice from within.

Oscar let out a breath, relieved. "It's Oscar de la Nuit." He opened the door slowly and saw Verity lying in the hospital bed, her legs covered in a thin hospital blanket. Her eyes were glazed with sleep, as if his knock had woken her.

"Oscar! What are you doing here?" Verity self-consciously smoothed her hair.

Oscar entered the room slowly. After what she'd been through, he wasn't sure what kind of state she would be in to receive guests.

"How are you feeling?" he asked.

She nodded. "A little better. My head's sore, but it's not so bad."

It was strange, seeing someone who was usually looking out for others in such a vulnerable position—it was probably best to let her know why he was there. He knew she was putting on a brave face. Her head was probably pounding, but he couldn't see any visible signs of what they'd done in surgery. He suspected it was a key hole procedure to tweak something, but it wasn't the reason for his visit, and it wasn't his place to ask.

"Caroline Taylor asked me to have a chat with you. If I knew what'd happened, I probably would've come by anyway."

"Really?"

Oscar thought about it and laughed. "No. Truth is, I probably would've considered it before convincing myself it was awkward and intrusive."

Verity laughed.

"So, how are you feeling, other than the headaches?"

Oscar sat by her bed so she didn't have to move.

"A bit shaken, I guess." She squinted against the light.

"Did you want me to turn the lights down?"

"No, that's okay."

"Caroline came by with me earlier, but you were in surgery."

"Yeah," she said apologetically. "Something with the cancer. I don't know. I couldn't really follow—I was too tired."

"I didn't know you had cancer—Detective Payneham told me."

"I haven't really told anyone. I wore a wig for a bit when I lost my hair. Sounds stupid, but I didn't want to see what the chemo was doing to me." She shrugged. "Stage four breast cancer. I mentioned it to the detective because I thought I'd seem less pushy asking them to put more resources into Ashlee's case if they knew."

Oscar nodded. He probably wouldn't tell anyone either. "You're doing what you can to kick it, right? That's all that matters. If you ever want to talk, I'm here."

She took a cup from a tray by her bed and sipped water. "It's hard to know which treatments are working and which aren't," she said. "I wish there were progress reports or something to let me know."

"Well, if there's anything I can do," said Oscar.

"Thanks." She smiled and placed the cup down. "You know, maybe you can help clear up some questions."

"Sure."

"Did Dale...did he survive the fall?"

Oscar saw the hesitation. Verity wasn't sure she wanted to know. If Dale was still out there, it meant he was still a threat, and if he was dead it meant she might not get the answers she needed.

Oscar paused before answering. It wasn't fun being the guy who had to deliver bad news. "He survived."

She looked disappointed. "Survived? Does he have a concussion too?"

Oscar looked apologetic—it seemed unfair that she had a head injury, and he got away with a broken leg.

When he told her, she looked dumbfounded. "That's it?"

"It's pinned up pretty good, if that helps."

She gave a half smile. "I guess it's something."

Oscar agreed and asked what happened on the roof.

"I don't remember falling, just the feeling of flying through the air before everything went dark."

She closed her eyes for a second and he knew she was reliving it. "Even inside the house, before the roof, everything was dark. He turned out the lights. Maybe he had smart lights he programmed." She opened her eyes and turned to Oscar. "Have you seen him?"

Oscar confirmed that he'd spoken with Dale while Verity was in surgery. "Caroline asked me to speak with you both, to try to figure out what happened up there," said Oscar, offering an explanation.

"Okay," said Verity weakly, holding a hand to her temple to block the worst of the light.

"I heard about your sister's disappearance. I'm sorry, for what it's worth."

"Thanks," said Verity.

"Caroline told me you might've gone home with Dale to find out what happened to her?"

Verity shrugged.

"I talked to Dale to get a feel for the sort of person he is," said Oscar.

"He took her. That's the sort of person he is." She looked at Oscar. Unblinking. Challenging him to disagree.

"Did you see something at Dale's house to make you believe that?"

"Isn't it enough that he locked me up? He would've killed me. He tried to throw me off the roof." She stopped, her brow creasing. "What day is it?"

"Monday, the eleventh of May."

"I went to Dale's over a week ago. Was I gone for that long?"

"You were unconscious when you arrived at the hospital. They found you around a week ago," said Oscar gently. "Do you remember?"

She shook her head.

"How did you end up at Dale's house?"

"I saw him at a bar. I was there on a date, but my date left when I went to the bathroom..." Her voice trailed off. "I was sitting there alone feeling a little sorry for myself, and then I saw Dale. At first I thought it was good luck, that maybe it was my chance to find out what happened to Ashlee. Serendipity. When the end of the night came, I had to choose whether to go back to his house." She covered her eyes with her hands—a memory, or a regret?

"You chose to go?"

"I was desperate to find Ashlee. I was just going to look around, make sure he wasn't keeping her there." She picked some lint from her top. "If I'm going to die I needed to know what happened to her, so I searched his house, looking for signs that she'd been there."

It made sense—if Oscar's time was limited, he'd want to know too.

"Do you remember what happened while you were inside the house?" asked Oscar.

"I don't remember everything, but I remember finding blood in the bathroom. It caught my attention because it was on the bottom edge of the cabinet. I think there was a little on the wall too, like someone had leaned against it while they were bleeding."

"Maybe it was from a shaving cut?"

"I don't think so. It was kind of streaked, but faint, like he had tried to clean it up." She swallowed hard before continuing. "I probably wouldn't have noticed it if I wasn't locked in there."

"You're sure it wasn't just lipstick or something?"

"Pretty sure," she said, but she was clearly humoring him; she sounded certain.

"The police are searching the house. If it's blood, they'll know."

Verity's shoulders shook gently, the only sign that she was crying. "What if it's Ashlee's?"

Oscar's expression darkened. There was a chance it was Ashlee's blood.

"I wish she'd just walk through the door now and say she was okay, that she just needed some time away from everything." She looked at Oscar with pleading eyes, like his

131

agreement could somehow make it true. "That's not going to happen, is it?" she asked.

"Probably not," he said. "But that's not a reason to stop searching."

18

Chapter 18

Verity

Then

"Why were you following me?" Dale asks. The anger in his voice is menacing and repressed, making me cower against the sofa. I look around the room. There's nowhere to escape if he lunges at me.

I stand quickly, moving backward toward the door with one foot falling behind the other, but he moves forward just as fast, his hand circling my waist so that I can't easily move around him. He's not ready to give up the game. I feel like a rabbit facing off with a fox.

"Following you?" I do my best to sound offended. "You approached me at the bar."

"Why were you there alone? The *real* reason." He does a good job of selling it as a compliment, but I'm not buying.

I consider lying, but don't want to get caught out. "I really was on a date. He had to leave early, and I stayed to finish my drink."

Dale looks me straight in the eye, deciding whether to believe me. "I saw you in the parking lot at my building. You were watching me from your car. I noticed you because when I entered you tried to sink down in your seat." My pulse pounds harder. "You waited until I left the lot before you followed me. I've had enough reporters do the same, but you're not a reporter, so what do you want?"

He holds me a little closer, getting up in my face. It's a warning he won't let go until I give him an answer. My throat turns dry as I stumble over a response. I could deny being in the parking lot, feign ignorance, but his tone suggests he knows more than he's saying. I don't know him well enough to predict what he'll do if I lie. I could say I was waiting for him to exit the building because I'm a fan of his work, but I don't think he'd believe me.

The words I want to say stick in my throat. *What did you do to my sister?*

"You *are* a reporter," he says, surprised to have gotten it wrong before.

"No."

He doesn't believe me. He tilts his head to the side as if he's disappointed in me for failing his test. "Why did you follow me?"

I don't answer. If I tell him why I came here it'll give him the chance to hide any evidence. I need to distract him a little longer, until I've had a proper look around.

His hand shoots out. I'm not expecting it, and he flings my drink away. I watch it fall from my grasp, the liquid sloshing over the sides as the glass clatters to the floor.

"Answer me."

I don't answer, and he strikes me with the back of his hand, an instant burn spreading like fire, running the length of my cheek, through to my jaw. "I should go…" I say, trying to mask the pain.

"It doesn't matter if you don't tell me now," he says, "I can make you talk." He moves forward, but this time I'm prepared and move away, glass crunching under my shoes.

I turn in a half circle. I'll never get past him and to the front door before he stops me. I notice a half-open door down the hall—I'm guessing it's a bathroom, maybe a bedroom. There's probably a lock on the inside. We're on the first floor, and by my calculations I have a chance of reaching that door and climbing out of the window before he can make his way around the side of the house to stop me.

I breathe in and count. *One. Two.* On three, I stomp down as hard as I can on his foot, channeling everything I hate about him into the attack before I run, taking advantage of his surprise. By the time he's figured out where I'm going, I'm already paces ahead and gaining speed.

I get there first and push the door open before sliding inside. I close the door behind me, blocking out the light from the hall that shows him exactly where I am. In the dark, I feel for a lock, aware that he could turn the handle at any time. If he wasn't angry enough to hurt me before, he will be now.

I suck in air, recovering from my sprint, my fingers desperate to find the lock in the darkness. I find it with a rush of triumph—a pin lock. I press the head of the pin in place just as he slams against the outside of the door like a charging bull. The pin keeps him out.

He raps on the door insistently, rattling the hinge. "You

can't hide in there forever."

It's difficult to see in the darkness, and I move my fingers across the wall, searching for a light switch. I find a section of smooth plastic with a little bump, and I know I've found it.

I flick the switch, illuminating the room in light. I'm in a large guest bathroom with a shower and tub. I don't know how long I'll be in here while I figure out how to escape, but at least there's water if I need a drink. I look for something to use as a weapon, in case he breaks down the door. There's a showerhead, but I doubt it's heavy enough to do more than slow him.

A cabinet under a stone basin draws my attention. There could be a pair of scissors or a nail file I can use in self-defense.

He bangs against the door again, startling me as I sift through the cupboard. "Open the door! You're only making this worse for yourself." I keep searching. There's the usual: toothpaste, body wash and a few unlabeled pill bottles that look like aspirin, but nothing sharp enough to use as a weapon.

A splotch of rusted maroon catches my attention on the edge of the cabinet, smeared horizontally. It could be an old nail polish stain, but the color is wrong, almost maroon. It looks like blood.

Ashlee.

I get closer to inspect it. A shaving cut? Maybe. With renewed energy, I search the cupboard, pushing my arm all the way to the back. My fingers grasp something. A chain? I picture myself wrapping it around Dale's throat.

I pull the chain forward. It's not the cheap, fake silver I was expecting to find in a bathroom, but a gold necklace with an intricate gold *A* in a fancy script.

The pendant is instantly recognizable to me.

Ashlee has one just like it.

19

Chapter 19

Oscar

Now

"I want to make sure Dale goes to jail for what he's done."

"Well, he held you at his house. He'll probably go away for that," said Oscar.

"It's not enough," she said. "I want people to know what he did to Ashlee."

Oscar understood. If Dale received a token amount of jail time when he should be locked away for good, it would feel like a consolation prize. Oscar had treated survivors of crime before, and he knew that, no matter the sentence, it was never enough.

Verity would need to find her own peace, because if Ashlee was dead, no punishment would ease the loss.

"I want to help you find her," said Oscar.

Verity nodded, grateful.

"Can you tell me what you remember?"

Her hand went to her throat as she told him about the necklace. "I found it while I was hiding in the bathroom. It had a charm on it—the letter *A*," said Verity. "Ashlee wore one just like it. She got it from our parents for her twenty-first birthday. She never took it off."

"Are you sure it was Ashlee's necklace, not just a similar one?"

"Yes," said Verity decisively.

"I can ask the detective whether they have it. Do they know about it? Where did you put it?"

She shook her head. "I didn't tell them about it. They came in just after I woke up. I was still dizzy. I can't even remember what I said to them."

Verity clasped her neck with her hand, as if expecting to find the necklace there. "I was wearing it while I was on the roof. When I found it, I put it around my neck. I should still be wearing it," she said.

"It's okay," said Oscar gently. "Someone probably removed it when you went into surgery. I'll check with the nurses."

"It might be all I have left of her," said Verity.

Oscar nodded. "I'll go ask now," he said, trying to ease her anxiety.

He left the room, Verity's thankyou faint behind him. He thought about what Verity and Dale had said, each blaming the other. Something didn't make sense. Dale was caught in his own lie, so why was he still trying to implicate Verity? Did he believe what he was saying? Or did he think she deserved what happened to her for snooping around and inconveniencing him?

Oscar waited at the desk outside until someone was free.

A nurse wearing bright eye makeup and a matching bar-rette scrolled a computer screen, completing her task before acknowledging Oscar.

Oscar went to her post and asked about the necklace.

The nurse sighed in exasperation. "I'll get someone to look into it and let her know myself." She went back to her computer screen.

"Thanks. How long should that take, just so I can let Verity know? The necklace belonged to her sister."

The nurse stood. "Okay. I'll see what I can find out, and I'll let her know."

Oscar smiled, wondering if he should tell Verity they were checking.

He still needed to visit his dad. He supposed he could message Steve and see if he was there yet. Steve could let Bill know he would visit him later. Maybe Steve could even tell him how Bill was doing, but it felt too impersonal, too lazy, asking Steve to pass on information so that Oscar could feel like he was being a good son.

Oscar poked his head inside Verity's doorway. "Hey. The nurse out the front is asking around now."

Oscar lingered outside. "I'm seeing what Payneham found at the house later today but I'll try to come by after to see how you're doing."

Verity thanked him. "Really," she said. "Not just for asking about the necklace, but for listening."

"Of course. Don't worry, I'm sure it'll turn up."

She looked at him as if she had an idea. "Maybe Dale took it. He was there when I fell. It'd prove that Ashlee was at the house. It makes sense he'd want to get rid of it."

Oscar folded his arms. "When do you think he took it?"

Verity tried to remember. "It would've been around my neck when I hit the ground, unless it flew off. Dale was falling under me—"

She stopped abruptly, but it was too late—she said Dale was under her. That meant he fell from the roof first, making it less likely that he'd pushed her. Maybe he lost his footing and fell. *Or maybe Verity pushed him off.*

"Did he notice you were wearing the necklace? Did he seem interested in it?"

"It was pretty dark, but I don't think so," she said. "Where was he when the ambulance arrived?"

"Semiconscious. His leg is broken. I don't think he could've crawled on it to take the necklace."

"Then he must've gotten it another way."

"Let's see what the nurse finds first."

She nodded.

"Is there someone I can call to keep you company? It might help to have someone here with you," said Oscar.

"There aren't many people I've stayed in contact with. After Ashlee went missing, I couldn't focus on anything else. Everyone wanted to keep my mind off what had happened. It was like they were afraid of saying the wrong thing, so they avoided talking about it."

Oscar nodded. It was the same after Riley died.

"But I can't avoid it. I think about her all the time. About what happened. I wonder what I could've done to stop her from going missing," said Verity.

"Don't do that to yourself. If there was something you could've done, you would've. This was one of those things that no one saw coming." He stepped inside, unable to leave her there alone when she looked so dejected. He checked the time—he could visit Bill later.

20

Chapter 20

Verity

Then

I hold the necklace in my hand. It could be a coincidence—a lot of people have necklaces with their initials, but Dale's initials are *DC* and the necklace looks more feminine than I'd imagine he's comfortable with. Maybe an old girlfriend left it and had since forgotten about it?

I can't convince myself. Something's telling me it's hers. I feel my legs melting beneath me, but I can't let myself break down. Now more than ever, I need to stay strong. If Ashlee's necklace is here, I must be close to finding her. She would never leave it behind.

"What are you doing in there?" calls Dale, his voice menacing. "Come out or I'll break the door down, I swear."

I know he means it but I stay crouched at the cupboard, hugging Ashlee's necklace to me like a lifeline.

I've heard that killers keep trinkets. Maybe Dale kept the necklace as a trophy, to remind him that he was more powerful than my kind, trusting sister. To Dale that probably seemed like a weakness to expose.

My grief gives way to long, racking sobs. I don't know how long I sit there, but I'm suddenly aware that Dale has grown quiet.

I strain my ears, listening for noise from outside of the door, but it is silent—too silent, as if he's left the house. My fear is rekindled, the quiet more threatening than his fist banging against the door. At least while he was making noise, I knew where he was. Now, he could be looking for something to tear down the door like he threatened he would.

He thinks I have no right to question him and what he might've done. He sees himself as untouchable, but he's entitled, taking whatever he wants. A self-ingratiating reward for being Dale Carmot. Does he really believe he can get away with murder?

I tiptoe to the door, keeping my head low in case he's waiting with a gun. I press my ear against it. The cold paint sends a shiver through me. Mindful of my own breathing I listen, trying to use the yoga techniques I'd learned to stay calm, but since being sick, I've skipped a few classes and my awareness of the silence outside elicits a rising panic.

I look around the bathroom, searching for an escape. There's a small, uncovered window close to the ceiling, but it looks barely big enough to fit my shoulders through, even if I could reach it.

I can't find another exit, and I imagine Dale waiting for me on the other side of the window, ready to grab me and drag me back inside as I try to wriggle my way out.

From my limited view from the bathroom, I can see the house hooks around like a "U", exposing the second story window across from the bathroom. There's a square window on the third story that looks like a loft window. It has outdoor shutters across the glass, just like the ones I noticed when I entered the house. But there's an uneven gap, slashed open like a wound between the window and the shutter. The shutter is broken, but it's too far away from the bathroom I've trapped myself in to use as an escape. Even if I got all the way to the third story, there would be plenty of time for Dale to intercept my escape.

I clutch Ashlee's necklace. Is this how she died? Huddled alone in the bathroom, waiting for Dale to break down the door?

I hope it was over before she realized what was happening.

Until now, I'd thought the cancer was the worst way I could die, but now I know I was wrong. A quick death that didn't give you a chance to say goodbye to the people you love and tell them the things you should've said was even worse.

Regardless of how I was going to die, not knowing what happened to Ashlee was worse.

I glance at the blood on the cabinet again, wishing there was a way to find out whether it's hers.

It comes to me slowly in the silence, the beginnings of a plan. I close my eyes, deciding whether I can go through with it. I would have to be fully committed to seeing it through—if I even hesitated for an instant it could give Dale the chance to end me. When I'm sure I can do it, I take Ashlee's necklace and wrap it around my neck, my fingers fiddling with the tiny clasp until I feel it hook onto the eye.

"I will not die here," I whisper to myself, needing to hear

the words out loud.

My voice makes me feel less alone, reminding me I'm still breathing, that I can still make choices.

I won't let Dale Carmot scare me. I won't be another silent victim, and I will *not* go quietly.

If I fight back, perhaps I can win. He's stronger, and knows the house better, but I have traits that can help me too. I'm level-headed, and I know he'll almost certainly underestimate me. I can use that to my advantage.

What he doesn't know is that when you're dying, the rules change—if I get out of here, I'm dead anyway.

I have nothing to lose.

I pull the showerhead loose from its holder. It's not enough to kill him, but it should stun him while I run to the kitchen and find something sharp to finish him with.

My hand rests on the door handle as I pull back the lock, releasing it gently so that Dale can't hear it open.

My voice is steadier, stronger as I call out, "Hello?"

There's no answer, but I can sense him there in the dark, waiting for me to come out so that his game can begin.

"Dale!" I call, answering his challenge by using his name. If a game is what he wants, I'll just have to win. If he leaves me with no other choice, I *will* kill him. "Let's talk about this."

Maybe I'll kill him anyway after everything he's put me through, to make sure he can't hurt anyone else.

I'm about to open the door when suddenly the room is pitched in darkness.

I snap the pin back in place, locking myself inside the bathroom again.

I know the lock won't keep him out if he wants to come in, but it's a barrier, and at least I can hear if he tries to get inside.

My hand finds the light switch in the dark and I flick it off and back on again to test it.

The darkness persists—he's cut the power.

I sit against the wall, thinking about what I should do next. The window's too high, and even if I managed to get it open, it'd probably be loud enough for him to stop me before I got very far.

I stroke the *A* of Ashlee's necklace. "Whatever he did to you, he won't get away with it," I whisper, kissing the pendant and sealing the promise.

When we were kids, Ashlee kept every promise she made to me, even if it meant getting into trouble, like the time she promised not to tell our mom that I broke her favorite mug. Even though Ashlee was punished for it, she took the rap until I came clean.

Dale's voice breaks through the silence. It's close enough that for a moment it feels as if his words are coming from inside my head.

"You can't stay in there forever, and I've got as long as it takes to wait for you to come out."

21

Chapter 21

Oscar

Now

"I didn't realize you went with Ashlee to the gala," said Oscar. Had she been vague on purpose?

Verity glanced at him. "Ashlee was angry with me. We fought in the car."

"Why?"

"It was stupid. She lost her temper, and I was too stubborn to set things right, so she went in alone while I sat in my car trying to figure out what to do next."

"Did you go inside?" asked Oscar.

Verity shrugged. "I was there as Ashlee's guest. I doubt I would've been allowed in without her to check our names off—I was probably listed as a plus-one, not even a name—so I waited in my car. It sounds ridiculous, but I was crying and I didn't want to drive until I had calmed down." She looked away, embarrassed.

"How long did you wait?"

"Maybe thirty minutes. I thought she might come back so we could sort out our fight. I was about to drive off when I saw her walk out of the front doors. Dale followed her onto the lawn. He walked outside right after she did and it looked like he was watching her."

"Did he talk to her?"

"When she walked toward my car, he called out to her. She turned and looked at him, but she didn't stop."

"Did you hear what he said?"

"No. He was too far away, but he might've been asking her something. I think she replied. I saw her mouth moving."

"What did she say?"

Verity shrugged helplessly. "I couldn't hear anything—"

"Was Ashlee smiling, or did she look upset when Dale spoke to her?"

"She was a little agitated maybe." She looked unsure. "I don't think Ashlee knew him very well. She got in my car and we joked about the guy following her, but I think he creeped her out. She kept looking back after she got in the car, and she didn't use his name when she talked about him. I know he's semi famous in the business world, but I didn't know who he was until Ashlee went missing."

"So that's why you think Dale knows where she is?"

"No."

"Okay," said Oscar, confused. "Then why do you think it was him?"

"Usually Ashlee would apologize and try to fix things, but she was...preoccupied."

Verity reached for a glass of water, the trolley just out of

149

range. Oscar handed it to her.

"Thanks," she said, taking a sip. "Dale watched her get into the car before he went back inside, and I joked that she had a secret admirer. She kind of laughed and said it was a creepy way to show you liked someone."

She stopped chewing on her thumbnail absently. "I thought our fight was forgotten, so I unclipped my seat belt, ready to go back inside with her, and she flipped out. She told me to go home. I offered to drop her back at her place, but she said she had to go back inside, and she'd call an Uber later." Verity stopped, taking a moment to compose herself. "I shouldn't have left her, but it felt like she suddenly didn't want me there. I think she came back to the car to tell me to go home. If I'd taken her home, she'd probably still be here."

"Ashlee's a grown woman," said Oscar, careful to use the present tense. "You can't make her do something she doesn't want to."

"Probably not," said Verity, "but I didn't even try. I was annoyed at her for storming off, only to come back and get annoyed with me all over again. So, when she got out of the car, I let her go, even though I wanted to talk to her and sort things out."

Verity looked suddenly tired and excused herself, saying she needed to rest.

Oscar wished he had something comforting to say, but the nurse hadn't returned with news about the necklace yet. "I'll ask Detective Payneham if he knows what happened to the necklace and see if the nurse found anything," said Oscar, closing the door on his way out.

His phone buzzed, the screen lighting up with a message from Steve.

Dad's awake. He's asking for you.

Oscar typed back, thumbs racing over the keys.

Where were you this morning?

Sorry, Oz. I guess I forgot.

Oscar had figured as much, but it didn't matter—Bill was awake.

Heading there now. See u soon.

He pocketed the phone and stopped at the front desk to ask if there was any news about the necklace. The nurse who had promised to investigate apologized and said they'd been busier than usual, that she'd looked in Verity's things and hadn't found it.

Oscar took the elevator to his dad's room, bracing himself for how Bill might look. It'd take more than a day for him to look like himself again, but part of Oscar expected to walk in there and see Bill sitting up in bed, telling them all to stop making such a fuss.

The lingering smell of hot pumpkin soup filled the room. The patients who were well enough to eat must've just finished lunch. Steve was already there, standing over their father, studying him as if trying to answer a perplexing question. Oscar noticed Bill's food tray was untouched.

"Oz, you made it," said Steve, shifting to make room.

Oscar watched Steve's elbow catch the tray, sending it off balance. Oscar tried to stop it from teetered over the edge, his gammy knee slowing him. On a regular day he would've caught it, but today the tray toppled to the floor, dumping soup and a plate of rice and green beans as it went.

Steve looked at his shoes, which had caught a lot of the mess, and tsked at Oscar. "These shoes are expensive, little brother."

Oscar was incredulous—it was just like Steve to worry about his shoes over Bill's lunch. "*You* knocked the tray."

Steve frowned and wiped his shoes down with a napkin.

Oscar forgot the spill as Bill's eyes fluttered open, a broken blue-gray without the golden hues of his own.

Chapter 22

Verity

Then

I wake suddenly, expecting to be at home in my own bed. As my eyes open, the sensation of the cold, ceramic sting of the bathroom tiles returns in a rush. How long have I been out for? My mouth is dry, my back stiff from lying down for too long. It feels like I might've been lying here passed out for days.

I move my hands beneath me, but the tiles from the bathroom are gone and all I feel is something soft. As my eyes adjust to the light I notice warm sheets and a pillow with a crisp case. I push myself up onto my hands, my head still spinning from whatever drugs Dale gave me. I wait until my head adjusts to being upright and the spinning stops a little before surveying the room.

The walls are bare and eggshell white. Other than the bed

with the luxurious sheets and cover, I could be inside an expensive display home. Outside, there are shutters on the window. They're drawn, casting a shadow across the inside of the room.

I don't have any way of checking what day it is, or the time, but my body clock is telling me that it's too late in the day to be sleeping.

I look instinctively toward the door, but that's shut too, and my first thought is to open it and make sure I can get outside. I notice a textured section of wall beside the door, thin lines engraved into the smooth surface. As I look closer, nausea rises in my throat. It isn't a texture...it looks like fingernails have been dragged across the wall, gouging the plaster. My stomach sinks.

I must have dozed off in the bathroom, and when I did, Dale came in and moved me here.

Why didn't I wake up?

I calculate how much I had to drink. It probably wasn't enough to knock me out, but Dale could've slipped something into my drink throughout the night.

I edge my way off the bed, trying to ignore a headache. The carpet is spongy under my bare feet. I look for my shoes, but they aren't under the bed, or anywhere else in the room. Maybe Dale took them?

I go to the door, wrapping my fingers tentatively around the handle with a wave of déjà vu. I remember Dale's threat from outside the bathroom. *You can't stay in there forever.* He must've had the key all along. He was playing with me, like a fox waiting to see if a rabbit will venture out of its burrow. Maybe he wanted to see if I'd try to escape?

I listen, hoping for a hint of noise to tell me where Dale is, but it's quiet. He probably has a key for this room too. The handle is cold in my hand and I'm worried that turning it will confirm I'm locked in. Why did he leave me here? Maybe he has decided to let me go, and the comfortable bed and some sleep were a peace offering.

I try again to remember what happened. I walked through the door hoping I would find out what happened to Ashlee, but my memory is hazy. I still feel hungover, and my headache intensifies when I try to think.

Whether the pain in my head is from last night or from the cancer, I can't tell.

I don't have time to worry about that now. The array of pills I'm supposed to take are in the medicine cabinet at home.

I close my eyes and listen, trying to guess what's happening outside of the room. Is Dale waiting patiently for me to wake up?

I could call out, see if he responds, but I don't want him to know I'm awake.

I look toward the door, but the little push lock is subtle and looks almost the same whether it's locked or unlocked.

If Dale has locked the door, it's probably locked from the outside. I get down on my knees and bring my head to the ground, trying to see through the gap under the door, searching for shoes, a shadow, anything to tell me what I'm up against. Something touches my foot and I jump away instinctively.

When I look down there's nothing there. I must've bumped the edge of the doorframe. I'm playing into his game. He doesn't need to be close to get at me—he's already inside my head.

When I think about all the ways he could hurt me, it's

another reminder that dying might not be the worst thing.

I breathe evenly, trying to steady my thumping heart, which feels as if it's lodged inside my throat, blocking my airway.

I reach around my neck and find Ashlee's chain. I hold the letter A while I gather the courage to turn the handle.

The handle yields and I open the door slowly, trying not to make too much noise. I peer outside, pulling myself through the crack in the door to get a better look.

The house is quiet. There's no sign of Dale in the hallway.

I trace the A under my fingertips, reminding myself I need to go on. Having her necklace helps me feel closer to her, giving me a purpose.

With false courage, I put one foot in front of the other until I'm running for the front door. I can see the outline ahead, the promise of freedom.

By the time I reach the front of the house, there's still no sign of Dale. I fall against the doorframe and try to work the handle, expecting it to give like the last one, but it doesn't budge.

I try freeing the lock and retry the handle. It's overridden by a dead lock; only the key will open it.

I'm trapped inside.

Fighting to keep my growing panic at bay, I search the house for an open window, but the windows I find are all securely locked and shuttered. I pick one at random—the living room—I need to break the glass.

Something about the room feels different from the night before. As I look around, I realize that all the pretty furnishings splashed with ambient light from the night before look plain in the daylight. For a moment I wonder if I'm in a different house, but the layout is the same. Perhaps the room looked elevated because Dale slipped something in my drink, altering my perception. Maybe that's why I'm having trouble remembering everything that happened.

I eye the closed window and raise my elbow, ready for the impact. I summon my strength and drive my elbow into the glass as hard as I can, but the window remains intact. Pain rips through my arm anyway, and I know there will be a bruise.

With the window plan a complete failure, I need a Plan B. I go through the other rooms one at a time, searching for something to use as a weapon, nervous and expecting to find Dale in one of them. My nerves don't settle when I reach the last room. It's as if he's gathered everything that could be used as a weapon and removed it, like the house has been prepared for this game, to stop me from escaping.

He never intended for me to leave.

As I move down the hallway I find one more bedroom with charcoal gray pillows and a matching cover. It is separate from the other rooms, and looks masculine and simple. The bed is made up—this is probably Dale's room. There is no sign of the Terminator collectibles he told me about. Maybe that was a lie too, or maybe he keeps them at another house. I look inside to see if his window is shuttered—if it *is* his room, I'm hoping he's kept the window open for some air. Disappointment overrides my hope when I see the familiar slats covering the glass. The window is lower in this room, larger. I try it anyway, but like the others, it's locked.

Men's clothing hangs in the closet. A suit, chinos, and a couple of shirts, finishing the display home look for an upmarket bachelor pad.

I take one of the shirts from a hanger and wrap it around my bare foot, wishing there were shoes I could borrow in the barren closet to protect myself from the impact. I steel myself and ram my foot into the glass, the two colliding with a heavy thud. The glass holds and I try again with the same result.

I let out a scream of frustration, kicking out at the reinforced glass over and over.

There's no way out. I'm trapped.

23

Chapter 23

Oscar

Now

"Dad?" said Oscar, unsure how close to stand at his father's bedside. Bill had never been an affectionate person, avoiding displays of sentimentality and emotional outbursts, and Oscar doubted a near-death experience would change that.

"Steve?" called Bill, ignoring Oscar.

"I'm here," said Steve, shooting Oscar a look as he stepped forward.

"What happened?" asked Bill, as if the day before was forgotten. "It can't be good if you've been here twice in as many days."

"You had a heart attack," said Steve matter-of-factly. "A pretty big one."

"Ahh," scoffed Bill. "It can't have been too bad, or I wouldn't still be here, would I?"

Steve shrugged, as if to say that was Bill's call.

A nurse entered the room, stopping short when she saw food across the floor. "Oh no," she said. "I'll get someone in to clean that up. Would you like something else to eat?"

"Yeah, I'll have a steak if you've got one hiding under those little plastic trays," said Bill, eliciting a laugh.

"I don't think it's on the menu today."

"Maybe tomorrow then," said Bill, as the nurse took his pulse and checked his vitals.

"How are you feeling? I think you gave everyone a bit of a scare."

"I feel good," said Bill. Oscar had never seen him admit to feeling sick, but he never said he felt good either, which meant he probably felt awful.

The nurse checked the graph on the machine that was monitoring Bill's heart rate and left.

"Well?" said Bill, his voice gravelly.

"Well, what?" asked Oscar while Steve was tapping on his phone, too distracted to notice that Bill was looking right at him.

Bill scoffed. "How the hell did I have a heart attack? I felt fine. Aren't you supposed to get pain shooting down your arm or something?"

"Not always." Oscar looked to Steve for help, but from the expression on his face, Steve was dealing with problems of his own.

"Everything okay?" asked Oscar, turning his attention to his brother.

"Yeah. Uh, it's just..."

He stopped, interrupted by a new face.

Oscar turned around, seeing the last person he expected

to see. His mother stood in the doorway, her face worn and defeated, breaking the timeless image he had kept from his childhood.

24

Chapter 24

Verity

Then

Eventually I give up, holding my foot gingerly, willing the throbbing to ease. Dale hasn't come running despite the noise, so maybe he's not home.

I circle the house like a caged lion, frustrated and trapped. I still can't hear Dale and there's no clock to know how long he's been gone. This wasn't a peace offering like I'd hoped—if he wanted to make up for last night, he would've left the door open and let me slip out quietly.

As time passes, I wonder if the blood in the bathroom was left by the girl before me. Maybe there were more before her too, and Ashlee and I are just a couple more in a line of many. I balk at the thought that if I don't make it out alive and tell someone, there could be more to come. The blood tells me that the last girl probably didn't survive the game, and I know it's only a matter of time before he kills me too.

I feel grief for the next girl if I don't stop the cycle now.

I'm at the bathroom door again, hesitating. The last time I was here, I ended up locked inside. I force myself to enter and go to the basin to splash my face and drink some water, cupping my hands as it spurts from the tap. My eyes are drawn to the blood on the cabinet again. It's a grim reminder that last night wasn't a dream. How could the police miss it, almost brown now but still obvious against the white?

If they test the blood and it's not Ashlee's, will they give up on her completely?

Irrationally, I wish if Dale was here to tell me who it belongs to. *If he's going to kill me, what does it matter what I know?*

I splash my face again with cool water. I have to stay calm and think. If I'm going to survive, I need to be one step ahead. Without Dale here, I have free rein of the house—there might be more than Ashlee's necklace and a smear of blood to find.

I need to leave a small clue that I was here, something Dale can't clean up after he kills me, but subtle enough that he won't know I've hidden it. That way, if the police search the house looking for me—or the next girl—they'll have a better chance of catching Dale.

I return to the bedroom with renewed purpose. He probably kept Ashlee here too.

I sit on the bed and hug the pillow, wondering what Ashlee would've done. Now that I'm here, now that I can see what she might've seen before she disappeared, I try to piece together the sequence of events. The pain permeates my whole body at the thought of her, much worse than the throbbing in my elbow and foot.

I thought that knowing what happened to her would make

it easier, but now that I know she was here, I have more questions than before. The closure I hoped I'd find seems further away.

Time passes and Dale still hasn't returned. My desire to know what happened is replaced with a need for retribution.

Ashlee's necklace proves she was here, not that Dale killed her. The police would probably write it off as a fling; she took it off along with the rest of her clothes and forgot about it.

I return to the bathroom to see what else I can find. The showerhead is lying inside the shower cubicle, off the holder, and I curse myself for not ripping it from the wall and pounding it against his head.

I step inside the shower, trying to pull it free. Without another option, it will have to suffice as a weapon. I'll wait behind the front door until he returns, and when he does, I'll strike him in the face.

I'll show Dale Carmot what it feels like to know you're dying, the despair and anticipating of it coming whether you're ready for it or not.

The bathroom door slams, the noise echoing through the shower. I hear the click of a lock. I'm back to where I was the night before.

"Hello?" I call. "Dale?"

He doesn't answer, but I can hear him moving around outside, his feet shuffling back and forth. How long has he been listening out there? He circles again, his presence ominous, like a skittish dog that could snap at any moment.

"What're you going to do with me?" I ask with false bravado. "What did you do to Ashlee?"

I don't expect an answer, but I ask anyway. Maybe his arrogance will encourage him to brag about what he's done.

The next words are heavy on my soul, a question I'm not sure I could ask if I wasn't running out of time. "Is she dead?"

The shuffling stops. I don't hear him for a while and then he taps on the door three times. "That's why you were in the parking lot. You want to know what happened to that dead girl everyone thinks I killed?"

I swallow, trying not to let his words get to me. *The dead girl.*

"You killed her, didn't you?"

His voice is still close, as if he's whispering in my ear despite the door between us. "Why do you care?"

I step back and fight the tears threatening to unravel me. He can't see my weak spots or he'll exploit them. I have to give him something to make him think he's broken me, but I won't give him my tears. I need to give him a reason to tell me what he did.

"She's my sister."

He snorts. "I didn't expect that."

"Are you going to kill me too?"

"That depends."

I swallow harder, but my throat has gone dry. He didn't deny it. He has almost admitted to killing her. Is he still trying to scare me, or does he want me to know that I'm going to die too?

"Depends on what?" I ask, hating myself for sounding hopeful, as if I can do something to make him spare me.

"On you."

25

Chapter 25

Oscar

Now

Oscar wasn't sure what to call Kiko—it'd been so long since he'd called her Mom, and she hadn't been a mother to him for more years than he'd been alive. She might be completely different to the mother he knew since he last saw her.

He looked at her, trying to figure out if she still saw him as a son, or if she gave up on being his mother when she walked out of his life.

Oscar shuffled out of the way, making a path for Kiko to reach Bill. Whatever Oscar felt, it wasn't his business if Bill spoke to her or not.

Bill sounded as surprised as Oscar felt when he saw Kiko, even managing a smile. "Well, this is unexpected," he said, and then under his breath, "but you shouldn't be here."

Kiko took a hold of Bill's hand, grasping it as if she never wanted to let go. "I didn't know if you were going to make it," she said, looking back at Oscar. "So, I had to see you."

Kiko hadn't tried to contact Oscar until he was grown, and by then it was too late. He ignored her calls, telling himself he didn't need her anymore. The truth was, he was afraid to invite her back into his life in case she left again.

Since he was eleven, Oscar had been building his own scaffolding, giving himself the things he couldn't rely on from his parents. He'd spent too much time trying to figure out why Kiko had left, wondering why he wasn't enough for her to stay.

Oscar's knee ached, threatening to buckle if he continued to stand. He had to get out of there, find somewhere to rest for a moment.

"You okay?" called Bill.

"Yeah," said Oscar. "Just need to find something to bandage my knee." He looked at the mess of food on the floor.

Kiko reached out as he passed, but he didn't stop, moving around her. He was relieved when the door to Bill's room closed softly behind him.

His knee became increasingly heavy as it seized, but he kept walking as Kiko opened the door to slip through. He cursed himself for looking behind, for making eye contact with her. He couldn't outpace her without looking like he was running from her.

Kiko's voice stopped him with the name she'd used when he was a boy. "Oscar-kun. How have you been?"

He had forgotten that's what she called him. He'd gotten good at blocking thoughts of his family, but it'd taken a long time to perfect.

"I know you're angry. You have every right to be upset, but

I left for your own good." She was looking at him, pleading with him to understand, but he set his jaw defiantly. "I don't expect you to understand that, but it's true."

"I was eleven. You left me with an alcoholic," said Oscar, choosing the parts of his dad that he could deal with, leaving out the violence and emotional outbursts usually directed at him.

She sighed. "You're right, but your dad did his best. Look how you turned out." She smiled, proud of the man her son had become.

"How did I turn out?" asked Oscar. His mother had no idea beyond superficial observations. She didn't know that he'd struggled through nights of despair, or that his son didn't survive infancy. There were things he'd needed a mother to help him get through. Things she wasn't there for.

His anger rose, fueled by everything she'd missed. Yes, he had a good career and a girlfriend he couldn't have imagined loving as much as he did, but before that, he'd been broken. What Kiko saw now mightn't have happened if Caroline hadn't stepped in and taught him he could be loved. Caroline became a mother to him, not out of a sense of biological responsibility, but because she chose to.

"He didn't raise me. I raised myself. I cleaned the house and made sure he ate. The kids at school don't understand when you say you can't go to the party because you have laundry to do, and a father who might pass out and die in his own vomit if you're not there to turn him over."

Oscar took a moment to reset—it wouldn't do any good to get angry about Kiko's failures as a mother. It was already too late. "He was worse after you left. He drank more. It was like he couldn't figure out why he was doing any of it. He gave up completely. It didn't matter that I was still there."

"I'm sorry," said Kiko softly, humbled by the truth. "I didn't know what else to do. I was so lost after Lila died. Everything fell apart."

"Maybe. But that didn't mean you should've left me there holding everything together." He wrapped a hand around his knee, trying to stop the ache.

Kiko watched, grimacing at his pain as if it were her own. "Is your knee still…"

"Yeah," he said. The car had clipped him when he'd tried to push Lila out of its path. He had gone flying across the street from the impact, his leg shattering when he landed. He'd downplayed his pain through the surgeries and physio as they tried to piece his knee back together, feeling like he had no right to talk about it, to even feel it, when Lila wasn't there to feel anything. The pain reminded him he was alive, that he'd fared better than Lila.

"Can we talk?" asked Kiko.

"We are talking."

"I mean, can we grab a coffee or something?"

If Oscar was going to have a conversation with Kiko, he'd have to ask the question that had plagued him since the day she packed up her things and walked out. "Why did you leave?"

"What?"

"Tell me why you and Steve left me there with Dad, and I'll have coffee with you."

Kiko looked at her son, the question hanging between them. Even now she couldn't answer.

"I deserve to know," said Oscar.

She tried to cover her hesitation by looking right at him. Oscar could feel her thinking—she was about to lie. "After

169

Lila died I was a mess. I needed to sort myself out, so I took my things and left," she said.

She *was* a mess after Lila died, but that wasn't why she'd left him there alone.

"You took Steve. Why him and not me? I needed you just as much as he did, maybe more because I was younger."

"I don't know why," said Kiko lamely. "I guess I thought he could take care of himself—he was two years older. You might've dealt with the disruption worse than he did, and he wasn't doing so well at school anyway. I didn't know where I was going, or where I'd end up. I didn't know how to care for you and still find work so I could feed you."

"What you did was worse," said Oscar.

"What I did was awful," she said, a rawness in her voice. "But you don't understand. I couldn't stay."

He turned and walked away, conscious of how difficult it was to ignore her words behind him, wondering how she'd been able to keep going when she abandoned him.

26

Chapter 26

Verity

Then

"What do you want from me?" I ask, watching the door handle, expecting it to jiggle and Dale to burst through.

The showerhead doesn't feel like a weapon in my hands anymore, just a weak imitation compared to the weapons Dale might have. I remember the pills I saw in the bathroom cabinet and have an idea—I can turn them into a more reliable weapon if I can get Dale to ingest some.

I need something to administer the mix with, but I have to move quickly. I place the showerhead on the side of the basin and sift through the cabinet. Grabbing the pills, I look for something I can use to administer them once I've crushed them, hoping he doesn't burst through the door.

"I want you to tell me what you think happened to your sister," says Dale, his voice cutting through the silence and startling me.

Keep him talking. Keep him out there.

I need to time my exit flawlessly, so that I can catch him by surprise and administer the concoction before he realizes what's happening. I don't want to talk to him about Ashlee right now but I need to know where he is, and that means keeping his attention so he doesn't wander too far away.

"You brought Ashlee here after the gala. She never spoke about you, so I doubt you were dating. Maybe you met through work?"

I wait for him to answer, but he doesn't. I know he's listening because I can hear his shoes pass by the door.

"She wouldn't have seen you for what you are because she was kind and too trusting. She never had the best survival instincts, but that's why you chose her, right?"

There are no syringes, but I recall a client explaining how they made a syringe out of things they found around the house when they needed a hit. I search the cabinet and find a pen, which should work perfectly. I empty the case as I talk before cutting a Q-tip at an angle with some nail scissors, testing its sharpness before fitting it over the plastic shaft.

He laughs at my assessment of Ashlee. "Your Ashlee sounds very nice, but that's not the Ashlee I knew."

I almost lose my hold on the syringe, catching it before it clatters to the ground.

It's the first time he's admitted to knowing Ashlee, and it doesn't sound like there's any love lost.

I find an earplug—rubbery and squishy—in the back of the cupboard. I try not to think about the noises he was trying to block out.

"Did she realize what you were going to do to her?" I ask.

My hands are shaking, but I cut the rubber carefully to fit the inside of the pen, stabbing the metal tip of the pen through to make a plunger. If I fill the pen too much, the rubber will probably move, so I need to put just enough in to administer.

He laughs, making what I'm about to do so much easier to justify.

I crush the pills with the end of the bottle and add water before I soak them up with the syringe. "I hope she gave you hell."

It's almost time.

"You're wrong about Ashlee," he says. "I didn't kill her."

"You don't expect me to believe you, do you?"

"I don't expect you to believe anything. You didn't know your sister like I did. She wasn't as innocent as you think."

"How did you know Ashlee?"

I clutch the syringe in my hand and get ready to turn the doorknob, fighting the fatigue that's creeping in.

I need to act soon, before I miss my opportunity to act at all.

27

Chapter 27

Oscar

Now

Oscar left Kiko standing there, their conversation unfinished, the same way she'd left him all those years ago. He focused on Verity—he'd made a promise to find out about Ashlee's necklace, and he was going to keep it.

When he was close to the exit, away from the echo of the hospital walls, he called Logan Payneham. Payneham answered on the fourth ring, just before Oscar gave up.

"Hello?" The detective sounded impatient, giving Oscar the impression he'd been interrupted.

"It's Oscar de la Nuit."

"Oscar, what can I do for you?" he asked, his tone hard to read.

"Verity asked me to follow up on a necklace she found at Dale Carmot's house. She thinks it belonged to Ashlee."

"There was no record of a necklace found at the scene," said Detective Payneham, the slight rustle of wind from his end suggesting he was outdoors walking against the breeze. "And Verity didn't mention it when we spoke with her."

"Are you sure it wasn't there?" asked Oscar.

"I've been through the inventory at least a dozen times."

"She was suffering a head injury. I'm surprised she remembered it this soon," said Oscar. "She said it was around her neck when she fell from the roof. She thought it might've been recovered as evidence. I'm wondering if the clasp came undone somewhere in the house?"

"There was definitely no necklace," the detective said, his tone firm. "She suffered a head injury. Maybe she imagined it."

Oscar ignored the detective's comment. "She wasn't wearing it when the ambulance arrived?"

"If she was, it would've been bagged. Look, I'm combing through Dale's house now, checking where they landed when they came off the roof. I can't believe we didn't know about this place. He didn't have it listed as an asset. He said he kept it quiet because of the reporters meddling in his personal life. Did you talk to him?"

"Yeah. I've talked with both of them, and I have a few questions."

"I might be here a while." The breeze rushed through the phone as the detective paused. "Can you get here in the next twenty minutes?"

"You don't want to do this over the phone?" asked Oscar, walking through the hospital entrance.

"We can if you like, but I'd still prefer if you came by. The address is 555 Leland Street."

Oscar put the directions into his phone and told Detective Payneham he'd be there in a few minutes, ending the call.

When he pulled up at the house, the outside looked clean and well kept except for a right-side gutter, askew from the fall.

Detective Payneham greeted Oscar outside with a quick handshake. "Doctor," he said.

"Detective," answered Oscar automatically. "How's the search going?"

"We found a couple of things we didn't expect. I've got people scouting the place to see what else they can find."

"What are they looking for?"

"We found blood in the bathroom. Over the cabinet and inside the shower. He tried to clean it up, but he's a shitty housekeeper. Made it look clean enough, but it's pretty hard to scrub away blood."

"Whose blood was it?"

"We don't know yet. We're waiting for the samples to come back from the lab. What'd Dale have to say? Did you get a confession out of him for me?" asked Detective Payneham.

They'd probably establish the blood type and see if it was a match with Ashlee. Hopefully she was one of the rarer types, and not O positive like thirty-five percent of the population—it was too common to draw conclusions.

Looking at the luxurious modern house, Oscar got a sense of just how much money Dale had, and this was just a holiday home. "He admits Verity was here, and that he threatened her. He says he was trying to scare her because she was spying on him, but that he wasn't going to kill her."

"Hard to prove anything else when she's still alive—why would he say otherwise, right?" said Detective Payneham.

"Yeah," agreed Oscar.

"What I want to know is how they ended up flying off the roof like a couple of penguins," said Detective Payneham skeptically.

Oscar had wondered the same. "Can I take a look inside?"

"What? You think you'll find something we couldn't?"

Oscar couldn't tell if he was joking.

"I was hoping to get a sense of the kind of person Dale is. You know, how he decorates his home, what he keeps," said Oscar. Seeing Dale's house could provide clues about Dale's intention.

The detective smiled. "I was hoping you'd say that," he said.

So that was why he'd asked Oscar to drive there.

Oscar stepped inside, imagining how Verity might've felt walking into the beautifully lit house that felt like it belonged to a movie set—it was pretty, but it lacked any warmth.

Dale was meticulous. From the distance between the chairs in the kitchen, to the layout of the lounge room, it was all optimized, with everything in a designated place. Oscar bet the lights ran on a timer and that Dale had the heating turn itself on before he arrived on wintry days.

"This isn't his primary residence. It most likely represents a piece of who he is," said Oscar, looking around at the bare walls and brand-new furniture. There was nothing personal, no pictures, just a 3D Star Wars model of Darth Vader's helmet artfully attached to the wall and a framed Terminator poster on the second floor. Was Dale's home as bare as his holiday house?

"Like an alter ego?"

"Something like that," said Oscar distractedly. What had

177

happened here? Why did Dale lock Verity inside? He wasn't sure if Ashlee was ever here, but he'd promised to try and find out, so he waded deeper into the house, feeling like he was moving into the center of a spider's web.

"This place looks pristine," said Oscar, noticing the shuttered windows. Verity would've searched for a way to escape, but there wasn't much to find. "I'm not sure it feels like somewhere he'd take someone if he was planning to kill them. I think it's somewhere he goes to feel powerful," said Oscar. "It's well-tended. I'd say it's more likely somewhere he takes dates for the weekend. There's a pool out the back and a tennis court."

"It looks pretty cold to me. The guy's a control freak," said Detective Payneham. "There's nothing to break, and there are outdoor shutters, so he can lock them in. Maybe the money's just not doing it for him anymore and he needed the next thrill—something his money couldn't buy."

The shutters could be a sign that he likes privacy, or maybe it was a security measure—it looked like the kind of place that would attract break-ins, and it sounded like it wasn't used very much.

"I think he's more likely to celebrate his successes here. The money and everything else that comes with it. He's not overly ornate, but still likes to show he has money. He's proud. I noticed it in photos. Not just the photo shoots, but the everyday snaps. His clothes are the same. Expensive. Mostly simple with a detail highlighting some flamboyance which shows his more temperamental and perhaps unpredictable side."

"You think he brings women here to impress them?"

Oscar shrugged. He wouldn't assume who Dale brought back

here, but the whole place was designed to impress—minimalistic luxury. Almost everything looked simple and elegant, but the furniture was clearly expensive and carefully selected, with featured accents highlighting his taste. The kitchen table was likely custom made for the space, shaped into a triangle with rounded corners. "Besides the necklace Verity mentioned and the blood in the bathroom, did you find anything to suggest that Ashlee was here?"

Detective Payneham scratched his nose with the back of a knuckle and hesitated, as if he'd shared everything he meant to and wasn't willing to give any more.

"Listen, I know you're busy, but Verity needs to know what happened to Ashlee before she dies," said Oscar.

"We're doing what we can."

"Is finding this place enough of a reason to put more resources into finding Ashlee? If Dale kidnapped her sister..." Oscar let the words hang.

"If she was here, something'll turn up. We're waiting to see what the blood sample tells us."

"Do you think it's Ashlee's?"

Air escaped between Detective Payneham's teeth, creating a whistle. "I wouldn't wanna say either way. Sometimes, you think a case'll turn out one way, and it turns up something different. Let's wait and see."

There was a lot more he needed to learn before Oscar would be satisfied with 'let's wait and see'. "Did anyone see Ashlee and Dale talking at the gala?"

"Yeah. Problem is, Ashlee spoke to a lot of people that night, so if we're going by that it could be anyone."

"But you talked to the party guests?"

"Yeah. At least the ones on the guest list and anyone they

179

brought with them."

Oscar had left early with Hayley, but the police hadn't called them, so he knew they'd skipped at least a few people. Maybe they'd ruled some guests out in other ways, but it made him wonder what else they'd missed.

"What stood out about Dale? Were there other suspects?"

The detective walked alongside Oscar. "We've had mixed messages about whether Dale and Ashlee left together. We got a tip just recently from someone saying they saw Dale and Ashlee leave around the same time."

"Together?"

"No. Within a few minutes of each other. But between then and the time she went missing, he probably knew where she was going, and he had the means to follow her."

"Do you think Ashlee left with Dale?" asked Oscar. He didn't get a chance to ask the last time they discussed it, but he was curious about the detective's theory.

"Looks like she caught a ride there with Verity, but we're not sure how she planned on getting home," said Detective Payneham. "All I can tell you is we're getting a lot of mixed messages. Most people are so focused on what they're doing that they don't really notice the details. The problem is they'd rather tell you anything than admit they don't know."

It didn't seem like Payneham knew what to think.

"Ashlee and Verity fought in the parking lot, so Verity never went inside," said Oscar, relaying what Verity had told him.

"That's what she says." Detective Payneham shrugged. "But that doesn't make it so."

"You don't believe her?"

"I didn't at first—we had to rule Verity out as a suspect. She said herself that they argued."

Since then, the detective's opinion seemed to have changed. "And now?"

"Verity's not a suspect anymore, but who knows what people are capable of? Verity's a bit..." He gestured with his hand, flat palm tipping back and forth like it was unbalanced. "I mean, who goes chasing after a murderer?"

Oscar came to a stop and looked the detective in the eye. "Someone with nothing to lose."

28

Chapter 28

Verity

Then

"Here's a little fact about your sister that I bet you didn't know," says Dale.

I listen through the door, terrified of what he might say.

"She sold drugs. Illegally."

The syringe almost falls from my hand. "No, Ashlee's a nurse. She wouldn't."

"That's why she was at my house. She was one of my reps, not officially, but she sold prescription drugs to people who couldn't get them from a GP. It's what we were discussing at the gala. I invited her to my house for the evening because she needed more product," said Dale. "We shared some wine, talked, and then she left."

He's lying. If that's all that happened, why was Ashlee's necklace in the back of his bathroom cabinet? You don't accidentally leave your jewelry at someone's house when you're visiting for an hour or two...unless you're setting them up.

I call him out on it, hoping he doesn't think well on his feet. He could still open the door at any moment, but he seems to enjoy making me squirm.

"You're saying you killed my sister over some pills? Ashlee doesn't sell drugs. She doesn't do drugs."

I don't say it, but I know that selling drugs illegally might be something she'd do if she thought she was helping people who needed them.

"You really don't know her, do you?" His laughter fills the hall. Pity laughter at my naivete. "Take the wrong kind of addict, looking for a high, and someone who has exactly what they want, and it's only a matter of time before something goes wrong, isn't it?"

He's lying.

If she really was selling drugs, I'd know. She didn't seem to have any extra cash, and she wasn't throwing money around or going on expensive trips.

"What were you supplying her with?" I ask, ignoring his comments. In my line of work, the best way to establish what really happened is to ask for details. Where were you before you fell down the stairs? How many times did they threaten to hit you before they followed through? How can you be sure the kids don't know that you take drugs when they're asleep?

"Just oxy."

He says it like I'm overreacting, like he's talking about buying milk and eggs. I look at the syringe in my hand, wondering if I've put enough in there for it to be effective. If he's selling drugs, he might be a user, which means he

183

might've built a tolerance. I could be preparing myself for a failed attack, but my eyes are growing heavy and if I don't do something, I've already lost.

I never told anyone I was meeting Wes for drinks. It would be too embarrassing to explain what happened if it went wrong, so no one knew where I went missing from. It seems insignificant now, but I hadn't wanted to admit to the friends I was too tired to talk to that I'd met someone on a dating site.

No one will look for me. The only people I see regularly enough to notice I'm gone are work colleagues and my doctor. How long would I be missing before someone realized it was anything more than a couple of sick days?

If I kill Dale and manage to escape, I'll either be a hero or a criminal. Will I still have a job, or will my clients jump ship so they don't have to be alone in a room with a murderer giving them advice on how to fix their problems? It doesn't matter—what matters is knowing that Dale won't be able to take from anyone else what he took from me.

"Why Ashlee? Why couldn't you find someone else to sell your drugs?"

"Why not Ashlee?"

What if I was wrong about Dale? Maybe a disgruntled customer killed her. But why would they do that if she was their link to the medication they wanted?

Why would Dale need to get rid of her?

Was she going to come clean and take him down too?

He probably won't tell me, but I ask anyway.

He denies killing her again, this time more emphatically. I don't expect a confession, but I'm hoping he'll give something away, that I can figure it out for myself.

He got her involved too deeply in something she couldn't

get out of, but why wouldn't the police tell me that if they knew what had happened? Did they have a deal with Dale? It would explain why Payneham wouldn't put more resources into finding her.

Dale surprises me by talking, offering information I didn't ask for. "The last time I saw Ashlee," said Dale, his voice shrinking, "was when she came to my house to get more product. I don't do that kind of business at my regular home." He stops and I wonder if he's walked away from the door, bored with the conversation. I strain my ears to listen for his footsteps, but I don't hear any. He starts speaking again. "She was great at selling, but she never wanted to follow the rules."

The Ashlee I knew always followed the rules. I can't imagine her breaking them.

"Any more questions before I open this door?" he asks, mocking me. I hear the lock click.

"Yeah," I say it in one long breath so I don't lose my nerve. "When were you planning on killing me?"

"I don't know," he says. "I'm enjoying our talk. Aren't you?"

I give him an answer he won't forget.

Chapter 29

Oscar

Now

"Who knows what people are capable of?"

The detective's comment seemed out of place given what Verity had been through. "What does that mean?"

Detective Payneham lifted his brows to his forehead in a quick gesture. "Well, she went home with the guy, didn't she? Even though she was convinced he killed her sister. I would've expected her to run the other way as soon as she saw him."

Oscar wondered what might be considered a standard way to act when your sister is missing and you know time's running out to find her.

What would he do in Verity's position if it had been his sister? He remembered Lila's braids dancing around her shoulders as she ran away squealing, avoiding being tagged. Despite being years younger, her speed always surprised him, weaving this way and that to avoid his outstretched hand.

"I told Verity to leave the policing to us," said Detective Payneham, suggesting that Oscar should do the same.

"She was worried about her sister. She doesn't know how long she has left to live, so she's probably panicking." Oscar had to open him up, make him see it from Verity's perspective. "Do you have family you're especially close with, Detective?"

"I guess that'd be my brother if anyone," said Detective Payneham.

"Okay. What would you do if he went missing?"

"That's different. I'm a cop. It's my job to get involved, find out what happened. It's what I'm trained to do."

"Verity is a case manager for a women's shelter. What do you think she's seen? She knows what people go through, the kinds of things that can happen at the hands of people you trust."

"Yeah, okay," conceded Detective Payneham. "I told her not to get involved. She's compromised the scene, and maybe the case we could've built against him."

Oscar cleared his throat. "You mightn't have known about the house if he didn't take her there. If anything, Verity led you to the answers."

The detective looked flustered. He couldn't decide whether to put his hands at his sides or on his hips. "If there was a crime committed and she contaminated the scene, she's probably ruined our case."

Oscar didn't respond—there was no point getting caught up in a discussion if Detective Payneham already had his mind made up.

"She might've set him up," said Detective Payneham.

"Why would she do that?" asked Oscar.

Detective Payneham walked, gesturing for Oscar to follow. "She was so sure he was guilty, that we should've charged him with Ashlee's murder. People will do pretty much anything to get what they want, especially when they think they're doing the right thing."

"I believe Verity when she says she wants to find her sister. If the wrong guy went to prison, it would mean that whoever was responsible would get away with it."

Oscar followed Detective Payneham to a bedroom that was thinly adorned. "We don't have a body," said Payneham. "There's no evidence that Ashlee's dead, just that she dis-appeared. I'm not a psychiatrist, but from what Verity said, I get the feeling she wants closure more than answers. She's running out of time—maybe she wants someone to pay for what happened."

Oscar looked around the room. Once. Twice. His eyes moved quickly. Too quickly. Like the rest of the house, the room looked unlived in, impersonal. If there weren't any blankets crumpled at the end of the bed, he'd have thought the room was unoccupied. "This is where Verity was," Oscar guessed.

"Yeah. She said she woke up here."

"Did you talk to her much before I interviewed her?" asked Oscar.

The detective shrugged. "I told her she could say as much as she wanted. She didn't say a lot, but she didn't seem bothered by me asking questions."

"Caroline said you wanted to make sure she was up for the task. Is that why you wanted an evaluation?"

"Something like that. We need to tick the boxes. Despite what Verity thinks, we want to solve this case. We're being cautious... not knowing what happened to her sister has affected Verity's recollection."

"Yeah," said Oscar absently. He wasn't sure that what happened to Ashlee had affected Verity's memory as much as the fall had.

"That, and, when you're dying..." Detective Payneham trailed off, letting Oscar fill in the blanks.

"Detective, are you hoping I'll be able to tell you whether Verity Casmere is capable of providing accurate information about her kidnapping, or do you want to know whether you should believe her account of what happened?"

"Can't we do both?"

"You're an experienced officer. You don't need my help to tell if someone's lying," said Oscar.

"Yeah, but I'm asking for a second opinion," said the detective. "Look around the room. Tell me what you see."

He wanted to know if Oscar was any good. He hadn't chosen Oscar himself, hadn't worked with him before—but Oscar had questions of his own he wanted answered.

"Do you think Dale's telling the truth?"

"He thinks Verity was setting him up," said Detective Payneham confidently.

"That's not what he said to me," said Oscar. "He said Verity was snooping around, so he wanted to scare her."

"If he told you Verity was there to set him up for Ashlee's murder, would you believe him?"

Oscar considered the question. He wasn't sure what he'd believe from Dale. "Is that what he said happened?"

"He said she tried to drug him."

"Did he also say he's addicted to oxy?" asked Oscar.

"How do you know?"

"I saw the pills when I talked to him. The sweats gave him

away. He was acting like he was in pain, but it didn't seem like pain. He wanted me to leave so he could get a hit. I had to end the interview because he couldn't focus."

What if the pills were a cover, and Dale was trying to avoid answering Oscar's questions? Oscar had seen avoidance tactics before. People used them to get their story together—cheating spouses were especially creative. He could probably get funding for a study on the correlation between creativity and propensity to cheat based on some of the stories he'd heard.

Oscar circled the room again in a soft arc, focusing on minute details. He stopped at the door when he saw what looked like scratch marks etched into the wall. "Did Verity do this?"

Detective Payneham shrugged. "I don't think so. It looks like they were here before."

"Ashlee?" asked Oscar.

The detective curled his lip. "Hard to say," he said. "We've swabbed it anyway."

Oscar placed his hands above the scratches, not quite touching the wall, angling his fingers to match the pattern until they fit perfectly. He drew attention to the fact that he looked like he was almost falling before his hand and the lines on the wall were in sync. "They look like scratches to me."

Detective Payneham sighed, glancing sideways at the wall.

"What if there were other women he kept locked up here?"

Detective Payneham's phone rang, killing the question.

He held up a finger. "Payneham," he said briskly into the receiver.

Oscar watched the detective's face change from a little bothered at the disruption to genuine surprise. "What?

Where?" He shot Oscar a look—*You're not gonna believe this.*

"Are you sure they're human?"

Logan Payneham's features dropped in resignation. He went to the wall, investigating the scratches more closely, looking at them with new eyes.

He didn't want to push, so Oscar waited until the call ended, giving Logan Payneham a chance to process whatever had just happened.

"I have to go," said the detective, his shoulders slumped more than before.

"Okay," said Oscar, already guessing what had happened before the detective confirmed it.

"They found a body."

30

Chapter 30

Verity

Then

It's silent outside the door. I poise my syringe. It is a snake, cornered and ready to strike, releasing its poison in a deadly display.

I might not make it, but I have to try. Dale doesn't know about my secret weapon—I just need to stick him with it before he sees it curled in my fist.

The handle turns and I throw the door open. He's waiting for me, lurching forward to catch my arm, anticipating that I'll try to run past him.

I don't.

I plunge the syringe into his upper arm, unable to reach his neck like I'd planned.

He cries out, surprised more than fearful as the makeshift syringe pierces his skin like an insect's stinger. The poison flows into his arm before he can swat the needle away.

I avoid eye contact, afraid I'll lose my nerve, and push past him. I know the front door's locked, that the probability of unlocking it before he catches me isn't good enough to try. I head for the stairs instead. If I saw what I think I did, then the upstairs window isn't shut properly, which means it might be the only way out of here.

I'm willing to shimmy my way down the gutter as far as I can and jump the rest of the way. I've seen videos of people landing similar jumps without serious injury and I have to believe I can do it too, because it might be my only option.

31

Chapter 31

Oscar

Now

"Is it Ashlee?"

Detective Payneham nodded slightly. "That's what they're thinking. I need to go to the morgue, so we're gonna have to call it for today."

Oscar scanned the room for the last time, placing everything in memory storage to process when he was alone.

"Mind if I come along?" he asked boldly.

"I don't know. I'm sure you've got lots to keep you occupied besides Verity Casmere and her sister. Could be good to focus on something else for a while," said Detective Payneham.

He was right—Oscar had been hyper focused on Dale, Verity, and Bill, and in the process he'd neglected Hayley. He'd already missed most of their weekend together, but these weren't usual work circumstances.

"When can you write up the report on Verity and Dale?" asked Payneham, interrupting Oscar's thoughts. "When Caroline said you'd be the right person for this job, I'll be honest with you, I wasn't sure. As far as I knew you were more interested in being a celebrity than being here on the ground. I saw you in the news. But I trust Caroline." He must be talking about the publicity he got after working with Jessica Green.

Oscar laughed at that, unable to help himself. He'd hated the publicity. He'd hated being a manager at Whitner too, at least the politics and the administration. He'd done it because he'd been nominated and he didn't want the job to go to the other candidate, who wanted the job for all the wrong reasons. It had never been a dream of his.

"I'm not done yet. I need to speak with them both again," said Oscar. So far, he only had a few hours of data to go by. It wasn't nearly enough to make a proper assessment for something this important.

"Isn't there a test or something you can do to find out if Dale's capable of killing?"

"There are a few," said Oscar. "No single test can tell me if someone's likely to have killed someone. It requires a considered assessment and a detailed personal history."

Oscar had the information that'd been gathered so far. He knew that Dale got into a bit of trouble when he was younger—mostly petty theft at his hometown convenience store in his teens, probably to see if he could get away with it rather than because he needed to for survival. After that, he straightened out and dabbled in a number of business ventures, amassing a fortune along the way.

He'd been taken to court a few times. Disgruntled employees claiming misconduct, and more recently, Ashlee's disappearance. So far, nothing had stuck, but if it *was* Ashlee's body they'd found, there'd be pressure on Payneham to provide answers.

Still, Oscar wasn't about to administer tests without the context to interpret the results just to make Payneham and the district attorney happy. He understood that Payneham was feeling the pinch, but hurrying things now for the sake of having them done wasn't going to help anyone—especially if they got it wrong.

"Well, what *can* you tell me?" asked Detective Payneham.

"Killers—if Dale is a killer—interpret things differently, but they don't necessarily know that. Standard self-report measures rely partly on the perception of the person answering the questions, but if their perception is off, and there's no incentive to answer honestly, it can skew the data."

"So, what are you going to do?" asked Payneham.

"I've got medical records and a general history. Once I've established a base line in his responses, probably an inkblot test and the revised Hare Psychopathy Checklist."

"You think he's a psychopath?"

"It's just the name of the scale," said Oscar. It still surprised him how many law enforcement officers and lawyers thought being a psychopath was a diagnosis. "I'm trying to find out whether Dale has antisocial tendencies, and figure out any behavioral patterns. That's all."

Oscar didn't know how they'd handled things when they were questioning Dale the first time, but this time he wanted a chance at some real answers for Verity's sake, even if it meant Payneham wouldn't ask him back as a consulting psychiatrist.

"Antisocial? You're trying to figure out if he doesn't like being around people?"

"It's more about how he treats other people," said Oscar. "But the trick to an accurate test is interpreting the results correctly."

"Okay," said the detective. "Then set up a time to get the information you need to interpret and let me know when you're done."

It was a classic knee-jerk reaction. When there was time no one wanted to rush things, but as soon as the pressure was on, the talk stopped and people started taking shortcuts.

"I warned Verity Casmere not to press Dale Carmot, and look where she ended up."

"Are you saying what he did was her fault?"

Detective Payneham looked uneasy. "It was stupid to chase after him. She should've known better, especially being sick. She's lucky he didn't...well, it could've been a lot worse."

"How do you think she got onto the roof if the house was locked up?"

"Looks like the shutter was broken."

"Couldn't have been easy getting to the loft in the first place," said Oscar.

"Retractable stairs. They were pulled down when we got here. It looks like she climbed up and got out through the window," said Detective Payneham.

Oscar went to the ladder and inspected it. It was half drawn, the rungs laid out. Oscar automatically looked for the string, but there wasn't one.

"How did she pull the ladder down?" he asked. "There's no cord."

"Not sure," said Detective Payneham, inspecting it himself. "She said she couldn't remember. Maybe it was already like that." He checked the time on his phone. "I really gotta go."

"Yeah," said Oscar, following him outside.

The detective turned around suddenly, as if something had just occurred to him. "She's hiding something." He waited for Oscar to respond, but soon gave up. "I guarantee it."

"They're both hiding something," said Oscar. "I just need more time to figure out what it is exactly."

Payneham hesitated. "You know what? It can't hurt to have you along. You're not getting that report to me today by the sound of it."

Oscar called Hayley to let her know he'd been held up. Her phone went to voicemail, and he ended the call without leaving a message. It wasn't like Hayley not to answer. Maybe she needed some space, or she was out on a run.

Before he could convince himself that something was wrong, Payneham was ushering him into his car before getting into his own car.

Oscar trailed Payneham, watching the loft window blinking against the cloud-lined sky, growing smaller in the rearview mirror as he drove away.

32

Chapter 32

Oscar

Now

The entrance to the morgue sat on the side of the building, hidden from plain view. Oscar might have missed it if he were alone, but Payneham found it easily and walked in purposefully, like he was going to do this no matter how terrible the news was awaiting him on the other side. Was that how he managed to come back each day and do his job?

Oscar walked in after. He much preferred talking to people when there was a chance of helping them, not when it was already too late. Payneham probably felt he was helping by bringing closure and justice to a situation like this, but Oscar already felt a heaviness in the air as he entered a sterile room of metal and tiles. A row of pull out trays for the bodies lined a wall. He tried not to imagine how many were occupied, instead focusing on the woman who greeted them in a white lab coat. She introduced herself with a contained smile. Amelia Sanchez. Her hair was dark, layered with rolling waves she had bound in a tight ponytail to contain them. Everything about her looked practical, from her plain black pants and sneakers to her digital wristwatch, which Oscar imagined was especially useful to manage calls and messages in her line of work. She was small, barely clearing five feet, her lab coat hiding the strength she'd built for the physical demands of her job. Her bronzed skin sported the kind of glow that came from the sun. Oscar guessed she liked to run—a sensible choice for someone who spent the majority of their work time inside.

Payneham introduced Oscar before moving on to business. Dr. Sanchez nodded and led them to a computer, where she opened up a file. Everything in the morgue looked like it was scraped down to its bare requirements. Even the stool Dr. Sanchez sat on looked like the top had been removed so that it was easy to clean and didn't take up extra space.

Oscar and Detective Payneham stood on either side of Dr. Sanchez. "We got her dental records from her mother. Our odontologist made a match. We'll need to run DNA and write a full report, but the preliminary findings from the dental records tell us it's her."

"I thought an ID might've taken longer," said Detective Payneham, clearing his throat. "Given how long she's been missing."

"So did I," said Dr. Sanchez, "but the thing is, the estimated time of death isn't as long ago as we were expecting. She died approximately ten days ago."

"Ten days? Then it couldn't be Ashlee, could it?" asked Oscar.

"I know. The dates don't seem to match up," agreed Dr.

Sanchez. Her calm tone achieved the right amount of empathy for someone responsible for comforting the grieving families of the dead.

"Hasn't she been missing for months?" Oscar moved closer.

"She has," said Dr. Sanchez.

"If she died ten days ago, that means—"

"That Verity was right. Ashlee was alive for a good part of our investigation," finished Detective Payneham, the frustration flaring his nostrils.

"The cause of death is yet to be determined," said Dr. Sanchez. "But, unofficially," she looked pointedly at Payneham, as if she'd forgotten to warn him before and suffered for it, "it looks like asphyxia by manual strangulation. It's more commonly seen with intimate partner violence. Often there's a struggle, but it doesn't look like she put up too much of a fight." She, like everyone else in New Haven, had probably seen the news, and knew that there was no known romantic partner to investigate.

Except, as Oscar had seen many times in his profession, people were notoriously good at hiding their entanglements, especially the ones they wanted to stay a secret.

"Maybe she wasn't in a position to fight. Or she was surprised by her attacker," said Detective Payneham darkly.

Oscar looked at Dr. Sanchez, who seemed to be thinking along the same lines.

"There was no evidence that she was restrained," she said, navigating to a different section of the file. Oscar glimpsed a photo of Ashlee, all cleaned up and lying on a metal table—probably in this very room—her discolored shoulders and neck peeking out from under a white sheet covering the rest of her body. It was hard to tell with her uneven skin tone, but Oscar thought he could make out some bruising around her neck. In the angle of the photograph, it might be a trick of the shadow extending from the darkness underneath her chin.

The room was silent as Oscar and the detective contemplated the doctor's revelation. If Ashlee wasn't restrained, then why didn't she fight back?

Payneham asked first. "Is the tox report back yet? Maybe he gave her a tranquilizer, or something to stop her from fighting. It would make it easier for him to kill her."

The way he said it suggested he thought Ashlee's killer was a coward, that they'd planned what they were going to do so that they could carry out her death with the least amount of trouble to themselves.

"Not yet. But that's what I'm wondering too," said Dr. Sanchez.

"So, it definitely wasn't an accidental death?" asked Oscar.

Dr. Sanchez pressed her lips together as if she didn't want to answer and turned to Oscar. "It's only preliminary information I'm providing, but an accidental death seems unlikely."

"It looks like Ashlee was murdered around the same time that Verity went to Dale Carmot's house," said Detective Payneham, typing something into his phone. "Around ten days ago." He looked at Dr. Sanchez for confirmation.

"It may have been a few days either side," said Dr. Sanchez.

"But that means both Verity and Dale were in the same place. Could Dale have killed Ashlee while Verity was locked inside without Verity noticing?"

Oscar didn't answer, watching as the detective played out various scenarios in his mind. From what he had relayed, it didn't seem likely that Dale was away from the house long enough to murder someone and dispose of the body.

Verity was going to be devastated. Oscar remembered how it was when someone you loved died prematurely.

Like when Lila died. He'd wanted to blame the world for taking her, but deep down he knew it was his fault. His father had confirmed it with his drunken temper, which seemed to emerge more often once Oscar had scared away the rest of their family. Oscar felt he deserved it. In a way, he was grateful to Bill for staying.

"What are you looking at?"

Bill lunged in a drunken rage, swaying from side to side as he crossed the room, moving toward Oscar.

He was ranting, the words slurred around the edges so Oscar couldn't understand them. Oscar wished he could've found his own anger and shouted back, but all he could find was guilt and pity. Pity that Bill hadn't found the strength to recover—that Kiko leaving wasn't the wake-up call he needed to get his life in order, but another blow to sink him.

His arm swung in Oscar's direction, but when you're eleven, you hope that'll be the time he changes his mind and doesn't connect the hit, and you stay put, trying not to flinch, placing your trust in your father reconsidering his actions.

The sound whooshed through his head as he waited for the dizziness to pass. He grabbed at his ear, willing himself not to cry, not to show Bill that it hurt.

"That wasn't even a tap. Do you want to see what pain feels like?" said Bill, but Oscar knew that the pain Bill was talking about couldn't be fixed with Advil.

"You should've been watching her. That's what you should've

done."

"Someone should tell Verity," said Oscar.

Detective Payneham cleared his throat. "I thought I'd do it tomorrow. I was hoping you'd agree to being there when I tell her."

According to public opinion, Payneham had already compromised the case, so now he was being extra careful. There was always an opinion on what'd gone wrong, and the media were happy to print it, whether it be because Dale was arrested or let go, or because the police didn't read the evidence well enough. "Sure. But why do you want me there?" he asked, curious whether the detective would give him the real reason.

Detective Payneham readjusted his shirt, as if suddenly aware it was uncomfortable. "I want you to pay attention to Verity's reaction and tell me if she seems surprised to hear Ashlee's dead."

"Am I paying attention to whether Verity's surprised her sister died *recently*, or if she's surprised that she's dead?"

Payneham still didn't trust Verity enough to deliver the news himself.

"Just... tell me what you notice."

* * *

Oscar pulled into his driveway later that night, his heart beating faster when he saw Hayley's car parked out front. He hadn't been expecting her, and he was afraid of what her impromptu visit could mean. He gathered his things and went inside. Hayley's dog, Artemis, greeted him with an enthusiastic tail wag and an invitation to pat her golden coat. "Art," he said, smiling at her enviable enthusiasm. "Where's Hayley?"

Artemis bounded into the kitchen, the edge of her clipped claws catching the wooden floor, creating the aural illusion that she was wearing a pair of plastic pumps. Oscar followed, expecting Artemis to lead him to Hayley, but when they reached the kitchen it was empty.

Two forks lay on the table. "When did you start using a fork, girl?" Oscar asked affectionately, ruffling Artemis's fur. "Hayley?" he called, walking deeper into the open-plan kitchen, expecting her to pop out from behind a cupboard.

A voice from the patio grew louder in the darkness, moving closer to the sliding door leading outside. Artemis followed the noise, greeting Hayley as she slid inside.

Oscar grinned when he saw her talking on her phone. "Hey," he mouthed.

"Hey," she returned, finishing up the call.

He went to her, the need to touch her, to make sure she was real overpowering his other senses. "I was worried. I came in and Arty was there but you didn't answer when I called." His voice sounded strained, a consequence of the kind of day he'd had.

"I'm fine," she said, folding her arms. She was clearly not fine, but it seemed like something he might regret pointing out.

"How's Verity?" asked Hayley, moving away from Oscar to usher Artemis outside to fetch her ball.

"She's recovering," said Oscar, aware of Hayley's distance.

"Then what's with the sad face?"

"They might've found her sister," said Oscar in a soft tone, as if it could take the sting out of the news.

"Where?" asked Hayley, widening her eyes.

Oscar took a steadying breath. "I've been at the morgue with Logan Payneham."

"Oh." With that, she seemed to forget what she was annoyed about, taking Oscar's hand in hers. "Steve came by looking for you. He was only here a few minutes," she said. "I think he enjoyed your night out and wanted to see if you were up for another sometime soon." Hayley shot Oscar a knowing smile. "Can't say I blame him. You're pretty good company," she said, trying to lighten his mood.

Oscar held her for a long time before he took a shower, scrubbing his skin raw to remove the tepid feel of the morgue from his body. He dried off and dressed before pouring them both a glass of wine. Usually he'd drink beer, but tonight he craved the red warmth the wine offered. He couldn't stomach food right now, so he curled up on the sofa with Hayley instead, folding her legs across his.

"How did they find Ashlee?" asked Hayley gently. Somehow she knew avoiding it wouldn't help—he was thinking about it anyway.

"Some kids playing in the woods found her. Well, they didn't. Their dog did. It ran off barking, so they followed it further in. It sniffed around a couple of trees and started digging, trying to get under a fallen log."

Oscar looked at Hayley. He was sure she knew where this story was going, but she listened attentively, taking hold of his hand and clasping it tightly, encouraging him to go on.

"When the kids called the dog to go home, it wouldn't leave. They had to wait until it stopped digging, and when it finished, they noticed a human hand sticking out of the dirt."

"The poor kids. That must've been horrible," said Hayley, bringing a hand to her throat as if she could taste their dread at finding human remains.

Oscar nodded. They both knew the kids would probably need therapy after what they'd seen. "They ran home to tell someone. They were pretty shaken up—a couple of nine-year-olds. Too young for phones, I guess."

"How do you think Verity's going to take it?" asked Hayley.

Oscar's expression said everything. Verity's reaction was what he was most worried about—she'd know where Ashlee was, but not who killed her. Walking into the lair of someone she thought was a killer suggested she was searching for a reason why her sister was targeted.

"I don't know," said Oscar. "I hope she'll be okay."

Hayley searched his face. It wouldn't be the first time she'd geared up to ask him a tough question, or said something she wasn't sure he was ready to hear. "This doesn't mean she'll stop looking for whoever did it," she said.

"Yeah," agreed Oscar. "But the thing is, Dale couldn't have murdered Ashlee. His leg is all busted up. I saw him—there's no way he could walk on it. Whoever did this, I don't think it was him."

"Didn't he break his leg recently, after Ashlee was already dead?" said Hayley.

"Payneham messaged me while I was driving home. He said Dale was out of town on business until the day before Verity went missing. His employees confirmed he was at the office most of the day catching up on work. There were people to corroborate his story. He's covered for the time when Ashlee was murdered. I don't think Dale Carmot did it. There was a small window of opportunity, but we're talking a couple of hours. It would've taken him longer than that to kill her and get rid of the body."

"Could he be working with someone? Maybe they finished what Dale couldn't," said Hayley.

"That's what I'm wondering too."

33

Chapter 33

Verity

Now

One day in the hospital bleeds into the next, an endless cycle of day and night. When I ask when I'll be allowed to go home, the answers are vague, whether it be from doctors, nurses, or Google. I know they're trying to fix my body without worrying me too much with the details, but they're making me afraid that my health is worse than I've imagined.

I focus on more immediate questions I need answers to instead, like finding Ashlee.

She should have had her whole life ahead of her. She should've lived on for the both of us. My head is a mess, flipping from the certainty that she must be dead to hoping she's alive. She's been missing for long enough that people are starting to give up on finding her, but if I'm being honest, a part of me is still hoping the signs are all wrong, that she's out there somewhere, waiting to be rescued.

I've been having dreams about falling from a rooftop. In the dream Ashlee's calling to me, cheering me on as if I'm about to attempt a harrowing dare like we did when we were kids.

I lie awake in the dark, fighting the sleep that pulls at my eyelids, hoping the dreams don't come, but eventually my eyes close and I'm swept away.

In the dream, my head feels like an exploding melon, pain pressing against the inside, searching for a way out of my skull. It feels like only a matter of time before the pressure explodes, shattering the bones on its way out.

Usually, Ashlee appears in the dream about now, and I ask where she is and what has happened to her.

She never answers, but I know I'll keep asking until she does.

Tonight I can't see her as I burst through the locked shutters and onto a rooftop that's so high the ground is invisible beneath it. My fingers slip against the window frame as the rain slams down, the droplets stinging my skin. I know the roof will be slippery even before I let go of the window frame, but there's nowhere else to go and I'm compelled forward to escape Dale, hoping he doesn't follow me. I know that if he catches me, I'm dead.

My knees bend as I try not to slip across the angled tiles. The roof moves like an earthquake under my feet, and all I can do is shift with it, because to fight it means throwing my balance off and falling to the ground.

Dale's shadow looms behind, larger than life. He's closing the distance between us.

Ashlee should've called out by now. I listen for her voice, expecting it to come from the loft window. A lock of blond hair peeks from behind the wall, and I realize she's hiding from Dale too. I stop. If I get too close, Dale might see her.

"Verity!" she calls, her voice struggling against the pounding rain. "Go! You can do it." Her voice grows faint. I try to hold on to it, but the rain grows thick, making it harder to breathe. The water fills my nose and my throat until it feels as if I'm drowning. I close my mouth to stop it, but it fills my ears instead, muting Ashlee's voice until it disappears and I'm ripped back to reality.

I wake in my hospital bed, but the feeling of suffocation persists.

Fear sinks in as I realize it isn't a dream and I'm still struggling for air as the dream fog lifts, my arms flailing.

I grab at my throat, trying to stop whatever's blocking it. Something soft and squishy is pressed over my face—a pillow, melted against me like toasted marshmallow, blocking the oxygen until I almost pass out.

I grab at it, struggling to find a grip. I hear myself calling for Ashlee, but my scream is nothing more than a muffled cry.

Instinct kicks in and my legs fly up, kicking until they find something solid.

A man stifles a grunt of pain as my feet strike him in what feels like his chest. The pillow loosens and I kick out again, hoping to find a soft spot in his belly to wind him.

Dale.

He couldn't kill me on the roof, but he's here now. Maybe he knows I found Ashlee's necklace—I can prove she was at his house, and he needs to bury the truth. He'd happily bury me with it.

I give one last kick, but there's nothing to hit—he's moved out of reach. I stop flailing and take hold of the pillow with both hands, throwing it with all my strength.

Air fills my lungs, crisp and nourishing.

I'm still calling for Ashlee when a nurse comes in, drawn by the commotion.

34

Chapter 34

Oscar

Now

Oscar soaked up the midmorning sun like a nourishing balm as he drove to the hospital to see Verity. Something about the warm rays on his skin felt comforting, making him reluctant to go inside. Detective Payneham hadn't arrived yet, so he stopped by Dale's room to see how he was doing.

He found Dale propped against pillows, his leg elevated. He looked out the window longingly. "Looks nice out there," he said.

"Yeah, it is." Oscar had never been good at small talk. Usually, he was too focused on the thoughts bouncing around his mind. At work it was easier. He could mostly skip the small talk, especially if he timed his lunch breaks. Socializing wasn't like working with patients, where his scrutiny was expected and taken as an indication he was doing his job rather than a rude quirk.

Oscar looked around the room. There were no police watching him. Dale was alone. If he could walk, would there be police stationed outside, keeping him out of trouble?

"How's the leg?" asked Oscar.

"Yeah, it's okay." Dale eyed his leg as if it was a faulty product he might return. Oscar imagined Dale used the same look on employees who didn't live up to his expectations.

"I'm surprised you're still here. Over a week for a broken ankle and an infection?" said Oscar.

Dale laughed with his mouth closed, muting the sound. "Well, it might be jail from here, and they can't care for it properly if I'm locked up."

"How much do you donate to this hospital?" asked Oscar, cutting through the illusion—plenty of people in jail had broken bones.

"Enough," said Dale. "No more than I donate to some of my other hospitals."

"The same ones you sell drugs to?"

"Pharmaceuticals," corrected Dale. "As part of our commitment to our patients, we fund the facilities our pharmaceuticals are available at, to give our patrons the best healthcare experience possible."

Oscar cleared his throat, surprised Dale was giving him the corporate social responsibility spiel. He needed to get Dale focused.

"How did you know Ashlee Casmere?" asked Oscar, trying to catch Dale off guard.

Dale's eyes peeled to his leg, grimacing as he shifted, avoiding any weight on it.

"You knew her, right? She was a nurse at the hospital

you held the gala for. You seem to hold a lot of galas and fundraisers—is that how you met her?"

"Events are part of my business. It's how we talk to the doctors and provide them with ongoing business opportunities. We have some great psychiatric medication that could help your patients," said Dale, smiling mildly.

By opportunities, he really means new drugs. It doesn't escape Oscar that he's avoiding the question. "And Ashlee, was she usually at these events?"

"I saw her around at work. I said hello because it was the polite thing to do. If I wasn't friendly to the hospital staff, I'd never sell anything. But I already told you, I didn't hurt her. I don't know what happened to her," said Dale.

He wasn't likely to come out and admit to doing anything illegal in the space of two conversations, so Oscar didn't push him yet.

"Why do you sell pharmaceuticals when you practically own the company? I would've thought you'd be too busy for the groundwork," said Oscar.

"I started out in sales, and I believe it's where you go to gauge the health of your business, not the boardroom. I always enjoyed selling. The conversations, getting to know what someone needs and finding something to help. So, I still spend time in the field selling."

Dale liked the hunt. When people were vulnerable and needed something to fix their pain, he was the guy with the solution. He was a hero.

"Why are you telling me this?" asked Oscar, suspicious that Dale was suddenly so talkative.

"Well, Dr. de la Nuit, I did some research since your last visit, and I found out some interesting things about you. I don't know how you helped that woman—what was her name, Jessica? It seemed like she'd spend the rest of her life in prison, but somehow you pulled it off. I guess I'm a combination of curious and hopeful that you'll do the same for me."

Oscar scratched the side of his head, uncomfortable with Dale talking about his previous patients. It was true; he had helped Jess, but she had been held in preventive detention based on circumstantial evidence.

He wasn't convinced Dale was worth helping. He'd admitted to kidnapping Verity, and he'd have a tough time convincing people—including Oscar—he hadn't planned on doing more.

"I helped Jess see a way forward. She did the rest," said Oscar. It was better than giving Dale an outright no.

"You helped her." Dale tilted his head, like he was tipping a cap, signaling his respect. "You're probably the only person that can help me."

"What makes you think I can help you?"

"Despite how it seems, I didn't do it. I didn't kill Ashlee Casmere, and if Verity hadn't been following me, I wouldn't have taken her home. Maybe you can help me show them that." He shrugged. "As it is, she *was* following me, and I wanted to know why. I thought she must've been a reporter, looking for a break."

Oscar didn't back down, and didn't mention what a stupid idea it was to hold someone captive if you believed their job was to report on drama like the kind of drama he'd caused. Either Dale wasn't thinking straight, or he was lying. "How about this? You weren't sure what you wanted to do with her when you took her home. You kept her there while you decided, only she got out before you had a chance to figure it out. If she hadn't, you would've killed her."

"That's not true," said Dale, growing agitated, pressing his fists into the mattress to shift his weight. "I didn't keep her there overnight. She's lying if she said I did. She knocked me out and put me in the loft. I went down to investigate because I woke up and heard someone still in the house. That's when she burst through the bathroom door holding a needle."

He held up his arm, presumably where the needle had pierced.

"I don't know what was in it, but after she stabbed me, she ran to the roof. I called after her, but she didn't slow. There was nowhere to run up there, except over the guttering. It was pouring rain outside but she climbed through the window anyway. She had completely lost it by then. She was calling for Ashlee. For a second it seemed like she thought I was her sister. I was worried she'd jump. I called her back, but she got too close to the edge. I went after her to pull her away from the edge, and that's when she pushed me off the roof. My arm caught her as I fell, and she went rolling toward the edge with me."

"You're saying you didn't keep Verity locked inside your house, that she stayed there so she could drug you?"

"I'm telling you what happened," said Dale defiantly.

Dale's tone made Oscar wonder if he was telling the truth, if maybe Dale had woken in a drug induced haze, a stranger in his own house.

Without speaking, Oscar pushed the button to call for a nurse.

Dale looked as if he was about to ask what Oscar was doing, but changed his mind and kept his mouth shut.

A flustered nurse bustled in moments later and reset the call button before acknowledging them. "Did you need something in here?" she asked with a smile.

"Yeah," said Oscar. "Dale was wondering if you could tell him what was in his system when the ambulance arrived?"

"Uh, I'm not sure," said the nurse, smiling at Dale. "I can find out for you if you like?"

"Yeah, that'd be great, thanks." Dale smiled back at the nurse, following Oscar's lead.

Once the nurse left, Dale's smile disappeared and his head swiveling, honing his attention on Oscar. "What the fuck was that?"

"Just seeing if your story adds up. If you're lying to me, I'll make my recommendation based on what I've observed, and you won't see me here again."

"And when the nurse comes back to tell you I'm telling the truth?"

Oscar thought about it, put off by Dale's confidence. If he was addicted to oxy, it'd show up in his system. He could easily blame Verity for that if he was saying she'd drugged him.

"We'll see," he said. If Verity drugged Dale, Oscar was counting on her not knowing how much she should administer.

Moments later, a doctor in a white coat and narrow, rectangular-framed glasses entered Dale's room. "Hi, I'm Dr. Palensche," he said, adjusting a stethoscope around his neck so that it sat evenly across his shoulders. It made him look like a pretend doctor in a Netflix series. "Belinda said you had a few questions?"

Oscar raised his eyebrows at Dale expectantly.

"Yeah," said Dale. "I was just wondering what was in my system when I came in."

The doctor looked at Oscar, and back to Dale, subtly asking whether they could talk freely with Oscar in the room.

Dale waved a hand dismissively. "It's okay. I'm pretty sure Dr. de la Nuit wants to hear this." He folded his arms defiantly. "He's my psychiatrist."

"Okay. Well, a police officer that was here when you arrived requested toxicology," he said, shifting uncomfortably. "Are you sure you want me to share the results?"

"I've got nothing to hide," said Dale, a stubborn lilt to his voice.

"We found narcotics."

Dale's jaw dropped. "What?"

"Can you be more specific?" asked Oscar.

Dr. Palensche looked at Dale, who nodded, seemingly just as eager to find out what they found.

"Oxycodone," said the doctor. "Which is a drug sometimes prescribed for pain relief, but there were larger amounts than I'd expect to find from filling a prescription," he said tentatively.

Dale guffawed. "Would you expect to find those levels if someone was drugged with oxycodone?"

"It's possible," said Dr. Palensche.

"Is it usual to find similar amounts in a patient suffering from an oxycodone addiction?" countered Oscar.

"It would make sense for levels to be elevated, especially if the patient overdosed. The respiratory system was compromised," said Dr. Palensche.

Oscar nodded. If Dale presented with high levels of oxy in his system and the pills Oscar saw him with before weren't from the hospital, then it was possible Dale was using Verity to cover his addiction.

"How were the drugs administered?" pressed Oscar, still unconvinced of Dale's innocence.

"Intravenously," said the doctor. "There was a makeshift needle found at the site."

Oscar knew that someone suffering from addiction would get a fix however they could. With his medical knowledge, Dale could easily fashion a needle.

"We think the needle used contributed to Dale's infection. It wasn't sterile."

"And it was administered into a vein?"

"It pierced the vein, yes."

"Did it look self-administered?" asked Oscar. It didn't seem likely that someone could rush at you with a needle and still pierce a vein. He watched for Dale's reaction, except Dale's expression was blank.

The doctor's brow furrowed. He looked at Dale, trying to figure out how much to say. Dale was an important contributor to the hospital, and the doctor was probably mindful that he was treading in dangerous territory.

"It's okay. Dr. de la Nuit is trying to establish whether I'm lying to him. Please," he gestured toward Oscar, "answer his questions."

"It was a homemade needle, but I believe someone else administered it, judging by the force with which it entered the site, and the fact that it wasn't sterilized. There was also fentanyl in his system."

"Is that unusual?" asked Oscar.

The doctor straightened his coat. "Street oxy, also called hillbilly heroin, sometimes has fentanyl in it. It's a more potent drug. Keeps customers coming back."

"Both drugs are also used in combination to treat cancer pain," said Dale. "Just to save you some time, if you were going to look it up later."

220

"Is that true?" asked Oscar.

Dr. Palensche nodded.

"Thank you," said Oscar.

Dr. Palensche did some checks while he was there before leaving the room.

"Do you have cancer?" Oscar asked, just to rule it out.

"I don't. So, Doctor. Do you believe me now?" asked Dale.

Oscar laced his fingers together, taking his time before answering.

"You might've set Verity up, like you said she did to you," said Oscar, wiping the smug smile off Dale's face. "You have more access than anyone to drugs. It's what you do. Maybe you should tell me why you've got street stuff in your cabinets. You say you want me to help you like I helped my previous patient, but this isn't the same."

"You're right, it's not the same. Because you know Verity, don't you?"

Oscar looked surprised, but there was no time to figure out how Dale knew that.

"So, you probably already know what she's capable of," continued Dale. He leaned forward. "Verity Casmere's lying. I didn't hold her hostage. She drugged me and tried to make it look like I was going to kill her. She pushed me off the roof. I think she had it planned all along. She was going to kill me and make it look like she was defending herself."

He stopped, his breathing fast and ragged. Oscar knew what anger looked like, he'd seen it enough to recognize the slow build or the sudden explosion, but his experience as a psychiatrist had trained him to identify other emotions too, enough to know that under the indignation, Dale wasn't really angry at all.

He was scared that no one would believe him.

"She's still playing the game, and everyone feels bad for her because of what happened to her sister. She's manipulative, and she had time to plan what she was going to do. If she hadn't caught me off guard, I would've seen it sooner," said Dale. "But I was already drunk by then."

"You really believe what you're saying, don't you?" said Oscar. Dale believed he was the victim, that Verity was the monster.

"It's the truth," said Dale vehemently.

35

Chapter 35

Oscar

Now

Verity was out of her hospital bed, stuffing clothes into a travel case, when Oscar arrived.

Detective Payneham was already there. At first, Oscar guessed she'd heard the news about Ashlee.

"Verity?" said Oscar, trying to get her attention. She didn't turn around. "How are you?"

The detective shot him a look, trying to tell him his questions were futile.

Verity spun around, relieved to see a friendly face. "Oscar! Someone was in my room last night. I think they might've been looking for Ashlee's necklace?"

"What do you mean?" asked Oscar in a soothing tone.

"Someone broke into my hospital room. They're trying to make me think I'm losing my mind. They tried to kill me, but gave up when I fought back."

"Okay, sit down for a second," said Oscar, leading her by the shoulder to the edge of the hospital bed.

"I'm going home," she said decisively. "I'm not waiting here for them to come back, especially when no one is doing anything about it."

Oscar heard the fear in her voice, could see the dark circles of stolen sleep around her eyes.

"We can talk about this," he said, sitting beside her. The bed frame shifted, the railing clicking into place under his leg.

Logan Payneham shrugged, as if the situation was just as confusing to him.

"Okay, now tell me what happened," said Oscar, ignoring everyone in the room except for Verity.

"Someone tried to suffocate me with a pillow," said Verity calmly. "I reported it, but everyone thinks I imagined it, or that it was a dream."

"Did you see who it was?"

Verity shook her head miserably. "It was dark, and they held a pillow over my face. I couldn't see anything."

"Excuse me," said a nurse, standing to the side of the commotion. "I was the first person to respond when I heard a scream, but I didn't see anyone in the room. I think it was probably another nightmare. She was struggling to breathe, and the pillow was thrown to the floor, but there was no one there. We would've heard someone come in. We would've heard the scream."

Verity shot the nurse a look. "You didn't hear me scream while they were in the room because there was a pillow over my face."

The nurse sighed. "It was long after visiting hours. No one

can get in. We have security measures to stop people from entering during the night.

Oscar looked at Detective Payneham for confirmation. The detective shrugged. "I can't find anything to suggest someone who shouldn't have been was here."

"Is there footage we can look over?"

"We don't record footage of the rooms. Privacy," said the nurse. "There are cameras at the exits—we could have someone check those if you like?" She stifled a yawn with the back of her hand, looking like she just wanted to go home. Her shift had probably finished hours ago, but Detective Payneham was still questioning the staff.

"I've been here for a couple of hours, trying to sort this out, but Verity's checking herself out and going home," said Detective Payneham, sounding fed up with the situation.

The corner of Oscar's mouth twitched at the irony of waiting around when Detective Payneham was already there.

"It was Dale," said Verity. "I know it."

Oscar clenched his jaw. He shouldn't have told Verity that Dale was in the hospital—it had probably made her more anxious knowing he was there.

She was going to kill me. Oscar wasn't sure he believed Dale. It seemed too far-fetched.

"I know his voice. I had to listen to it while I was locked inside his house. He made me tell him what I thought had happened to Ashlee, like my suffering was entertaining to him. It was him," said Verity confidently. "So don't tell me it wasn't, because you weren't there."

"Is it possible it was a dream? They can seem pretty real," said Oscar gently, still ignoring the others.

"It wasn't a dream," said Verity. "I couldn't breathe. I was asleep, but then I woke up with a pillow over my face, and when I tried to remove it, someone held it there. I kicked out and it must've hurt them, so they let go."

The nurse shook her head. "Verity has been talking in her sleep since she arrived."

"What does she say?" asked Oscar.

"She calls out a name. Ashlee. Sometimes she screams, like she's having a nightmare. Usually, she settles herself back to sleep so we don't wake her."

"Are you sure she was sleeping?" asked Oscar from his post on the edge of the bed.

"No one saw anyone enter her room," said the nurse, squinting against the heavy sunlight winking through the window.

"Verity," said Oscar gently, "Dale Carmot's ankle is broken. He couldn't have gotten in here without someone noticing."

"I kicked him and he let go of the pillow. Maybe I got the son of a bitch in the leg."

"What happened after he let go?"

Verity sighed, as if an explanation was futile. She could see they didn't believe her, but Oscar's job was to talk through the facts and help her draw her own conclusions.

"He left," said Verity, sounding less sure of this detail.

Detective Payneham paced back and forth, listening. Oscar would bet he was the sort of person who went for a drive to think, someone who had to act to feel like he was making progress.

"Did you see Dale leave?" asked Oscar.

"By the time I'd moved the pillow and caught my breath, he was gone," she said.

"So, you never saw him?" said Detective Payneham.

"No," snapped Verity. "I didn't see him, but I *heard* him."

"Did you hear crutches? They make a kind of stomping sound," said Payneham.

Verity glared at him.

This time, Oscar was certain Dale hadn't done it—there was no way he could walk on that leg and go undetected, but Detective Payneham's heavy-handed approach wasn't getting them anywhere.

"Can we have a moment?" asked Oscar, eager to defuse the situation. He waited for everyone to exit.

The nurse nodded, relieved to finally be able to leave. She slipped through the door with a quick wave.

"Fine," said the detective, adjusting the back of his pants as he went. He was almost gone when he spun around and added in a low voice, "Feel free to tell Verity. Probably better you than me."

His attempt at subtlety was poor and Verity tensed. "Tell me what? Did Dale say something? It was him in my room. What does he have to do before you believe me?"

Oscar folded his hands. "Let's just...take a breather."

"Why is everyone protecting him? He tried to kill me. Doesn't anyone care that he'll do it again, maybe to someone else next time?"

"Did you find Ashlee's necklace?" asked Oscar.

Verity gripped the bed, her feet dangling over the edge. "A nurse told me they couldn't find it. They said I wasn't wearing it when I came in."

"Payneham didn't see it at the house either, but I'm not sure how much I'd trust him to notice a piece of jewelry," joked Oscar.

"I had it on, Oscar. Dale took I because it *proves* she was at his house. The police won't look for her unless I can show them it was there."

Oscar cleared his throat, hating Payneham for leaving this to him. "Verity, I have something to tell you."

It was never easy giving someone bad news, and Oscar was worried how she'd take it; it wasn't the best timing, and he suspected her focus on finding Ashlee was a way to cope with her own sickness. He might be taking away a lot more than her hope, but he couldn't keep it from her any longer.

"What is it?"

"They found Ashlee."

"What? Is she—"

Oscar shook his head. "I'm sorry."

"She's dead?"

Oscar nodded.

He waited as Verity's eyes filled with tears, her hands trembling as the news sank in. There was nothing more he could say to make it any easier.

"When did they find her?"

He told her, watching as her face crumpled into the unmistakable defeat that comes with grief.

"Maybe you can ask Detective Payneham for the details when you're up to it. For now, just take some time to grieve."

He sat with her, an arm around her shoulder, until her sobs subsided.

36

Chapter 36

Verity

Now

Nothing can prepare you for the news that someone you love is dead. I listened to Oscar, my stomach sinking as he told me Ashlee was gone. He held me as I cried for the life Ashlee wouldn't live, for the horrible things she might've suffered before the end.

I wanted to ask him how it happened, but I wasn't ready for that, could barely form the words to ask. Instead, I asked if they were sure it was her, just in case.

By my request, no one visited while I was in the hospital. My mother wanted to, but I asked her not to come. I didn't tell my work colleagues the real reason for my time off, but somehow, they found out anyway and sent a "get well soon" basket of snacks, nail polish, and magazines to keep me occupied during my stay. Amy snuck a bottle of Shiraz into the basket, with a note saying I might need a little something for after and not to drink it without her.

Eventually, Oscar leaves, and I feel more alone than I ever have before. I offer him his pick from the "get well" basket, but he declines and heads for the door somberly, promising to accompany me to the station if I want him to, once I've had time to decide what I want to ask. It feels like a warning—choose carefully because once you know, you can't unknow.

I don't need to think too hard. The detective can't tell me anything I want to know. Only Dale Carmot can do that.

With Oscar gone, I pack up and sign the discharge papers, ready to go home. The wheels of my travel case trail behind me as I leave the room that's been my cage for almost two weeks. I'm thankful I was unconscious for some of it.

I reconsider whether Payneham can answer my questions as I leave. He can't tell me who hurt Ashlee, or why they chose her. He won't tell me much more than Oscar already has, and he doesn't trust me—probably still wonders if I had something to do with her death.

If I want answers, I need to find Dale Carmot. I already know he's somewhere in this hospital.

I make a stop at the bathroom first, where I tidy my hair and splash my face. Next, I make my way to the information desk located on the first floor. I pass watery-eyed visitors carrying flowers, visiting their loved ones.

I know it's a risk, but it'll be worth it if it pays off.

A woman at the front desk smiles as I approach. She has short blond hair that looks as stiff as her uniform. "Hi. How can I help?" she asks.

"Hi," I say, the wheels of my luggage stopping behind my

heels. "I was wondering if you know how to get to room... " I pretend to search for a misplaced paper containing the information I need. "Sorry," I say. "I had it right here. My husband broke his leg pretty badly. It was a whole thing." I flip my hair, pretending to be flustered. "He needed some new clothes," I say, flicking the handle of the luggage.

"Sure," says the information clerk, sizing me up while I talk. "What's his name?"

"Dale Carmot." I hope she doesn't recognize his name.

She does a quick search, and lowers her voice, like we're sharing a secret. "He's on ward D, level 3."

"You're amazing. Thank you so much," I say as a wave of nausea passes through me. His room must've been just above mine.

I catch the next elevator to Dale's floor and walk right through, past the nurses' station.

Dale's sitting in bed, scrolling through his phone. I close the door behind me and walk straight toward him.

He stops when he sees me, reaching for the buzzer to call the nurse, but I'm faster and I pull it from his hand, sending it to the floor, like the pillow he tried to suffocate me with.

"I know it was you in my room," I say. "It's the last time you'll ever come near me."

"What are you talking about?" he says. "I haven't been near you since you pushed me off the roof." He gestures to his ankle and I notice the pins sticking out of it, like a pincushion. "I can't even walk."

"You tried to suffocate me last night," I growl, less confident than before, placing my fingers around his ankle. If he moves, I'll make good on the threat and crush it. "Where did you put Ashlee's necklace?"

"Necklace?" he says, looking at me like I've lost my mind. I almost believe he doesn't know what I'm talking about.

"I know Ashlee was at your house. Don't say she wasn't, because I found her necklace in your bathroom. I was wearing it when you threw me off the roof, but when I woke up, it was gone."

"When I threw you off the roof?" he says indignantly. "I thought you were going to jump—I was trying to stop you." He shifts his foot slowly, trying to move away from my grasp.

Is this how he justifies the sort of person he is, by pretending he's one of the good guys? I'm tempted to push one of the pins, but I don't want to risk him calling out to a nurse. I could probably hurt him before anyone got there, but if he's in too much pain, he won't be able to tell me what I need to know.

He leaves his foot where it is, shooting me a look. "I'm going to call for a nurse now," he says deliberately.

"Do it, and I'll pull out these pins before they can get here," I threaten. I put light pressure on his ankle, showing I'm serious. He winces, and I can see his pain is real. If he's not faking, if it really is that painful, maybe it wasn't him who tried to suffocate me.

That means whoever tried to kill me is still out there.

Maybe Ashlee's killer is still out there too.

37

Chapter 37

Oscar

Now

Oscar was waiting for Detective Payneham at a hastily decided bar later that afternoon when his phone buzzed. He looked at the screen. It was his dad. He could list the number of times his father had contacted him in the last year on one hand, with one of them being an accidental pocket dial. So when he received a message from Bill saying he needed to talk—in person—Oscar couldn't imagine why.

If he left now, he didn't know when he'd catch Payneham again, so he stayed and ordered a beer and a serving of onion rings—his first meal since breakfast—and returned Bill's message.

Sorry, can't. I'm working. Will call when I can. O.

Oscar felt the slight sting of guilt as he slid his phone into his pocket. If it was urgent, Bill would message back. Oscar still wanted to clarify the details about Ashlee's death so he could give Verity enough detail and reassure her the police would focus on finding her killer now.

Oscar took his phone from his pocket and found Hayley's name at the top of his recent messages.

Hey, just meeting with Payneham. Home for dinner. Head to my place around 7. I'll have something delicious waiting xx

Detective Payneham arrived in time for hot, crispy onion rings, taking two when Oscar offered.

"You didn't go for the buffalo wings?" he asked as if it were a no-brainer. "Their wings are the best. You don't know what you're missing."

Oscar smiled—he hadn't even considered wings. When he was with Hayley, he avoided ordering meat. "I'll remember that for next time," he said.

Payneham took two more onion rings and sat back in his chair to enjoy them, one leg folded over the other. "Did you tell Verity about Ashlee?"

"I did."

"How'd she take it?"

He skipped the part where she cried for almost an hour. "She went home. I'll check in on her later—I don't think she has much of a social network to see her through this."

"Yeah, I kinda got that," said Payneham. "It's a pity. She could do with someone to talk her out of going after murderers."

Oscar suspected Ashlee might've been that person. "How are the kids who found Ashlee doing?" he asked.

"Shaken. Probably won't be going that way through the park any time soon," said Detective Payneham, opening a bag and fishing out a folder. He threw it on the table. "Are you trying to drum up some business? I can give 'em your card?"

"No, that's okay," said Oscar uncomfortably, watching Detective Payneham lay out a manilla folder.

"Pictures of Ashlee," explained the detective.

"The precinct hasn't gone digital?" asked Oscar, matching the detective's jesting tone.

"Sure. Sometimes it helps to look at things more organically, re-create a section of the scene to figure out where the murder took place, why they left the body where they did."

Oscar nodded. He understood. Sometimes it helped him if he re-created a situation a patient was explaining in his mind.

"What'd you find?" asked Oscar.

"Well, we still don't know who killed her, or where she was while she was missing, but I want you to look at the photos and tell me what you see."

Oscar agreed hesitantly. "I'm not a crime scene expert."

"Sure," said Detective Payneham, "but your job is about perception and detail. Tell me what you see." He flicked open the folder and ruffled through the pictures until he found what he was looking for.

Gently, he placed the image of a dead girl in front of Oscar. She looked as if she'd been pulled from a riverbed, her skin discolored, hair wet and grimy with mud.

"Was she found underwater?"

"They buried her after some heavy rain. The soil was still damp and muddy underneath."

Somehow, Oscar had been expecting the detective to show him a picture of Ashlee after they cleaned her up, once a mortician had tried restoring her to the Ashlee she was in life. In this image, her eyes were partially open—the same shade as Verity's. He was glad Verity hadn't gone to the morgue to identify her; their likeness in death might've reminded Verity of her ailing health.

Oscar turned the photo, noticing something glinting around her neck. He lifted the picture and looked closer. A thin chain with an ornate letter hung around her bare neck, the middle of the letter filled with mud. Under the mud was the letter *A*. It was the necklace Verity claimed to be wearing when she fell from the roof.

"That's it. That's the necklace Verity was looking for, the one she thought was stolen from her room."

Detective Payneham closed his eyes—just a flicker, but long enough to show it wasn't the news he'd hoped for. "How did it end up on a dead girl if Verity was wearing it?"

Oscar studied the picture, pressing the cold beer to his face to help him think. "The rest of the necklace is pitted with mud—but the letter is filled perfectly, almost neatly. It looks like someone did it purposefully," he said, turning the photo on an angle, following the outline of the letter. Dirt sat in the triangular middle of the *A*, so that the outer shape formed a fancy caret.

Detective Payneham leaned on his arms, bringing himself closer to the image he'd probably seen a hundred times.

Was it supposed to be a mathematical symbol? Oscar put the beer down on the table, away from the pictures. The detective's anticipation told Oscar he had touched on something the detective noticed too.

"Did someone at the station scrape the rest of the mud to see what it is?"

"Yeah. It's a letter *A*," he confirmed.

"It looks like they've turned it into a caret. Do you have a pen?"

The detective took a pen from the folder and a sheet of paper, placing it in front of Oscar, who drew the symbol.

^

"It's used in math to denote an exponent. I don't understand what it means here. Maybe they're saying they're square now, like maybe they're even?"

"Maybe it's an arrow," said Detective Payneham, looking more closely at the image. "It's pointing upward. It could refer to a higher power, or maybe going to a better place?"

Oscar focused on the symbol—the detective had a point.

"Maybe whoever killed Ashlee took the necklace from Verity. There's a chance she wasn't lying," said Payneham as if he couldn't believe it.

"They would have had to take it while she was lying on the ground, unconscious," said Oscar incredulously. How could someone do that? Whoever it was, it wasn't Dale—he would've been lying next to her, unable to move.

"Do you think Dale saw who it was?" asked Detective Payneham.

"I don't know."

"What kind of person would do that?" asked Payneham. Oscar didn't respond. It was a moral question, not a psychological one.

From years of listening to people's thoughts, the ones that seemed so unthinkable you stopped them before they were fully formed, Oscar knew the answer to the detective's question was "more people than you'd think." With the right motivation, people were capable of almost anything.

"Someone who thought the benefit outweighed the risk of taking it," said Oscar.

He'd seen a lot of things come down to risk and reward.

When the reward outweighed the risk or effort required, that was when someone usually took action. The problem was, it wasn't always easy to unravel because people were great at false reasoning.

If I stopped smoking, it'd probably kill me. If I steal something, no one really gets hurt. If I take the necklace... He didn't know what the reward was yet, but he'd work on figuring it out.

"Dale fell off that roof, the same as Verity," said Detective Payneham.

"What if she wasn't wearing it on the roof like she thought?" said Oscar. "Memory isn't always reliable. It's possible she was wearing the necklace at some point, but it fell off, or someone removed it. She might've even imagined she was wearing it because it brought her comfort in an emotionally charged situation."

"Yeah, I've heard of that happening. Some detectives went to a seminar. I remember them talking about a bunch of people remembering Nelson Mandela dying in the eighties or something, but he didn't really die."

Oscar finished his beer and eyed the last few onion rings, which had grown cold and greasy. "You're talking about the Mandela Effect," he said. "A group of people recollecting the same false memory."

"Yeah, that's the one," said Detective Payneham. "Are you gonna eat those?" He pointed at the onion rings.

Oscar offered him the basket.

Detective Payneham scooped them up, not fussed about the cold grease.

"I was talking about the misinformation effect," said Oscar. "Where the ability to recall information is compromised by things that occur after the event. It can cause people to recall memories that are flawed, or create false memories."

"So, you think the necklace is just a false memory?" asked Detective Payneham, licking the onion ring grease from his thumb.

Oscar's lip curved in disagreement. "I'm just saying, it's possible the circumstances compromised what she thinks she remembered because she was in a stressful situation. Even mild stress can inhibit memory."

"That's why we rely on evidence," said Detective Payneham. "No feelings or opinions to compromise it."

Oscar gave a short laugh, eliciting an amused look from the detective. "Does the evidence explain what it means?" asked Oscar.

Logan Payneham finished his beer, ignoring Oscar's sarcasm. "Come on, man," he said, setting the bottle down with a thud when he was done.

"Someone has to interpret the evidence and they aren't immune to incorrect interpretation," said Oscar.

"Yeah, I guess. At first, it looked like Dale was going to be our guy, right? And now...we have a dead girl who was probably murdered while he was incapacitated."

"Unless he murdered her before he broke his ankle," said Oscar.

"That's what I'm wondering." The detective sat back in his chair, his posture tense, like a runner who forgot to warm up. His phone beeped and he sighed, scooping it up to answer it. "Yeah, this is Logan Payneham."

Oscar tried to listen to the voice on the other end, but couldn't quite hear.

"Son of a..." said Detective Payneham, trailing off. He gave the table a rap with closed knuckles. "The blood results are in.

Ashlee Casmere was in Dale's bathroom."

38

Chapter 38

Verity

Now

When I walk in, Ashlee's apartment feels strange and barren because now I know she isn't coming back. I set my bag down with a thud, silence permeating the room as it did the first day I stayed here, when I still hoped she'd come home.

I look around, no longer seeing the place where Ashlee and I watched movies and talked over generous glasses of wine, testing the limits of the brim as we walked carefully to the sofa.

She was missing for months before they found her. Where was she all that time? Why hadn't she come home? My imagination swims with possible reasons. Was someone stopping her from reaching out? I close my eyes tight, each question spurring another.

I remember how it felt, being locked inside Dale's house,

knowing I might die if I couldn't find an escape. I would've lost my mind if I was locked up for weeks.

Had Ashlee been locked inside too? The police didn't know about the house he took me to. Did he have other homes where he kept other girls? The thought is humbling, the unnamed women who might've died without anyone knowing what happened to them. Was this a hobby to him, something to fill the lonely nights; a form of entertainment for the man who could buy almost anything he wanted, but hungered for forbidden things. He likes knowing he holds their lives in his hands, that there's nothing between death and the people he locks up except his will. The guy has a god complex.

My thoughts are different this time. There is less conviction, less certainty Dale is all of these things. After seeing him in the hospital, his leg pinned to the extreme like a Meccano enthusiast's project, I have to admit he probably didn't try to suffocate me. Still, he kept me locked up, and I'm sure he would've killed me eventually.

If Ashlee was at the house while I was there, I'm sure I would've heard her, but I was so busy looking for a way to escape; it is possible I went right past her while she sat hidden in a room or in the basement? *Basement.* I hadn't even thought to check for a basement or a cellar opening. I close my eyes, trying to remember if I saw either, but all I can see is myself falling from the roof, Ashlee's necklace swimming through the air in front of me, the metal cold around my neck.

What if I went with Dale to the wrong house while Ashlee was trapped somewhere else, hoping someone'd find her? My stomach contracts. Who was looking after Ashlee, making sure she had food and water while Dale was with me?

I remind myself that there are still other possibilities. Maybe she went on the self-discovery holiday she'd always talked about, soaking up the sun and indulging in pedicures before a horrible accident occurred.

I press my fingers to my temple, still trying to hold on to a plausible reason for Ashlee's extended absence. Eventually I have to acknowledge that it seems unlikely she was missing for so long because she wanted some time to mull things over. Dale's assessment of Ashlee haunts me. Maybe she really was in trouble, and that's why she took time away. She might've been too ashamed to tell me she was hiding from someone.

You really don't know her, do you?

What other secrets had Ashlee kept?

I sit on the sofa, where Ashlee used to sit. If she were here, she'd be telling me to scooch over. I close my eyes, giving in to exhaustion. At the hospital there was always a machine beeping to let someone know that someone needs something, or someone calling out instructions—never a moment of unbroken silence to rest.

I fall asleep quickly, and the next thing I'm aware of is my hand at my throat as I jolt awake, feeling for Ashlee's necklace. As I become more consciously awake, I remember it's gone, that someone probably took it while I lay in the grass. It couldn't have been Dale, but what if someone had helped him—someone who knew his secrets? I imagine the secrets they share with each other must be horrifying if they would risk jail to protect them.

What else were they willing to do? If they could kill Ashlee, then breaking into an apartment would probably be nothing to them. But wouldn't the police notice that someone had broken in to search for the necklace?

Unless Dale's accomplice arrived before the ambulance got there.

I set my keys down on the table, pressing my hands against the cold surface. I hadn't thought about it before, but I notice the tabletop looks like real marble, not the cheap, fake version. If she was selling prescription drugs on the black market, maybe she made a little extra.

I go to Ashlee's room, open her wardrobe, and pull up a chair to reach the top shelf. My fingers find a jewelry box that I clamp onto with both hands and pull from the shelf. I open it, expecting to find her most prized belongings, but it's empty.

I know she kept old letters, but there is nothing in the box. Maybe someone went through it, looking for things to sell. My organized sister wouldn't just keep an empty box that was taking up space. I look closer. The hinge is broken, like the box has been forced open.

Someone was in the apartment.

A shiver ripples up my spine at the thought of someone going through Ashlee's things. Maybe they were here while I was in the hospital, which would mean they went through my things too.

I look around the living room, but there's no sign of a break in. Slowly, I realize everything feels just a little off, which could be why the space felt strange when I first walked in. It looks like whoever was in here took the time to cover their tracks, but the couch isn't quite aligned with the rug. Ashlee would've noticed it right away, but I'm not as pedantic as my sister.

A thought nudges at my conscious, tiny and unsure, but still wanting to be heard. What if Ashlee sold the jewelry? I hate myself for thinking it, but if what Dale said was true, and Ashlee was selling pharmaceuticals illegally, maybe she needed money.

Since I've been in the hospital, I've kept my phone switched off. I turn it on now, ready to notify the police about Ashlee's missing items. As the screen comes to life a slew of notifications flash.

I flick through the social media notifications and move on to messages and emails, closing the majority without reading them. I read the news headlines next to find out what I've missed when a notification pops up with a message from Wes. I want to ignore it, to pretend I don't care what it says, but curiosity wins out and I hit open and start reading.

Verity,

I wasn't going to send this, but I thought you should know that I really enjoyed our date...until your boyfriend asked me to leave. Obviously I left, but I was thinking, what if you were separated, or he was just some guy who wanted to ask you out?

Anyway, I'm sorry. If you want to grab a coffee, let me know.

Wes

xx

My cheeks flush and I message him back to let him know I'd like that, but for now I need to sleep, to grieve, and I resign myself to a day of tumultuous emotion. I cry for Ashlee, and then I allow myself some pitying tears for my failing health, the pain that radiates through my side serving as a reminder of my body working against me.

The doctor has signed me out with a bottle of OxyContin, but despite the pain, I'm hesitant to take it, remembering the makeshift syringe in my hand in Dale's bathroom.

Eventually, the pain wins out and I wash the pill down with a glass of water.

I awake to a knock on the door, my senses firing up. I wasn't expecting anyone, and I'm tempted to ignore it, hoping whoever it is will go away. The knock comes again, gentle but insistent. A question.

I'm not sure I can make it to the door just yet, my mind still fuzzy. I pull the covers up as my phone buzzes on the bedside table.

Oscar.

My fingers find the phone and I edge it toward me to answer the call.

"I'm at your door. I just wanted to see how you were."

"It's open," I say, horrified to realize I'd forgotten to lock it. I run a hand through my hair self-consciously, knowing it probably looks like a nest after my nap.

The door opens and closes with a soft click as I pull myself up and slide from the bed, shuffling out to meet Oscar, who's standing at the door as if he's unsure where to go now that he's opened it. He looks around my apartment—Ashlee's apartment. He hasn't been here before, and it's strange seeing him in my personal space. I've never been a private person, but since I've been sick I've avoided social situations, unsure whether I'll be too tired to show up.

We make small talk, with Oscar complimenting the bold splashes of color in the apartment.

"Ashlee had good taste," I say. "She liked decorating."

His outline jogs my memory as he moves deeper into the kitchen, and I see him now as I saw him then, moving through the gala entrance. This time he's not watching Ashlee. His eyes are centered on mine.

"Verity, what's wrong?" he asks.

"Nothing," I say, a little too quickly.

My mind is playing a cruel trick on me. Oscar said that while he was at the gala, he was with Hayley, but maybe I saw him alone, just for a moment.

I can picture it. Oscar's profile, his straight nose, the line of his mouth, watching Ashlee at the gala. Watching *me.* But that doesn't make sense—it was Dale watching us from the entrance, not Oscar.

But the more I think about it, the less it makes sense. If Dale and Ashlee knew each other like Dale claimed, then why would she pretend she didn't know him? Maybe it was her way of hiding their connection. If Ashlee sold drugs, she wouldn't want me to find out her supplier was a pharmaceutical mogul.

"There's something you need to know." Oscar's tone scares me. Whatever he is about to say is the real reason for his visit, and he looks like he wants to avoid this entire conversation, making me want to tell him to turn around and go home. What could be worse than the things he's already told me?

"I found Ashlee's necklace," he says.

"What? Do you have it with you?" I expect him to pluck something from his pocket, but he looks away and starts again.

"Detective Payneham showed me some photographs... Ashlee was wearing it."

He doesn't need to say it for me to know the pictures were taken after she died.

My breath catches in my throat, a lump forming. "How? I was wearing it when I fell from the roof. That means... someone must have taken it after I fell, and..."

"I know. I'm sorry to bring it up like this." He pauses, and I nod, not trusting my voice to make the right sounds. "The

247

blood was also a match. They don't think it contributed to her death. It looks like it was there some time before. Maybe a shaving cut she was fixing up or something. Maybe they were dating at some point. It would explain why her necklace was in the cabinet."

He's right. It seems more possible now that I know Ashlee had a whole life I didn't know about. Maybe it was one of Ashlee's secrets. She couldn't tell me she was dating her supplier, because I might ask uncomfortable questions like how they met, and I could always tell when Ashlee was lying.

"Can you remember anything from when you were locked up? Footsteps? Did you smell a specific type of cologne?"

A new theory occurs to me. Could Ashlee have come back for her necklace? Even as I think it, I know that it's ridiculous. Ashlee wouldn't have left me there, passed out, possibly dying, while she took the chain from my neck.

The idea of me having the necklace at Dale's house must seem implausible to Oscar. Does he think I was imagining it, or that I'm somehow involved in Ashlee's death and the necklace was just a cowardly way of confessing?

A headache builds, starting deep in the back of my skull, and I place my hand on the sore spot, trying to calm the pain before it's raging.

I watch Oscar swipe and pinch the screen of his phone. When he's achieved what he wants, he holds it out and shows me a zoomed image of a necklace caked with dirt.

From the picture, the symbol around her neck could be an upside down *V*, but the ornateness of the outside of the letter tells me it's Ashlee's *A*, set against her skin. I try not to notice that her skin is mottled in death and peppered with dirt, like she's been wading through mud. I realize with a sick feeling that someone must've buried her, that digging her up couldn't dislodge all the dirt. I have a horrible image of Ashlee, alive when they put her in the earth, her orifices filling with wet soil.

"That's the same necklace," I confirm, pressing a hand against my temple, as if holding in the horror of it all. "Where did they find her?"

Oscar looks at me pityingly. "In the woods. Is that somewhere she might've gone? To exercise maybe?"

The way Oscar refers to her, like she's someone who used to be part of the world, but isn't any longer, hits like a physical blow. "I don't know," I say weakly. "Maybe."

When I close my eyes, I see Ashlee as she was the last time I saw her—tense and distracted despite being dressed like a princess.

The Ashlee in my memory is replaced with the image of someone watching from the gala entrance. As they cross the lawn, I notice that it isn't Dale or Oscar. I feel embarrassed for thinking it could have been Oscar, even if it was only for a moment, but he's approximately the same height, the same build. With sickening clarity, I realize I'm seeing Wes.

He has an intensely focused stare, but I must be imagining it because I was never close enough to see his face. My eyes close tighter as I hold on to the memory, struggling to see more detail. I want to get out of my car and demand to know what he's done with her. I want to make him feel the pain I'm feeling.

"Do you want to talk about it?" asks Oscar, and I look away, ashamed.

A sudden, desperate thought overcomes me. What if I could get Wes to confess? It would give me something tangible to go to the police with. They would never believe me—not when I'd accused Dale and gotten it wrong.

Even if they believed me, and the case went to trial, I probably wouldn't be here to see it out; I'd die without knowing if Wes got away with killing Ashlee.

I'm out of time.

"It's fine. It's nothing," I say, forcing myself to smile so he won't guess what I'm really thinking.

"Are you sure? You look like you need a moment. Come and sit," he says, leading me to the sofa. He leaves me there while he goes to the kitchen for a glass of water. When he returns, he sits beside me and waits until I've had a sip.

"Tell me," he says gently, "what happened just now?"

I need to ask, just to rule it out, to show myself it's not true, that it wasn't Oscar watching Ashlee at the gala.

"Were you at the hospital fundraiser?" I ask casually.

He looks unsure, his brow creasing.

"The gala that Ashlee was at that night. Were you there?"

"You know I was there, on behalf of the psychiatric wing at Whitner." I mustn't look satisfied with his answer, because he continues. "I went with Hayley. We didn't stay long because we both had work the next morning. I'm sorry I never got to meet Ashlee."

Oscar waits for me to pick up the conversation as I work through the details of that night. "When I dropped Ashlee off, there was someone standing outside the doors, right at the entrance, among the smokers. I assumed it was Dale, but I think there was someone standing behind him. I think I remembered Dale because his name was everywhere, the philanthropist giving to the hospital, and then the police questioned him. He was the main suspect, and he looked a lot like the person I really saw. I got them confused." I sip some water, coughing as it struggles down my throat.

I try again. "The other guy was in the background, so I didn't really pay him much attention." It rushes back and I tell him what I saw, waiting for his response, to see how crazy I sound.

Oscar takes the glass from my hand and sets it down on the coffee table. He waits patiently as I catch my breath, smiling at my embarrassed apology. He makes a joke, coaxing a smile from me.

My voice is still coarse as I pick up the conversation. "I must've caught him out of the corner of my eye. I assumed he'd slipped outside for a cigarette, but when he noticed me watching, he went inside. Dale stayed out front and they kind of became the same person when I woke up in the hospital. All this time I thought it was Dale, but maybe I was wrong."

"Just because this guy was watching Ashlee doesn't mean he killed her," says Oscar, sounding worried that I'm about to get myself into more trouble.

"I don't think he was watching just Ashlee. He was watching me too," I say.

"Do you know his name? Have you seen him before?"

"Maybe," I say weakly.

Oscar asks who it was, and why I think they were watching, but I brush off the question, not ready to tell him what I think I saw until I can find out whether it's true.

Dale's an asshole, but he probably didn't murder Ashlee. If Ashlee was selling drugs for him, killing her could bring him a lot of unwanted attention.

Maybe Wes was selling too.

Or he was one of Ashlee's customers.

I need to find out if Wes uses prescription medication, and I need to do it without him suspecting what I know.

39

Chapter 39

Oscar

Now

Verity looked tired when Oscar arrived, soft pillows of fatigue lining her eyes. Her mind was probably tricking her, blurring the faces she'd seen recently into one.

Dale. The person whose name she wouldn't give him. From the way she was looking at him, he questioned if she thought *he* might've killed Ashlee.

Maybe she was experiencing the misinformation effect and the events since she last saw Ashlee were impacting what she thought she'd seen. To be fair, it wasn't every day you got kidnapped and had a fall from a roof, hitting your head. He could forgive a foggy memory.

Verity had seen him at the gala, probably when he and Hayley had first arrived. They'd gone through the front doors, but they hadn't lingered, so it wasn't likely that Verity saw him outside like she thought she had.

Oscar had spent the hour he was at the gala with Hayley, fulfilling his social duties as the then head of psychiatry at Whitner Psychiatric Hospital. Those events were mostly for networking and professional development and sometimes for headhunting a doctor who had published something noteworthy. As soon as it was socially acceptable, Oscar had excused himself and gone home to prepare for work the next day.

How much of Verity's account had changed while Detective Payneham questioned her? Was that why Payneham was hesitant to discuss Ashlee's disappearance with Verity? Her version of events was shaky at best, and from what Oscar could tell, she was trying to convince herself that one of them was true because she needed to believe there was a reason for Ashlee's disappearance.

"Who did you see, Verity?" he asked gently.

She hesitated, her lips pressed together while she considered her answer. "It was probably nothing," she said, but the way she straightened her shoulders, the determination in her eyes told Oscar she didn't believe it was nothing. Whoever she thought she'd seen, she didn't want to tell him.

Was she hiding their identity, or was she worried she might be wrong?

Oscar refilled Verity's glass with water.

Was it someone she knew?

He changed tack. "Does Payneham know you dropped Ashlee off at the gala?"

"I think so," she said, taking the water with a grateful smile. "I must've told him."

Oscar looked around Ashlee's apartment, trying not to make it obvious he was assessing what kind of person Ashlee was.

The inside was tidy, with an empty fruit bowl sitting on the kitchen island. He wondered if it was always empty, or if Verity's stint in the hospital meant she hadn't gone grocery shopping. She must be exhausted. Had she eaten at all that evening?

"Are you hungry? I can find you something to eat if you like?"

She shook her head. "No, thanks. I ate earlier."

"I can pick up some groceries tomorrow?"

"That's okay." She smiled. "I'll have some delivered and save you the trouble."

"It's no trouble," he said.

Her smile widened. "You don't need a reason to stop by. You're welcome anytime."

Oscar returned the smile. He wasn't really a drop-by kind of guy, unless he had a solid reason. "Well, let me know if you need anything," he said.

"While you're here, there might be something you can help me with," said Verity with a note of uncertainty.

"Sure. What is it?"

She sighed, and he wasn't sure if she was trying to prepare him or herself for what was coming. "Could you ask Detective Payneham to drop the kidnapping charges against Dale?"

Oscar hesitated. She had been so sure Dale hurt her sister and now she was going to let him get away with kidnapping her? "Why would you want to do that?" he asked gently.

Verity looked straight at Oscar, as if she was confiding something intimate. "My mother used to say you should pick your battles," said Verity. "When I was a teenager I didn't understand what she meant, but I think I get it now. She was telling me to choose what I spend time worrying over, and to let go of the rest."

Oscar nodded. He'd always liked that saying, because when he was a kid, it always felt like there were too many battles to fight.

Verity took a deep breath. "I could go through a potential court case. But it'd mean sitting inside a stuffy courtroom, listening to other people's opinions and accounts of what I went through before they decide whether Dale should be punished for what he did."

She threw her hands in the air. "I don't know how long I have left, but I know I don't want to spend my last days like that." She shrugged.

Oscar matched her expression, and she laughed.

"I want to spend the time I have left living. I've already wasted enough time in the hospital," she said regretfully. "If I waste my energy on punishing Dale, I'd be like keeping myself locked up in that house."

She was right. She might waste what little time she had left if she pursued it, and some people found the process more traumatic, especially when there were no results to show for it. The justice system wasn't always kind.

Oscar looked at the clock on his phone. It was almost seven, and he'd promised Hayley he'd have dinner ready. Except he hadn't shopped for groceries yet, and the pantry was running low on supplies.

"I'll talk to Detective Payneham," Oscar promised. "But only if you're sure?"

"I am," she said, unwavering.

Oscar said goodbye and left. If he hurried, he might be able to get the ingredients to throw together a salad. He'd been so busy with everyone else that he'd neglected his own life.

He'd be lucky if Hayley wanted to have dinner with him at this point.

He checked his phone, in case she'd messaged back, but she hadn't confirmed she'd be there yet.

It was just after seven—definitely not enough time to pick up groceries. On his way home, he stopped at Carnivals, Hayley's favorite burger place, and ordered burgers and fries instead. He messaged to let her know he was running a little late, but that he'd make up for it by bringing something delicious.

His heart sank when he pulled into the driveway and didn't see Hayley's car. Maybe she'd been held up at work too—she was busy with...

He didn't know what was happening at Whitner lately, but he knew there was always something to keep you busy.

Oscar fished in his pocket for the house key, unlocked the door and went in to set the burgers down on the table, hoping maybe she'd just gone out for a bit, that Arty would bound up to greet him. "Hello?" he called.

Hayley was probably exhausted. She worked hard. He plucked his phone from his pocket and sent a message.

Have food. Offering a one time delivery service if you're stuck at work? Also redeemable for home delivery if you prefer. Feel free to tip your delivery driver with a kiss. Xx

The smell of grilled onion wafted from the bag, tempting him. He ate a fry while he waited for a reply. He photographed one, half-eaten and dressed up with ketchup eyes and mouth, and sent a closeup with the caption: *You have one minute before I finish the fry. Can't promise there'll be any left after ten minutes.*

Still no reply. Usually, she'd laugh at that. Maybe she was out for after-work drinks. He didn't want to bother her, so he let loose on the fries. Alone. Usually, Artemis would slide around the floor, going too fast for her own feet, begging for a bite from the big table.

As he ate, Oscar realized his message mightn't be received well, especially if Hayley was upset with him for neglecting her over the last few days.

He finished his burger and tidied up, putting Hayley's burger in the fridge, just in case.

His hand lingered over a beer on the top shelf of the refrigerator. He'd already had one today with Payneham—another would mean breaking a promise he'd made to himself.

Oscar lit up the screen of his phone with a strike of his thumb, bringing it to life. He checked his messages again, the refrigerator door still open. Still no reply. He plucked a beer from the shelf, his hand constricting around its cold middle.

He took the beer outside and sat, looking out across his yard. The first gulp sent cold liquid racing down his throat. The evening chill had picked up, the cold prickling his skin so that he was just uncomfortable enough to pick through his own thoughts.

When Verity fell from the roof, she thought Ashlee's chain was around her neck. He remembered the dirt that filled the A, the way it lay against Ashlee's throat, transforming it into a caret. The lawn dimmed as the sky darkened, but Oscar ignored the fading light, still thinking.

What if he and Detective Payneham were wrong about it being like an arrow or a mathematical symbol? What if the caret was an editing tool, used to show there was something being added in? That could mean that Ashlee was an addendum, an afterthought to a different end game.

Verity had said the person at the gala was watching her and Ashlee. Maybe Verity was the target all along, and that's why they'd tried to suffocate her. That would mean they were still out there, waiting for an opportunity to eliminate her.

How had they gotten in and out of the hospital room undetected? They must be good at blending in, or they had access to the hospital. Could it be one of the staff?

He finished his beer and went for another, resuming his post in the brisk air.

Had Ashlee stumbled across her killer, thinking she was protecting her sister, or was she oblivious to who it was and what they were capable of?

If they were willing to break into Verity's hospital room, they probably wouldn't think much of paying her a home visit.

Oscar dialed Verity's number, hoping to catch her before she fell asleep.

She answered after the second ring.

"Verity, is there somewhere you can go tonight?"

"Wes?"

"It's Oscar." He paced the grass, the movement helping him steady his thoughts.

"Oh," she said, sounding embarrassed. "Sorry. What's wrong?"

"I don't think it's safe to stay at your apartment, or Ashlee's," said Oscar.

"What? Why?" Her voice crackled with sleep.

"I believe you—when you said someone tried to suffocate you, I don't think it was a dream. I think they might keep trying."

"Are you saying I should go to the police?"

He paused, considering what it would take for Detective

Payneham to treat this seriously. Right now, all he had was a hunch backed up by a theory. He didn't have any proof. "For now, I'm saying you should stay somewhere else."

"Okay. I can go to a hotel for a while?"

"Yeah, that works," said Oscar, feeling uneasy. The hospital was a pretty public place to attack someone, but it hadn't stopped them from trying. A hotel wasn't somewhere they were likely to have access to, and it should keep Verity safe while he thought about it some more.

"For how long?"

"I don't know," he said, realizing he hadn't thought out the details in his rush to make sure she was safe.

"Oscar, is everything okay?"

"Yeah," he said, finding himself eyeing the gutters around the edge of his roof. He imagined the dizzying feeling of falling from the top, the impact of landing. Verity was lucky to have survived.

"In the pictures of Ashlee, the letter *A* was filled with dirt, so that it looked like a caret," he said. "I don't know if that was an accident. Do you know what that symbol might mean? Does it have any significance to you or Ashlee? Could it be a message or a warning?"

"It's a symbol on a keyboard, right? What *would* it mean?"

"That's what I'm trying to figure out. You said you saw someone watching you at the gala. What can you tell me about them? Were they your age? Did they have a feature that stood out? What were they wearing?" asked Oscar.

"I'm not even sure I saw who I thought I did," said Verity. "I'm sorry I can't be more helpful."

"Just promise you'll stay somewhere else tonight," he said.

"I will," said Verity, ending the call.

40

Chapter 40

Verity

Now

My call with Oscar ends with me making a promise I know I won't keep.

I'll die sooner than I'd like anyway, as the cells in my body grow in bizarre ways. The irony of it strikes me—cells growing at a rate my body can't keep up with, proliferating, thriving beyond my capacity to sustain them. So if Wes wants to pay me a visit, I'm ready to find out why he killed Ashlee.

While she was missing, I thought I'd be satisfied once I knew where she was, but I was wrong. The need to find out why she was killed has replaced the need to find her.

Oscar's call has left me shaken. I don't know what the caret means, but I keep picturing the gold chain around her neck like a noose, the charm suffocating with dirt. Maybe it doesn't mean anything. After lying in the dirt for days, maybe that's how the mud settled.

My phone beeps and I find a message from Wes. It's as if he heard me thinking about him. He's suggested a time and place to meet—a coffee shop this time, cozy and intimate, the kind of place that's small enough to eavesdrop on other people's problems. I want to talk somewhere we'll be able to speak freely, to see who he really is when it's just the two of us. I want to know if it was him I saw at the gala, or another trick my mind is playing.

I need to ask questions without someone listening in. I was wrong about Dale, and this time I need to be certain. There's no time to waste on another dead end.

I type quickly and send the message. *What are you doing now?*

He answers immediately. *Not a lot. How about you?*

Me too. I'm kinda bored.

My pulse is racing. I feel it in my throat like a trapped butterfly, eager to escape. I punch in the next message before I lose my nerve, before the truth slips away again.

You want to come over?

I wait a couple of minutes before my phone dings with a reply. *I'd love to, but I can't. :(Early morning start at work.*

I check my calendar, an idea forming. It's Wednesday. Holding off for a day would give me time to get things ready so that I can confront him.

I tap a message. *How about tomorrow? I'll cook us up something.*

41

Chapter 41

Oscar

Now

Oscar awoke Thursday morning with a searing pain in his knee. The deep throb inside the joint told him it was going to be a bad day.

His knee had knitted back together a long time ago, but it felt like something had never really returned to normal. He reached for the oxy he kept in the drawer next to his bed.

It used to take the edge off his thoughts, but he only used it for pain now, after missing a visit to his son's grave too many times in a row, too hopped up on pain medication to drive.

He'd built himself up slowly, one day at a time, until he felt ready to visit Riley. Sometimes, he talked about the kind of day they might've had together if Riley was here. He told Riley about things he thought might interest him—a new scooter he saw, a PC game they could've played together.

His leg hadn't been bad enough to take painkillers for a while, but today he held the bottle in his hand, trying to imagine what the day would be like without them. If it'd just be a bad day he'd go without, but if it was going to be too difficult to walk he'd need them.

The morning light was harsh, casting a bright arc across Oscar's face, placing him under an unwanted spotlight. He rolled away from the glare, starting his morning with reluctant acceptance. But he couldn't forget. It was the anniversary of Lila's death. The years had dulled the pain, but every year Oscar wondered what kind of person she would have grown into. He'd never find out. Instead, she'd always be his little sister, her long braids falling down her back.

Oscar checked his phone, trying to distract himself from the pain in his leg.

No messages from Hayley. He felt a little heavier knowing she hadn't called. He took his time making breakfast while he decided whether to message her or give her space. Eventually, he decided to wait until she wanted to talk. He needed to meet with a nurse Ashlee had worked with today, to find out what she knew that he didn't. He had a feeling that Verity's account of Ashlee was marred; Verity saw her sister as an innocent victim. Oscar was curious how everyone else saw her.

He arrived at Bayswater Hospital midmorning, while Mercy was taking a break. She was the only nurse who had agreed to talk with him, but they were meeting at her workplace—maybe to show that she had nothing to hide. She led him through to the staff room and invited him to sit at a round table.

She sized him up while she made them coffee on an industrial sized, automated machine, asking Oscar how he took his coffee as she went. "The machine's courtesy of a few nurses pitching in. We were sick of instant and decided the night shift staff needed this. It's pretty close to barista made café coffee."

"Do you work night shifts?" asked Oscar.

"Most of the nursing staff work on rotating rosters, but I was lucky enough to secure a permanent afternoon shift so I can drop my kids off at school in the mornings." She shrugged and handed Oscar a blue-lipped ceramic mug. "If you want more sugar," she said, pointing out a canister on the kitchen island, "help yourself."

"No, thanks. This is fine."

He took a hesitant sip. Drinkable, but the hastily roasted beans compromised the overall taste. He took another sip and set his mug down.

"What do you want to know about Ashlee?" asked Mercy, settling down in a chair and sipping her own brew.

"What was she like? Did you know her well?" he asked.

"She was one of the rotating roster girls, but we worked together a lot. We did some training together too, sometimes caught up for drinks with a few of the girls. We used to go out on weekends until recently."

"So, you were friends?"

"Yeah, we were." The way she said 'were' suggested the friendship had broken down. Mercy cupped her mug with both hands, stroking the side with her thumb. "Ashlee made you feel like you could tell her anything without being judged. When my boyfriend and I broke up, I was a mess, but Ashlee made me feel like it was an opportunity to head in a new direction." She paused, smiling softly to herself, remembering her friend. "She was vibrant. She lived life the

265

way it's meant to be lived."

"How do you mean?" asked Oscar.

Mercy's smile deepened, her eyes crinkling at the corners. "She just didn't let the little things get to her." She cleared her throat. "Do you think they'll find her?"

Oscar hadn't counted on being asked questions, and he wasn't sure whether the police were telling people they'd found her body yet, or if they were keeping it from the public. The hope in Mercy's eyes almost made him look away. Maybe he shouldn't say anything, but people were bound to find out now that Ashlee's death had been confirmed.

He told Mercy as carefully as he could—Ashlee's body had been recovered. No, unfortunately, she wasn't okay. He gave Mercy a moment to process what he'd said before resuming his questions. "Had Ashlee's behavior changed much in the weeks before she disappeared?"

Mercy shook her head. "No. She seemed good. Some people thought maybe she had just taken off for an impromptu vacation. After a month, it was pretty clear she wasn't coming back. I visited her that first week to see if she was okay. I took soup with me in case she was sick, but she wasn't home. Her sister answered the door and told me Ashlee was missing."

"Why did people think she was on vacation?" asked Oscar.

"I was on during her last shift. I remember her saying 'See you when I see you' before she left. It felt like a strange thing to say, kind of like she knew she wasn't coming back." Mercy peered into her mug. "It was about a week, I think, before the police questioned me and some of the other nurses."

"Did you ask Ashlee about her comment?"

"No. I thought she was joking until she didn't show up for her next shift. When I called to remind her she was on the next day, her phone went to voice mail. I thought she might've been sick then, but I really didn't have time to check up on her until later—I had two double shifts that week, kids to drop at school, and errands to take care of," said Mercy, her tone thick with regret.

"There's nothing you could've done, if that's what you're thinking," Oscar said gently, catching her eye.

"If I'd visited her earlier, maybe I could've done something, but I was so busy with my own life that I barely thought about Ash until it was too late," said Mercy. "How is her sister? I felt so bad for her. She seemed to be just waiting for Ash to come home."

"How did Ashlee's sister seem when you spoke to her?" asked Oscar.

Mercy shrugged. "She was upset—kind of standoffish, like she didn't want to talk. I asked questions because I wanted to help, but I get the feeling her sister thought I was being nosy."

Oscar moved to his next question, hoping they'd been good enough friends to share secrets. "Was Ashlee seeing anyone? Or socializing with people she didn't usually socialize with?"

Mercy's thumb stopped moving across the mug. "Uh, I don't know," she said, the inflection unnatural, making Oscar wonder if she was lying.

"I want to find whoever did this," said Oscar. "Otherwise, they get away with it, and Ashlee's still gone. Keeping her secrets won't help her."

Mercy looked at the floor and swallowed hard, a worried expression on her face.

She knew something.

There was no reason to keep her secrets now—Ashlee couldn't be upset with her. Maybe there was a bigger threat.

267

Was Mercy involved in whatever trouble had gotten Ashlee killed?

Oscar lowered his voice. "Listen, I'm not here to make trouble for you. I just want to know how we can help find Ashlee's killer and stop someone else from getting hurt."

Mercy looked around, surveying the employees in the staff room. Satisfied, she lowered her voice to match Oscar's. "Ashlee was going through a reckless phase. When she found out her sister had cancer, her carefree attitude became more of a 'who cares.' She was struggling—she and her sister were close, and Ashlee dealt with her sister's illness by avoiding it. She started partying a lot."

"Partying? Was she taking drugs?"

"Maybe. She was going out most nights. Drinking."

"Who was she partying with?"

"Friends from work," she said. "Sometimes she went alone. I went a couple of times, but she ditched me when she met a random guy, and sometimes she'd just disappear for a while and show up again like nothing had happened. So, I stopped going."

"Was that usual behavior for Ashlee?"

"No. We used to go out dancing, maybe have a few drinks. We usually shared a cab home, exhausted at three in the morning." She smiled, remembering. "We'd call each other the next day to compare hangovers. It was supposed to be a girls' night thing, not a hookup."

She pressed her knuckles against her lip, giving Oscar the impression there was something she wasn't saying.

Oscar sipped his coffee. "Is there another reason you stopped going out with Ashlee?"

Mercy shifted uncomfortably. She didn't want to rat out her

friend.

"I'm just trying to get a picture of Ashlee before she died," said Oscar, "So that I can put together what happened to her, maybe give her family some answers."

"One time, she bought some drugs. I don't know if she got messed up with a dealer or what. I didn't ask questions about where she got it. She offered me a pill, but I couldn't do that. I had kids to go home to." Mercy shifted again and looked around, lowering her voice. "She really wanted the two of us to try them together, so I eventually agreed."

"What did you take?"

Mercy shook her head. "I don't know. It was kind of surreal. Lights were flashing. We were drinking. Then Ashlee was trying to put this pill in my mouth, and I told her I couldn't. That *we* couldn't. We're *nurses*. We see people OD all the time." She looked embarrassed despite the artificial pink stain covering her slender cheekbones, the natural pink underneath blooming down her neck.

"Did she do drugs often?" asked Oscar.

"I really couldn't say. I don't think so."

"Did Ashlee know Dale Carmot?" asked Oscar, hoping to find out whether Ashlee had a relationship she hadn't discussed with Verity.

"If she did, she never talked to me about it. Do they still think it was him?"

"The police are still piecing together what happened," said Oscar carefully. "I need to know what was happening with Ashlee before she went missing—it could tell us what kind of state of mind she was in, and where she might've gone that night."

Mercy was still keeping something. Was she worried about

tarnishing Ashlee's reputation? It wasn't uncommon for people to feel bad about speaking ill of the dead. "Is there anything else I should know?" asked Oscar.

Mercy sighed, shifting the mug in her hands.

"She was my friend, mostly. Someone who was always there for me. My colleague. But I think toward the end Ashlee became someone I didn't know so well."

"How so?"

"She was moodier," said Mercy. "Her usual bubbliness disappeared. I get that she was struggling with her sister's illness, but she started making mistakes at work. Nothing big, but she stopped following protocol. It was like she was just showing up. She'd take long lunch breaks and disappear mid-shift. I covered for her a couple of times, but when I told her she was putting extra pressure on everyone else, she brushed it off like she didn't care."

Oscar continued working through his coffee, listening attentively.

Mercy raised an eyebrow. "She laughed and said it was just a job. We argued, and I told her that people's lives were in our hands, and we needed to have our heads in the game, but she just...walked away."

It was a brave thing to open up about your last moments with someone, especially when they weren't happy memories.

"At first I wondered if Ashlee might've hurt herself."

"Suicide?" asked Oscar gently.

"Yeah."

42

Chapter 42

Oscar

Now

Oscar left his meeting with Mercy wondering whether Verity had noticed her sister's increasing melancholy. Maybe Ashlee had hidden it from Verity, afraid of what it'd do to her declining health.

Oscar's phone buzzed. He pulled it from his pocket and answered.

"Is this Mr. de la Nuit?" asked a serious voice from the other end. He tried to place it, but it didn't sound like anyone he knew.

"It is," said Oscar warily, hoping what followed wasn't a spam caller trying to sell him the greatest insurance in the world.

"This is Dr. Alex Larson. I'm calling in regard to your father, Bill," said a calm voice—too calm—muted by dim hospital noise in the background.

The tone put Oscar on edge. No one delivered good news that somberly. "Is he all right?" asked Oscar automatically.

"I'm afraid not. He's had a second myocardial infarction."

The anticipation of Alex's next words threatened to empty the contents of Oscar's stomach. "Is he…" He let the words hang, unable to finish the sentence. Bill wasn't perfect, but he was the only family Oscar had growing up. The thought of losing him put his nerves on edge.

"He's in surgery at the moment, but it could go either way."

"Okay, I'm on my way." Oscar walked faster, ignoring the pain in his leg. Gritting his teeth, he broke into a run, hoping to get there in time to speak to his dad one last time if it came to that, regretting that he hadn't followed up on Bill's message. Maybe Bill really did need to talk to him. What if this time, Bill knew he wasn't going to make it?

* * *

Kiko was already waiting when Oscar arrived, crumpled in a steel-framed chair with a hard white back, her head bent.

She stood when she saw Oscar, and instinctively, he hugged her. "How is he?"

Kiko shook her head. Oscar could see she'd been crying. "They haven't told me anything. I think he's still in surgery."

"Where's Steve?" asked Oscar, looking around the waiting room for his brother. "Someone should tell him what happened. He should be here."

Kiko's voice was resigned. "He knows. He can't come. He's

at work."

Oscar had forgotten the soothing tones of his mother's voice. She had a way of making it sound like things would work out in the end. That belief had left with her when she went, replaced by a pending sense of dread that something else was bound to go wrong.

"Can't he leave early? People will still want to buy whatever he's selling tomorrow. I'll call him."

Oscar needed to do something useful. He was used to fixing things, but this time there was nothing to do except wait. Calling Steve wouldn't really make anything better, but at least he'd feel like he was doing something useful.

"It's probably better if you don't," said Kiko.

Oscar renewed his argument with fresh points. "If Dad doesn't make it, Steve will hate himself for not being here. Let me call him."

"Don't worry yourself with that now," said Kiko, leading Oscar to a chair. She took the seat next to him, looking miserable.

Oscar felt a pang of sympathy for her. If Bill died, it meant that all the things his parents had avoided discussing would die with him.

"Steve needs his work, and his patients need their prescriptions."

"Patients?" Oscar said, confused. Kiko was mistaken—Oscar saw patients. Steve handled customers. It'd been so long since Oscar had seen Kiko that he couldn't tell whether she was experiencing a slight memory lapse or something more.

Kiko ignored Oscar's tone. "Let's just focus on Bill. He's been in there for a while. The doctor should be out with news soon."

Footsteps echoed across the waiting room. Oscar turned, dreading who might enter and what they would say. A nurse stopped by a woman who was bouncing a young child on her knee and whispered something Oscar couldn't hear. The woman nodded silently and stood, hoisting the child on her hip and following the nurse through a corridor to the right.

As she passed, Oscar could see the relief in her expression, like the surface tension of a pool breaking. She must've received good news.

Kiko was watching too, but now that they were alone, her attention went back to their conversation. "I was visiting your father when it happened. We were talking." She pressed her lips together.

"What were you talking about?" asked Oscar.

"You." She looked away. "He got upset. He wanted to tell you something, and I didn't think it was a good idea. He was very insistent. Maybe he knew he was going to—"

Oscar remembered the call, the way he'd fobbed Bill off.

Kiko continued. "He said he didn't feel great today."

"Then maybe it wasn't the day to upset him." Oscar snapped, but the hurt expression on Kiko's face made him apologize immediately. The tension of the day was getting to him.

Kiko nodded. "That's why I promised him I'd tell you."

Oscar wasn't sure he wanted to know if it had been bad enough to put Bill back on the operating table.

"Knowing won't change anything. It doesn't change me leaving, or that you had to grow up without a mother, but Bill wanted you to know anyway."

"Why now?" asked Oscar.

"Because I'm afraid that if he doesn't make it, I'll lose my courage," said Kiko.

Her expression scared Oscar—what she was about to reveal might burden them both more than either of them could handle just now.

"I was trying to protect you. I hope you understand why I didn't tell you back then."

It was hard to focus on Kiko's words when he knew his dad was fighting for his life, but Oscar did his best to listen.

Too many things were already wrong. He still hadn't heard from Hayley, and he wasn't sure Verity would be okay, or if she'd even stay at a hotel like she'd promised. And Steve wasn't here like he should be.

With a sudden burst of resolve, he stood. "Steve should be here. I'm calling him."

"That's what I'm trying to tell you. I know you must feel like I chose Steve."

"You have no idea how I feel. It's not like you came back to see how I was, or find out what I was doing."

He found Steve's name in his contact list, ready to hit dial.

"Wait," said Kiko forcefully. "Don't call."

"What if Dad doesn't make it?"

"I lied," said Kiko.

"What do you mean?"

"I didn't call Steve," said Kiko.

"Why would you keep him from being here?"

"Bill didn't want him here. They never had the best relationship." Kiko knitted her hands together, clearly rattled by Oscar's anger.

"Let me explain," she pleaded.

"You know what?" said Oscar dismissively. "Keep your excuses. I'm calling, and we'll let him decide if he wants to be here." He brushed by Kiko, stopping short when her hand clutched his arm.

"I was protecting you," she said. "Bill and I decided it was the best thing for everyone, even if it meant being away from each other."

Oscar was unmoved by her display. It was a huge decision to make without at least asking what he wanted, and Oscar had to deal with the fallout all by himself.

"It's hard for me too, seeing Bill here, seeing you. It reminds me what I've missed out on. You're all grown up." Kiko loosened her grip on his shirt, holding on just enough that he had to stay and listen, or risk toppling her slight frame.

"Steve can't help who he is," said Kiko. "He was born that way. Maybe that's my fault. Maybe it was just the way he was meant to be, but I couldn't let you suffer for it. Your father's stubborn and stuck in his ways, but he loves you."

Oscar wasn't sure Bill loved anyone, except maybe Kiko. She was referring to a side of Bill he saved only for her.

"That's why he agreed to let me take Steve. He blamed Steve for the way he is. Bill wanted to change him. He thought your brother needed discipline to get better. Bill offered to take Steve away so that I could stay with you. I didn't want to leave you, so I almost agreed."

Had his mom really left to keep Steve at a safe distance? Was she trying to protect Oscar? Steve was his brother. What did he need saving from?

Kiko was crying now. She reached out, resting her palm across her son's face. "If Bill had gone instead of me, they would have killed each other. So, I made the best choice I could. It was the hardest decision of my life."

Oscar could see in the lines of her face, the sacrifices she'd made, and what it'd cost her. What he couldn't understand was why she stayed away—even if Kiko believed Steve was dangerous, Oscar wasn't a kid that needed protecting any more.

"You could've come back," said Oscar, still not sure what she was protecting him from.

"Steve never changed. I didn't want him to come back. I know you idolized him when you were a boy. You never saw the bad in anyone, especially your big brother, but he was just so jealous of you. He thought you were the golden boy, the favorite."

She smiled wistfully at her son. "You had a way with people, because you were kind. Steve just didn't understand how to be like that. He didn't feel it like you did."

It seemed unfair, blaming Steve for the choices she'd made. He felt a sudden anger emerging, one he'd worked hard to contain, petrified that if he didn't, he'd end up like Bill. "You left without saying anything. I thought you blamed me for Lila's accident. I hated myself for it. I went over and over what I should've done differently until I was too numb to do anything at all, in case I stuffed up again. I know I was supposed to be watching Lila, but I couldn't stop the car from coming toward her."

Kiko looked pained. "I know."

"I thought I broke our family apart because you couldn't stand being there with me, and Dad was so angry. Once you left, he was even worse."

Kiko took Oscar's hand. "Not once did I think what happened to Lila was your fault," she said firmly. "You risked your life to save her."

Oscar looked at the floor, unable to meet her eyes.

"Oscar, I was afraid you'd take the hit for Steve too. That he'd keep letting you and, eventually, you'd end up buried next to Lila."

43

Chapter 43

Verity

Now

Waiting is the worst. All that wasted energy worrying about something I can't predict.

Will I find out why Ashlee had to die? Will I survive the night?

Before Wes arrives, I paint my face with makeup, trying to recolor the parts that look faded from sickness. First, I apply a dewy glow to my skin before using a plumping gloss to restore my lips to the rose petal pink they were before. Next, I highlight my eyes, lengthening and darkening my lashes with a mascara wand. When I'm finished, I look like I've regained some vibrance. My hair is freshly dyed, the ends glowing like red embers.

I check the time; he's still not here.

What if he doesn't show?

I go over my plan. One item at a time. First, I'll need to confirm that it was Wes at the gala. Then, I'll need to find out if he takes oxy, and where he gets it from.

Whether he got it from Ashlee.

Seven o'clock comes and goes, with no sign of Wes. Time slows painfully, the minutes struggling to move, until I hear footsteps in the hall.

Moments later there's a knock at the door.

I throw it open. Wes has made an effort to look nice, his hair washed and styled and I wonder if the effort's for me. His dark eyes, like coffee liqueur, catch mine and I smile, trying to hide my nerves, hoping he mistakes them for date jitters and nothing more.

I have all night to figure out why you killed Ashlee.

He compliments my hair, and eyes the dress I'm wearing. I offer him a drink which he accepts gratefully, watching me pour two glasses of Shiraz. I don't intend to finish mine. He waits for me to bring the glass to my mouth before he drinks. An outdated show of chivalry, or a subtle sign he doesn't trust me?

Playing along, I let the red liquid wash over my lower lip, richer than the pink of my lip gloss.

We make small talk about everyday things until I address the elephant in the room—how our last date ended.

We sit on the sofa, waiting for the ding of the oven to tell us dinner's ready. I've made roast beef and vegetables, an unassuming dish to start a difficult conversation over.

"So, the guy who told you he was my boyfriend was lying, but I guess you figured that out, right?" I conceal a shy laugh behind my wineglass, marring my expression.

Wes looks embarrassed. "Yeah. Sorry about that. I was so

shocked that I walked right out of there. You know, I actually considered staying," he said. "But then he sat right next to me. I don't think he had any intention of leaving. You were going to walk out of the bathroom at any moment and find him there, so I figured it was better to stay out of it. It was kind of creepy. He was so close he was almost touching me."

I try to laugh but it sounds forced. The thought of Dale Carmot pretending to be my boyfriend is repulsive, but it confirms that he set me up, that when I saw him walk in, he had probably staged it so that I'd see him. In approaching Wes, Dale had essentially created a witness to verify where we were that night.

A witness for him, or for me?

Was he afraid of what I'd do to him, making sure someone knew who to look for if things turned bad?

A third option crosses my mind.

Dale didn't tell Wes he was my boyfriend at all. Wes made that up. He lied about it so that he could leave, and the ex-boyfriend story was the first excuse he thought of.

"My god," I say, curling a piece of hair around my finger. "What did he say?"

Wes looks as if he's been caught by surprise, but he's quick to recover. "He asked if we were on a date and said he was your boyfriend." He shrugs as if he's as confused by Dale's comment as I should be.

"Hmm."

"What?" There's a defensive edge to his voice, but I pretend not to notice and follow my plan.

"It's just strange that Dale Carmot of all people would say that."

"Who?"

"The guy who said he was my boyfriend. He owns a pharmaceutical company. It makes me kinda mad," I say. "They overcharge people for medicine, and half the time they're just ripping off someone else's product."

I remember the days when I started researching chemo and the relief I felt when I learned that my insurance covered at least a few rounds. Not everyone is that lucky—especially by round five or six.

"Yeah," says Wes awkwardly.

"You don't agree?" My tone is teasing.

"No, I actually do. It's just that I work for one of those companies, selling pharmaceuticals to hospitals, so I guess that makes me just as bad," he says sheepishly.

The oven dings. "Be right back," I say, but not before I shoot him a look to suggest I want a rundown when I get back.

I open the oven door, the aroma of roasted herbs escaping. I linger over the food longer than I need to, keeping my back turned to him to process what he said.

So that's how he met Ashlee. He was a sales rep. He's not a teacher like he claimed. I imagine his severed head in the roasting pan, cooking slowly.

"It's ready," I announce, arranging potatoes and roast beef onto plates. I wait for Wes to wash up and return before apologizing. "I didn't mean it like that. Medicine helps people."

"No, it's okay. Some of those companies have too much say over the market. I'm just the guy who gives people what they need to stay healthy."

Wes slices the meat and tastes it. "This is great," he says. "I don't cook very often; work keeps me away from the kitchen."

"Thanks," I say, my fork stabbing a potato, pushing it

around my plate as I watch Wes eat.

I sense that he'd happily eat in silence, but I didn't invite him here for a free meal.

"Dale was also accused of murdering my sister," I say.

His expression doesn't change. "Jesus. That's how I know his name. I remember hearing something about that a couple of months ago.

I stop myself from asking where exactly he heard about it. If I ask too many questions too soon, he might realize that I know who he is and why I really invited him here.

"That was your sister?" He does his best to look surprised, and he's pretty good.

"Yeah. Ashlee," I say, letting her name hang in the air.

"I'm sorry, that must've been difficult." He drags a chunk of potato through the gravy distractedly.

"Not knowing what happened to her was awful." I let the words hang in the air, testing his response. "At least now I have some answers," I say.

He looks at me. "Answers?"

I could be imagining it, but he seems more interested now.

"I'm sorry. I didn't invite you here to unload my problems."

He forces a smile, his enthusiasm for the food forgotten. The way he's looking at me, eyes narrowed in thought, suggests he's realized that I know more than I'm saying.

Does he regret killing her and burying her among the trees, thinking no one would find her in the dirt? Or is he afraid he's about to get caught and go to jail for killing her?

He doesn't look sorry at all. He looks afraid, like the wolf who's suddenly lost its teeth.

"They found her body," I say, hoping he can't tell how nervous I am.

He's looking at me openly now, and I feel any pretense slipping. His head is tilted, and I realize he's deciding whether to silence me.

44

Chapter 44

Oscar

Now

The things Oscar hadn't dared to think about his brother were true. He sat heavily, a white-backed chair catching him. He let the chair take his weight and closed his eyes, remembering the day Lila died.

He saw Kiko burst through the front door to see what the commotion was. Steve had pointed to Oscar, who was lying on the road, trying to crawl to Lila. He was clutching his leg, dragging it along.

The stunned driver had jumped out of her vehicle, her straight dark hair and tailored clothes a contrast to the chaos before her. She was screaming that Lila came out of nowhere. Then she screamed an apology to God, but no one was really listening as she continued to wail. All eyes were on Lila, lying lifeless across the road.

All this time he'd thought that Lila fell into the road, that it was an accident. But somewhere deep down he knew what Steve could do to him if he told anyone he saw Steve nudge her.

"Steve pushed Lila," Oscar said, his hands holding on to the edge of his seat.

Steve had pretended it was an accident. Had Kiko known all along that Steve did it on purpose? Is that why she took him away?

Oscar racked his brain, trying to remember why Steve was annoyed with Lila that day. She'd come outside to see what they were doing, and to tell them their snacks were ready. Lila hadn't been outside long enough to upset Steve.

The roaring engine had approached quickly, barreling down their street. Lila had backed away from Steve as he approached her. Oscar saw her moving toward the road, but he was too far away to get there in time.

By the time he reached her, the engine was hot in his ears and it was too late to get her out of the way.

Kiko looked at her son, apologizing silently. "I'm sorry I wasn't there for you like I should've been. I was blind in my grief, and afraid of what Steve would do. I was terrified you'd be next."

"Why didn't you get Steve some help?"

"Because," said Kiko, resigned, "he can't help what he is. If I took him to a psychiatrist, they would've locked him up. How would that help him? There's no fixing it. He just *is*."

"So, you let him get away with what he did to Lila?"

"No," said Kiko. "I tried to stop it from happening again. I took him away."

Something in the way she said it made Oscar wonder if she

meant to do more than that. "He needed treatment," he said. "From someone that was trained to help."

"He wouldn't do it again," said Kiko. "What happened to Lila was a horrible, horrible mistake. He can't help his temper. He just needed to go somewhere for a while so he couldn't take it out on anyone else."

"If he could do that to his own sister, he could do that to anyone."

Kiko looked wounded. "Steve was my responsibility. I brought him into the world."

Oscar stood his ground. "He needs help."

"What would you do? If your child did such a terrible thing, if it would ruin their life? Would you tell the world, shame them for their mistakes? Or would you help them realize it was a mistake and give them some time to understand that they can make better choices?"

"What if you're wrong?" Oscar countered. "What if he does it again and all you've done is show him he can get away with it? What if it's too late, and he's already killed someone else?"

A doctor wearing a disposable hair cap pushed through a set of doors, sending an echo through the hall. He stopped when he reached Kiko and Oscar, their nervous energy bringing them to their feet. A tag hanging from his clothing identified him as Dr. Alex Larson. His movements were quiet, considered, like his tone had been when Oscar spoke with him on the phone. "Mrs. de la Nuit?"

"Yes," said Kiko, anxiously clutching her hands.

Oscar was surprised she still went by de la Nuit after all these years.

There was genuine concern in her voice—maybe even love—as she asked about Bill. "Is he okay?"

287

45

Chapter 45

Verity

Now

I have a little bottle of pills sitting on the table, hoping to catch Wes's reaction when he sees them.

Finally, he notices, but the thirst I expected isn't there as he looks past them.

I push harder. "They're for a slipped disk in my back." I pretend I'm embarrassed, but not so much so that I wouldn't want to talk about it. He doesn't ask questions, but I continue anyway. "They're so expensive. I mean, at least they used to be. It's probably why I sounded so annoyed at pharmaceutical companies before."

He raises an eyebrow and looks at the little bottle again. "Does it help? With the pain, I mean."

I shrug a shoulder, noncommittal, and load the dishwasher while Wes finishes his drink. "I guess. I buy them off-market.

It's cheaper than filling a prescription."

When I'm done loading dishes, I serve two chocolate tarts, each with a dollop of whipped cream and half a strawberry, knowing I won't be able to eat mine. The chocolate is too rich, and my stomach feels agitated by the stress of the evening.

"Have you ever tried oxy? It really takes the edge off," I say.

He smiles, maybe imagining me as a potential customer. "I haven't needed to—just lucky I guess."

I know he's lying, because he isn't reacting to the large amount I put in his food before serving it, which tells me he's built a tolerance.

"Really?" I ask, feigning surprise. "Not even recreation-ally?"

"No," he says, his grin wide.

I lean forward, my arms flat across the tabletop. "See, I thought that might've been why you were watching my sister at the hospital gala."

"What?"

"She was in my car, and you were outside with a bunch of smokers, but you didn't have a cigarette. I thought maybe you were watching her because you liked her or something. She was the girl in the pale pink gown."

Ashlee looked like the kind of person you could start a conversation with. She was a good listener and enjoyed talking with people. It wasn't difficult to imagine her smiling at Wes, capturing his attention.

"I don't know what you mean," says Wes, playing the part of the ignorant bystander perfectly.

Except I remember now. Seeing Wes here, away from the hazy light of the bar, his features cleaner, more focused.

I imagine what happened after she climbed out of my car.

289

Had Wes continued watching her, waiting for her to leave, or did he talk to her before then? Would Ashlee have noticed that something was off if she wasn't busy being angry at me?

"Why were you watching us?" I ask.

Wes smooshes the strawberry with the back of his fork and sighs, as if he's bored with my questions. His demeanor changes and his features harden, his tone more brisk. "See, the thing is, I wasn't watching Ashlee. I was just trying to figure out whether she'd hold up her part of our deal, but I realized when I saw you with her that it was probably up to you."

"Me?"

"People have attachments to things, to other people," Wes says, as if it's a disease. "It holds them back from achieving anything meaningful. It stains their lives and stops them from moving forward and letting go of the past."

Is he talking about Ashlee, or my inability to let her go?

"You didn't find my dating profile by chance, did you?" I ask.

"I was doing research," he says, as if I was nothing more than a project.

"What do you want from me?" I demand. "What did you want from Ashlee?"

He turns his dessert and slices the tartlet. I want to demand that he answer my questions, but I wait, watching for any sudden movements, reminding myself that this situation is different to the night at Dale's house. This time I'm prepared. I know the environment, and I have a knife taped under the table if I need it.

"I wanted to find out what Ashlee had told you. I wasn't sure what you knew, but you were with her at the gala. She never mentioned she had a sister, but she wouldn't have taken you with her if you didn't mean something to her. I was waiting for you to walk in with her, but it seems she didn't expect me to be there, and I spooked her. She was hiding you from me, which means you're important to her. She was very secretive like that, our Ashlee."

The way he refers to her as "our Ashlee" makes my skin prickle. My fingers twitch on the table, wanting to take the knife, but I won't let myself. *Not yet.*

"What did you want from Ashlee?" I ask, feeling my heart rise in my throat.

He made a flourish with his hand, like a magician. "I wanted her to disappear."

46

Chapter 46

Oscar

Now

Dr. Larson shook his head, an edge to his calm tone as he removed the hospital cap, revealing a head of dark hair, a few sprouts of gray starting to infiltrate. "I'm sorry. Bill had a massive MI. We tried to clear the blockage and put in a stent, but it was unsuccessful."

How could Bill be dead? Oscar had seen him after the first heart attack. He looked like he'd been through an ordeal, like maybe he needed a good rest, but he didn't look like someone who was about to die. If his heart was gearing up for another attack, wouldn't there be a warning?

Maybe there was, but Oscar was too busy worrying about Verity and what'd happened to Ashlee to notice.

Bill wasn't the only person he hadn't made time for. He'd ignored Hayley even more. She still hadn't messaged, and he didn't blame her for not returning his calls when he'd been so distracted. If she let him, he'd fix it. Not with a token quick fix like chocolate or flowers, but with something personal that would matter to her. He'd take her out to a new vegan restaurant and talk about whatever she wanted.

Oscar caught Kiko in his arms just as she crumpled, her slight weight falling against him. He wanted to say something comforting, but all he could think was that he hadn't even had a chance to say goodbye. His hope of one day resolving their differences was lost now.

For all his problems, Bill had stuck with Oscar. It wasn't enough, but being there was more than Kiko had done.

Oscar would feel his own emotions later. For now, he let Kiko cry quietly into his shoulder, her grief raw and fresh, a cacophony of regret.

Had Kiko really thought she was protecting him by leaving? It had been worse than his worst fear as a child—that something would happen and rob him of his family. He had never imagined back then that she'd choose to go...and then she was gone.

47

Chapter 47

Verity

Now

How easy I've made it for Wes. If I wasn't so hurt, I'd feel humiliated, but now isn't the time for emotions.

"Did Ashlee do something to you? Is that why you wanted her to disappear?"

"It's complicated," he says, running his fork through the chocolate.

"Try me," I say, hoping the oxy-laced dinner loosens his tongue.

"She was supposed to leave with her money, but she couldn't leave you. She came back. I think she was going to tell you everything."

"She was missing for almost two months. I didn't see her once during that time. She didn't come back for me."

I know he's probably lying to win my trust. If he wanted

Ashlee to disappear, he must want me to do the same.

"You killed her because she might tell me something you don't want me to know. I guess there's no point in asking you what it was?" Once I know, it'll be harder to convince him not to kill me, but I have to find out what made him kill her.

His lips form a thin line. "You already know too much." He says it with a note of apology in his voice, as if I've forced his hand. "Do you want to know?"

"You're going to kill me either way." Panic rises, adrenaline kicking in, prepping me for the moment I'll need to run for my life.

"If I left you here, you'd wait until I walked out of that door," he says, gesturing toward my front door, "and call the police."

"I don't care about the police," I say, thinking how they've been so far, hoping to convey the disdain in my voice. *Hoping it'll be enough to get him to talk.*

"I just want to know why you killed Ashlee."

"She gave me no choice."

"She *made* you kill her?" I lay the skepticism on thick. What he's implying is ridiculous.

"She ignored my advice. I couldn't risk my share of the money. Dale couldn't risk it."

Dale.

He knows Dale. Were they in on this together, or is Wes using a trick to misdirect me?

"Did Dale tell you to kill her? I saw her blood in his bathroom. She was there."

"Dale didn't tell me to kill her, but I *do* know why her blood was there." He smiles, as if it's a funny story. "She was robbed. It was someone that knew she was a dealer. Her nose was bloodied pretty badly. She called Dale and he helped clean her

295

up. She was worried he'd blame her for the supply they stole. After that, he gave Ashlee her money, and as far as he was concerned, their transaction was complete."

I remember Ashlee's bruised nose months ago. She told me she'd got it from falling from the circuit bike at the gym.

"Does Dale know you killed her?"

"I'm sure he suspects—"

I think of Dale in the hospital, and for a moment I wish I'd smothered him with a pillow, or released some poison into his IV. But that's not who I am. I wouldn't have been able to do it then.

Dale mightn't have killed Ashlee, but he didn't stop what happened to her either. He could've tipped off the police and given them enough reason to investigate Wes.

No, I couldn't have killed Dale, but Wes has just admitted to killing Ashlee.

Underneath, my anger is a raw, burning loss that I would usually talk to Ashlee about. What would she have said if I told her how satisfying it would be to show Wes the same end he'd shown her?

She'd probably tell me that Wes isn't worth going to jail over—but she'd be wrong. Once he kills me, there'll be no one left to stop him from killing again; no one to know what he's done.

I think about my last moments. I see myself trying to give in and let go, but my last thought is Wes's face, a satisfied smirk at knowing he's gotten away with murder, that he'll get away with doing it again because the truth will die with me.

Ashlee's voice echoes inside my head, watery and distant. For a moment I wonder if I'm beginning to forget what she sounds like, but it's definitely her, speaking in a reassuring tone.

He'll go to jail. Someone will figure it out.

She's sure the police will find something to prove that Wes killed her; killed me. But what if they can't? Or what if, after serving years in prison, they let him out, older and wiser, having learned new skills to do it again and get away with it?

"When they found Ashlee's body, it looked like the A on her necklace had been filled in with dirt to make a caret," I say, remembering Oscar's questions. "What does it mean?"

Wes laughs and it feels like he's enjoying this. "Maybe it means nothing—just a bit of dirt. It happens when a body is buried in soil."

He knows where she was buried because he killed her. I remind myself, letting my rage burn hot. I use the anger to prepare for what's coming, steeling myself against the pain.

"I'm impressed anyone noticed that," he says. "That message was just between me and, well, you. I never thought you'd notice." He places a hand over his heart, as if it's touching that I'd noticed.

I don't trust my anger not to explode, so I stay quiet. Each word he speaks fills me with loathing. How was the message meant for me?

"It was a little joke. I wanted to show you what you made me do to Ashlee. And you *didn't* give me a choice. You would've kept looking, and when Ashlee turned up, who knows how loose her tongue might've been."

I know it's in his best interest to make me doubt myself, but I can't help feeling responsible for getting Ashlee killed. I can't let that feeling win out, or Wes gets away with taking her life.

"Ashlee was selling drugs for Dale?" I say.

"Pharmaceuticals. Off the books. It was good money. I don't know why she didn't just take the bonus and leave, like we'd planned. The police were getting too close, watching what was happening with the accounts. We needed things to cool off for a while, so Dale offered her a job abroad. She took it, she even got to check it out in a private jet, but she couldn't stay away."

A private jet. That explained why there was no record of her leaving the country—Ashlee's presence on the plane was probably undeclared.

It makes sense now why he left our date when he saw Dale.

"You didn't want Dale to see you talking to me at the bar."

"If he came over, you would've known I was there to find out what Ashlee told you. I was seeing if I could spare you," he says, as if I should be grateful.

"Ashlee didn't tell me anything," I say, still unsure whether to believe that my careful sister was part of an illegal drug ring, or just someone who got in the way. "I didn't know she was selling. She was a *nurse*. She was supposed to help people."

He looks at me knowingly, waiting for something to click, taking satisfaction in my despair when he tells me. "She wanted to help with your treatment."

Nausea washes through me. He's right. Helping me might've been her motivation. She knew I was struggling to pay for the latest rounds, that my insurance didn't cover everything. She convinced me to do the last round, sure it'd be the one that saved me.

"I waited to see if Dale left. I would've come back in and said I had a call or something," he says. "But then you went home with him, so I followed. I didn't have any intention of killing you. At least not at first."

Wes seems too relaxed, and I'm not sure if he's unfazed by the situation, or if the drugs in his food are contributing to his blasé attitude.

Interesting that he says he didn't intend on killing me, but he tried to do it anyway. I ask about it, hoping to catch his lie.

"You got caught up in a game. I was making sure Dale paid me the money he owed. Then Ashlee came back."

He relays the story, but I don't know whether it's another lie. He says he thought I'd seen her, so he kept Dale and I locked up to give himself time to decide what to do with us.

"Why would she go to Dale's house if she came back?" I ask, dreading the answer.

"For a locket? It's like I told you—people can't let go of sentimental baggage. It gets people killed. You helped me figure that out when you and Dale tackled each other from the roof." He laughs, as if reminiscing. "Ashlee saw you both fall. I think she planned to sneak in unseen to retrieve it. She didn't know you were there but when she saw you fall off the roof, it was too much. She ran to the edge to catch you. It was a nice little touch that she came back for the necklace when she did. Of course, she had no choice but to stop by once I told her I had you locked up. She thought I wouldn't know she was back in the country. I'm sure she thought about going to the police, but she couldn't exactly do that without risking jail, could she?"

And this time, I know he's not lying, because I heard her voice, not just in my dream.

He is suddenly cold, the laugh ending abruptly. "I would've sent her down to join you, but she was fast, and the roof was slippery. I stopped her before she got out the door."

"Were Ashlee and Dale dating?"

Wes shrugs indifferently. "Maybe. I think Ashlee was going to come clean. She didn't know she'd caused a whole drama by disappearing, because she wasn't in the country. If she had told you what she had done, neither of us would've gotten our money—he was paying us in installments."

It turns out Dale is a control freak. He wanted to make sure Ashlee and Wes followed his instructions step by step before he paid. "I didn't feel so bad when I saw him fall. When I saw you fall with him, I thought it was an easy answer to a complicated problem. Then, I just had to take care of Ashlee, and take her cut too."

He looks at me as if my being alive is a conscious attempt to irritate him.

This whole time I'd assumed it was Dale who locked me up.

When I say it out loud, he smiles. "I realized that when you kept screaming for Dale to let you out. I drugged him with his own street stuff. He had a lot in his system. Enough to think you attacked him, apparently. He didn't realize I'd blindfolded him and moved him to the loft. I hoped he'd kill you himself. Neither of you would've noticed me if you'd walked right past. You were so focused on hating each other."

That didn't explain the shutters covering the windows. I thought Dale had them to stop the neighbors from seeing who he had inside. Wes laughs when I ask about it and says they're a security measure because Dale isn't around much and there's always someone wanting a fix.

"How do you know?"

Wes doesn't miss a beat. "Locker talk."

I ask him if he's really a teacher. If he lies about that now, he's probably lying about everything else.

He tells me he's not without hesitation.

He googled my name the night he messaged me. I feel stupid all over again, wondering if I'd been this gullible when I wasn't sick.

"Don't be upset with me for killing your sister. She made that choice by coming back."

"No. You made that choice."

"If you hadn't been looking for her in the first place, she might've just stayed away. At that point, it was you or her, and since you survived the fall, I had no choice. I couldn't go out there and finish the job without risking someone seeing me." He runs a hand through his hair. "Besides, for all anyone knew, Ashlee was already dead, so when she came back, it wasn't a tough choice."

Somehow, it feels like he's blaming Ashlee and me for what happened. *If you hadn't been looking for her... It wasn't a tough choice...*

"How did you kill her?" I ask. In a strange way, it feels like the least I can do, to know how she died. If I couldn't be there for her, the least I can do now is know what Wes put her through. "Was it quick?"

He sits himself comfortably back in the chair. He's not going to make this easy. He wants to make me suffer, and he's going to draw it out. He's enjoying having something I want. He makes a show of pretending to think about it, squinting his eyes as if he's looking directly at the sun.

Eventually he speaks, and it feels like he's addressing an audience. "Ashlee was lucky I was in a hurry. She showed up unexpected and I had to get rid of her without any evidence she'd been there, so I couldn't use a knife or something convenient."

I don't dare say it, but secretly I'm glad that she made things difficult for him. I get the sense that if he wasn't in a hurry, he might've tortured her for being such an inconvenience.

"I had to use my bare hands. Not an easy task. She almost got away, as slippery as an eel, our Ashlee."

I had hoped her death was quick, but he has taken that illusion from me.

"What are you going to do with me?" We both know the answer, but I need to hear it out loud if I'm going to be able to justify fighting as unfairly as he will.

"Whatever I have to."

48

Chapter 48

Verity

Now

"Hello?"

I almost respond before I realize Wes is speaking into his phone, the earbud almost invisible. I can't hear who it is. Maybe he has someone to help him dispose of my body once he's ended my life.

Dale?

My arms are off the table now, reaching for the knife underneath. My hand moves toward the edge I taped it under, but it's not where it should be. My heart speeds up—my carefully laid plan isn't off to a good start.

I peek under the table, expecting to see the blade lying on the floor, but it's not there. For a horrifying moment I wonder if Wes has managed to get the knife, but I can't see it in his hand and I can't dip under the table to get a better look without seeming suspicious.

Wes stands and I jump to my feet so that we're facing each other, neither of us sure what the other will do next. I realize he's waiting for me to run. He thinks he's the apex predator and I'm his prey.

He watches me, still on his phone, and I see the knife glinting in his hand.

He must've managed to free it from under the table. *He knew why I asked him here tonight.*

He looks unconcerned, like it's nothing more than a slight inconvenience. He doesn't see me as a threat, just some business he needs to take care of to get to his end goal.

I try to sidestep him to get to the door, but he blocks me. I weigh up my options. I could call for help from the person on the phone, but he's close enough to silence my cries with one quick stab of the knife. As if he can sense what I'm planning, he holds a finger to his lips.

The phone call ends and his attention turns back to me. He's gripping the knife, ready to strike—it's not just a warning. He holds it, ready to thrust it into me if he needs to. I have no doubt. If I play this wrong, I'm dead.

I try to move away slowly, drifting farther from his reach, avoiding any large movements, which he might see as threatening.

"You broke into my hospital room. The nurses thought I imagined it, but you were there," I say.

It's a relief to know it really happened. The sensation of the pillow smothering me wasn't a dream or a panic attack. The disease working its way through my body hasn't ruined my mind.

A coolness lingers in Wes's expression. I wonder if it was

there at the bar. He seemed so warm and genuine, but maybe I'd been so caught up in the excitement of going out and having fun that I hadn't seen what he truly was.

"I didn't break in," he says derisively. "Your door was unlocked, so I went inside. It's as if you were inviting me in. I was there to visit someone else. My visit to you was an afterthought."

He sounds crazy, but I don't dare tell him that.

My eyes don't leave the knife. I watch it move in his hand, expecting him to try to catch me off guard. I want to be ready when he tries to use it.

"I didn't know it was you that locked me in Dale's house. I would never have figured it out. I was convinced it was Dale. Why couldn't you just leave it alone?"

I was so embarrassed about being stood up by Wes. My cheeks flush at the memory. I'd been certain Wes left because I'd said the wrong thing, or broken some unwritten dating rule I wasn't aware of. When he messaged saying why he'd left, it was almost a relief.

I'd been so concerned with finding out the truth and making sure Dale was punished for what he did that I'd missed what was really going on. Now, it would cost me my life. Wes had a plan. I had to keep him talking while I figured out what it was and how I could stop him.

Just when I think he's forgotten my question, he answers, a lazy lilt to his voice. "Loose ends ruin plans. You were a loose end. Dale wouldn't talk. He was stupid enough to think you pushed him off the roof, that you knocked him out in his own home because you were grieving for your sister. He didn't even know I was here. You were both drunk. It made things a lot easier for me."

Wes tilts his head, studying me. I can't believe I mistook the gesture for concern for my missing sister on our date. "You're tenacious. You got so close to discovering what happened. If I thought you'd let it go, I could've done the same, but even on our date, you brought it up. You wouldn't've let it go, would you?"

"No," I say. There's no point lying about it now, not when he already knows the truth.

He looks as if he's won a secret bet with himself, and I realize I've sealed my fate.

49

Chapter 49

Oscar

Now

Oscar drove from the hospital to Hayley's house, killing the engine out front. There weren't any lights on inside—maybe she went to bed early? She hadn't responded to his messages. Would she answer if he knocked on the door? He wasn't sure he wanted to find out and he didn't want to wake her, but he needed to see her.

He unlocked his phone with a pass code, thinking maybe he'd call. But before he did that, someone should probably tell Steve about Bill. It seemed unfair to keep it from him.

Oscar expected the phone to ring out, but Steve answered, sounding flustered. Oscar explained what had happened and apologized.

"What?"

"Mom said you were working, but I thought you should

know." Oscar told him about Bill and waited as Steve took an audible breath.

"I knew he went in..." said Steve, sounding shocked.

"If you want to, you know, talk or anything—" said Oscar. Kiko might've warned him about Steve, but he was still his brother.

"I thought everything went well."

"It did. But he had another attack. It was just too much."

"Shit."

Did Steve have any attachment to the father he hadn't spoken to since he was a kid? Or had he let him go?

"Steve?"

"Yeah?"

"You okay?" asked Oscar.

"Yeah. I'm, uh, are you?"

"I'll be all right," said Oscar.

"Does everyone know?"

"Mom was there when the cardiologist told us."

Oscar glanced at Hayley's window. He couldn't sit in his car much longer without going in.

"How is she?" asked Steve.

"Mom? She seemed more upset than I expected. They haven't been together for a long time."

"I think she loved him. God knows why, but she did," said Steve.

From the little he'd seen, Oscar agreed. "Well, if you want to grab a beer or something, give me a call."

"Sure," said Steve in a tone reserved for when he had no intention of following through.

The call ended and Oscar looked at the evening sky, taking a moment to think about how Bill had been before Lila was gone, before Steve and Kiko left. He'd always had a temper, but he could be a lot of fun too. He was usually the first to suggest a camping trip or a round of baseball in the front yard, but his good moods could sour without warning.

After Kiko and Steve left, Bill never spoke about them. He never seemed curious about what Steve was up to, or how he turned out when he had grown up. It had always irked Oscar. He couldn't imagine being that blasé about your son. One time he'd asked where they'd gone, but Bill flew into a rage, asking Oscar how he was supposed to know.

Now Oscar wondered if Bill and Kiko had secretly stayed in touch.

Oscar stepped out of the car, away from his old memories. He needed to see Hayley, even if it was just to find out how she was and let her know about Bill.

He knocked on the door and stuffed his hands in his pockets while he waited. There was no movement inside. "Hello?" Artemis barked a greeting at his presence from the back of the house.

"Where's Hayley, Art?" called Oscar. Her car was in the driveway—she must've gone for a walk.

He sat on the doorstep and waited, eventually giving up and going back to the car. The minutes trickled by.

Fumbling his keys out of his pocket, Oscar jammed them in the engine lock and started the car. He still had to make sure Verity had gone to that hotel like she promised. He'd drop by after to see if Hayley was home yet.

Driving to Verity's house, he thought about Hayley, convincing himself that she would at least let him know if she wanted some space. She had probably just been too busy to call him back yet.

He pulled up outside Verity's apartment, threw his keys in his pocket, and pushed his thoughts aside.

He knocked on the door and waited listening to the slight hum of voices filtering through from the other side.

50

Chapter 50

Verity

Now

There's a knock at the front door.

"Are you expecting someone?" Wes asks, his tone low and foreboding.

I have no idea who it is, but I recognize the chance to escape.

"Coming!" I call in a strained tone as Wes moves forward to stop me. His expression is murderous—if whoever it is at the door heard me, they know I'm inside and that I'm alive.

My energy is waning, but I rally and throw the little I have left into reaching the door before Wes can stop me. He tries to block me but falls short as my legs pump, my hand grabbing the handle to swing the door open.

It's a relief to see a familiar face. In my hurry to exit, I almost tumble into Oscar's arms. Wes is still behind me, but I'm dreading what comes next.

"Oscar?" Wes sounds uncertain, testing Oscar's name.

"What are you doing here?" asks Oscar. At first I think he's talking to me because I broke my promise to find somewhere to stay, but he's looking at Wes like he's seen him before. *They know each other.*

"He's holding a knife," I say, but when I turn, there's nothing in Wes's hand and his dark expression has disappeared, making me wonder if I've imagined the whole thing.

"We were just having dinner," he says for Oscar's benefit. "The knife's in the sink," he tells me, keeping his tone casual.

I do a quick calculation. There was no time to cross to the sink and set the knife down—he still has it somewhere, probably hidden up his sleeve or tucked into the waist of his pants.

Oscar half smiles, as if he's not sure what he's walked into, but I can see him thinking, trying to decide how Wes and I might know each other. He seems to like Wes and for a moment I wonder whether he's Wes's reinforcement from the phone call before, here to help Wes silence me.

It's too late to take back my accusation about the knife—I wouldn't have thought Oscar was the type to kill, and I can't believe it now—I could maybe take on one of them, but my chances against two of them aren't great.

My plan to drug Wes and get to the truth about Ashlee is in pieces.

"Verity and I were kind of on a date," says Wes, doing a good job of sounding just embarrassed enough. If he's explaining to Oscar why he's here, then maybe Oscar isn't the person from the phone call.

I feel a little steadier as I practice breathing, keeping my distance while I watch both of them, just in case.

Oscar apologizes, looking sheepish. It sounds like he means it. Whatever Wes has planned for me, it doesn't sound like Oscar's part of it. I want to tell him he probably saved my life, that Wes was going to kill me, but he's looking at me as if I'm fragile and I'm not sure he'd believe me.

"Come inside," Wes says smoothly, opening the door for Oscar.

I'm stuck in the middle, not quite inside but not outside either. I look around for a neighbor or someone passing by to call out to, but there's no one close enough to hear me.

I try to protest, but Oscar goes inside before I can stop him. I think about running, putting as much distance between Wes and me as possible, but my legs are jelly, and I know he'd catch me easily. Once my back is turned, it's over. The knife will slide from his sleeve and he'll kill me. Once he's done, he'll go inside and finish Oscar.

I can't be responsible for that.

Wes has his hand on my arm and I realize that inviting Oscar inside has positioned him close enough to make sure I go inside too. He uses a gentle push to guide me, making it seem like a warm gesture, but the feel of his hand makes me react as if an open flame has touched my skin. I need to let Oscar know what's really going on without seeming hysterical. I try to match Wes's calm, collected approach, but I'm tired. He should be feeling the oxy by now, but he seems unaffected.

Wes is a talented actor. The easy smile. The pretense that everything is fine. He's so good that I'm not sure Oscar would side with me if I were to tell him the truth. If someone told me that Wes was a murderer, would I believe it? I'm ashamed to admit that I'd find it hard to believe given how *normal* Wes is acting.

Oscar rests a hand on my arm, and turns me so that his back is facing Wes. I try not to look at him over Oscar's shoulder as he asks if I'm okay. "I came by to see if you found your way to that hotel. I guess you didn't quite get there," he says.

I look away, hoping Wes isn't paying attention to my expression, that he can't hear our conversation. If only there was a way to warn Oscar to be careful about what he said—that the person he was trying to keep me safe from was standing a few feet away.

"How did you two meet?" asks Oscar, a hint of doubt in his tone.

I wait for Wes to answer, curious if he'll answer honestly.

"At a bar." The lie comes easily from Wes, just as I say, "On a dating site."

Oscar turns to look at Wes. "Really?" I can tell by his expression that something isn't quite adding up.

Perhaps I can tell him the *rest* of the story. "He found my profile on a dating site," I say, "and used it to contact me. I didn't know at the time, but he was looking for me because of Ashlee." My words sound thin and uncertain, knowing it sounds unbelievable after all the wrong turns I've taken. If Oscar knows Wes, the chances of him believing what I'm saying over what he already knows about him are low.

Wes tilts his head and looks at me from under his brow, as if he plans on watching me unravel myself. His silence is menacing, making me look as unstable as I was afraid I would.

Oscar tenses, his senses ready for whatever comes next. His eyes don't leave Wes. Now might be my chance to show him what happened. "Wes killed Ashlee," I say.

"What's going on, Steve?"

I feel the color leach from my face. *Steve?*

314

"We actually met on a dating site," says Wes, as if that explains the name. He doesn't seem to care that I just told Oscar he killed my sister. "That part's true."

I want to scream that he's lying. That he admitted to it just a moment ago, but that's what he wants me to do. I realize that Wes could probably get away with it right now, because when he speaks, he sounds reasonable and rational, as if he's confident that what he's saying is true.

The stress is showing in my demeanor as the cracks thicken and crumble, revealing deep ravines. I'm not sure what I can say from here to convince Oscar to listen, so I stand there watching as they face each other like two bulls ready to charge. The mood has changed from the friendly greeting Oscar gave Wes just a few minutes ago to an ominous storm breaking over us.

"How do you know each other?" I ask, already putting together the answer as I look from one to the other. They have the same bowed lips, their eyes make the same contours, but Oscar's are wider, a complex labyrinth of blue-gray with a golden hue in the center. Wes's—*Steve's*—are a syrupy brown. I didn't realize it when I first saw him, but Wes reminds me of a shinier imitation of Oscar.

Oscar answers first.

"He's my brother."

The hope that Oscar will help me is crushed by his words.

Brothers.

Oscar de la Nuit's brother killed Ashlee, and I have to prove he admitted to it in a confession that no one else heard. Oscar won't believe my word over his own brother. That's why Wes—Steve—told me. He knew he could deny it. People don't just confess to murder. And they definitely don't accuse other people of it without solid proof.

Who would I tell anyway?

Detective Payneham? Not after I'd accused Dale of killing Ashlee. He might ban me from contacting the police ever again if I called with another claim. He already knows I'm desperate to find answers before I die.

With Ashlee gone, the only other person I might've considered telling is in this room. I can only imagine what he would've said if I went to him, showing him the photo of Wes from his dating profile as evidence he really exists, not realizing it was his brother.

We watch each other, waiting for someone to make the first move.

"You gave me a fake name?" I ask, knowing he can't lie with Oscar there to call him out on it.

He shrugs. "No one gives their real name on their dating profile."

No one gives their real name on their hook up profile. But he made it seem like he hadn't messaged just for a hook up, especially when he followed up to see me again. I soothe my anger with thoughts that he can't be too smart, because if he had killed me, there was still proof of our conversations because I kept his messages.

A fake name on a dating side hardly shows that he's a murderer. Maybe he would've talked his way out of it, convinced the police he had nothing to do with mine or Ashlee's death. Except, I'm still here and now I need to convince Oscar that his brother is a killer.

51

Chapter 51

Oscar

Now

When Oscar arrived at Verity's house, he knew something was wrong. She took too long to answer the door, despite the whispering voices he heard from inside. Maybe she knew it was him and didn't want to explain why she wasn't at a hotel like she'd promised.

She wouldn't be the only person avoiding him, but he couldn't think about why Hayley wasn't speaking to him now—he needed to make sure Verity was all right.

When the door opened, a flustered Verity looked relieved to see him. At first, Oscar thought he'd interrupted a date—the table was set for two and the smell of food wafted through the house.

And then he saw Steve.

It's just a coincidence, he told himself. What would his

brother be doing at one of his patient's houses?

Oscar watched their interaction. Every time Steve moved closer, Verity took a step back, as if she was afraid.

Maybe Oscar had interrupted a fight when he knocked on the door, or maybe Verity was just jumpy from everything she'd been through?

He stepped closer to Verity to test her fear response, but she didn't move. It was only when Steve approached that she recoiled.

When they were kids, Steve had been at least a foot taller than Oscar, but Oscar had caught up and eventually overtaken him. Now, they were almost eye level.

He remembered what Kiko had said about leaving, about taking Steve with her—how she was worried that Oscar might end up like Lila.

Steve acted before he thought things through sometimes, forgetting the consequences. Kiko knew what Steve was capable of, that his carelessness might cause another accident, but Oscar had never really believed that Steve hurt Lila intentionally—he had always believed it was a horrible accident, something Steve would struggle with throughout his life. Steve used to be the guy that Oscar looked up to, his big brother.

Now, he was only just seeing the guy who could get angry enough to push a child intentionally onto the road, still unable to quite accept that Steve knew there was a car coming, that it wouldn't be able to stop in time to save Lila.

With a sinking feeling, Oscar remembered something else. It was the anniversary of Lila's death. She'd been gone for too many years, forever a child. Lila had loved swimming, so every year, Oscar took flowers to the beach and floated them out onto the water. Sometimes he sent them over the pier and watched them drift away until they were far on the horizon, hidden by the choppy ocean. Then he'd stay and listen to the water lapping against the pillars in a comforting rhythm until the sun went down.

After Lila died, Bill kept her picture on the wall, her dark plaits glistening like licorice across her shoulders. He told Oscar it was to remind them they were lucky to be alive, but to eleven-year-old Oscar, it was a reminder that he had lived, but Lila wasn't so lucky. He had wondered why it had to be her... why not him?

Now, knowing that Steve had pushed her into the path of the speeding car, Oscar wasn't sure what to say to his brother.

"Why don't you go home, Steve? I need to talk to Verity." It wasn't what he'd planned to say, but Oscar wanted Steve out of Verity's house. The look on Verity's face, the nervous tension, told him enough.

"Shouldn't you be home, playing house with your girl-friend?" asked Steve, a teasing note in his voice.

"Hayley's not answering my calls," admitted Oscar.

"Really?" Something in Steve's tone told Oscar he wasn't particularly sorry to hear it. "Trouble in paradise?"

Was it obvious something was wrong? Maybe Steve had picked up on it when they went out for a beer, before Oscar had figured it out himself.

God, Oscar wished if he could talk to Hayley now. She'd know what to do. Instead, he'd have to figure it out for himself and wait until Steve decided to leave.

"You look tired," Oscar said to Verity pointedly.

She nodded, playing along. "It's been a long day."

"Maybe we should go?" suggested Oscar, trying a different

approach, waiting for Steve to move first.

Oscar caught Verity moving out of the corner of his eye, arcing toward Steve. She went by the kitchen island and pulled a knife from the knife block.

Steve kept his eyes trained on Oscar, almost ignoring her until she sprang forward, a silver blade pointed at Steve's throat.

Oscar intercepted her attack, taking the knife as he pulled her away from Steve. He couldn't let Verity kill someone. She'd never forgive herself.

"He killed Ashlee. He was going to kill me," she said desperately.

"She's crazy," said Steve. "You saw her, she would've stabbed me."

Oscar gripped the knife, holding his ground. "Why would Verity think you killed her sister?"

"How am I supposed to know?" said Steve indignantly.

"You thought Dale killed Ashlee too. Why are you so sure it was Steve?" asked Oscar, still watching his brother.

"He confessed," said Verity, explaining to Oscar how they were illegally selling prescription drugs, how Ashlee didn't leave quietly like she was supposed to, and how it got her killed.

"Is that what you meant when you said you were in sales?"

"I'm in pharmaceutical sales," said Steve icily. "I work for a pharmaceutical company."

"Selling drugs illegally?"

"No." Steve sounded wounded that his own brother would ask such a question. His eyes dropped to the knife in Oscar's hand.

"They were selling modified oxy," said Verity in a resigned

tone. "I found some in Dale's bathroom and used it to drug him."

"How do you know it was modified?" asked Oscar.

"The pills should've been pale blue, but they were royal blue, not like the regular prescription stuff I've seen at the shelter. I know some of the women buy drugs illegally. You can tell when it's fake, because the colors aren't quite right. These women have no other way to manage injuries, and no money to pay a doctor's bill and meds on top of that.

Steve shot Verity a look.

"The only difference between you and me is you're lucky enough to get a prescription for what you need. Not everyone has that luxury. Not everyone who needs medicine can afford it, but you don't care about that, because it doesn't affect you. A piece of paper saying you're allowed to manage your pain doesn't make you any less of a user."

Oscar flinched. Steve was right. He had things under control now, but he never used to. Steve had a way of knowing things, but Oscar wasn't sure how he knew *that*.

"If you're in trouble, or you need help with something, tell me," said Oscar. "I'll do what I can."

Steve sneered. "Of course you will."

"What's that supposed to mean?"

"That's your thing, isn't it? You 'help' people less fortunate than yourself."

Oscar sighed, realizing how his words might've come across. "I didn't mean it like that."

"What does helping look like to you? You lock me up so that people like you can decide what's wrong with me? You analyze my life, my childhood, except you know what that was like because you were there—at least for some of it,—right?"

Oscar waited for Steve's anger to pass, but he was just getting started. "You know that when I was there, Dad seemed like this good guy, because I took the brunt of it. I took more than a couple of hits for the both of you, but I guess you already know that."

Oscar had suspected, but he didn't know for sure. He'd seen Steve take a hit and get back up, never admitting it hurt, but that didn't give him the right to do what he'd done. "Do you think that makes it okay? To do what you did to Ashlee, to Lila?" asked Oscar, knowing Verity was right this time. Steve was definitely capable of killing.

"I didn't do anything to Ashlee," said Steve. "I wouldn't."

"Except you would," said Oscar. "You did. When you pushed Lila—it wasn't an accident, was it?"

"Is that what you believe?" asked Steve.

"I want to know why. What did she do to make you so angry?"

"Nothing," said Steve. "It was a horrible accident." He said it with the same smooth tone he used when he was lying, to keep things calm during conflict and deflect attention from whatever he'd done wrong this time.

What Steve didn't count on was Oscar seeing through the act. And right now, Steve was showing the wrong emotions for the situation. There was no regret. No sadness.

Oscar's phone buzzed. He slid it from his pocket, in case it was important.

In case it was Hayley.

Her name flashed on his screen. Finally, she'd messaged.

"Are you okay?" asked Verity.

"Yeah," said Oscar, reading the message again. "Just Hayley."

Hepp eme. Ste

Her message looked like gibberish, but as he read it again, he realized she must've been typing quickly.

Ste? Steve?

"Really?" asked Steve. "Maybe she's ready to talk."

"Yeah," said Oscar, hitting the dial button, willing her to answer.

"What'd she say?" asked Steve.

Oscar ignored him, listening as an automated message told him that Hayley was unavailable. He tried again.

"What are you doing?" asked Steve with amusement.

"Calling her." Oscar kept his attention divided between the call and Steve.

The message repeated in his ear, but Oscar spoke over it.

"Hayley! Where are you?"

Oscar waited for the inevitable—if his hunch was right, he needed to be ready to react at just the right time.

52

Chapter 52

Oscar

Now

Steve lunged at Oscar. It looked like he was going for the knife, but he swung a punch at the last minute, his fist connecting with Oscar's nose.

The knife flew from Oscar's hand. He held tight to the phone, the only thing tethering him to Hayley, even if he couldn't really reach her.

Sharp pain seared through Oscar's face. Bright red blood trickled from his nose, but he didn't have time to assess the damage as Steve lunged again, trying to tackle him to the floor.

Oscar thought he had a few more seconds; he'd mistimed the attack, and now Steve had a hold of his throat, pressing the air from it. Struggling to break free, Oscar knocked over a chair in Verity's dining area, his compromised balance giving Steve the leverage he needed to push Oscar onto the table, slamming his bad knee against the surface.

He cried out in pain, but continued their struggle, unwilling to give in.

"Oscar," called Verity, but there was no way to stop Steve, and no way past him to get to the door.

With Steve's weight leveraged against him, Oscar couldn't angle his feet enough to use them to kick free from his position on the table.

Steve warned Verity to stay back, his voice loud and close in Oscar's face. "What did Hayley say?"

Oscar did the only thing he could, letting his body go limp to slide closer to the edge of the dining table, rolling himself to the floor and out from under Steve. His phone clattered to the floor as Steve struggled to keep hold of him. The sound of glass shattering filled Oscar's ears.

"Where's Hayley?" Oscar demanded, gripping his brother in a headlock. When they were kids, Steve used to do the same to him, just for fun.

"What did Hayley say?" Steve asked again, flinching as Oscar pulled his arm farther behind his back, making sure he felt it.

"Where is she? Tell me," said Oscar.

"Or what?" asked Steve. "You'll kill me? If you don't let my arm go, I can promise you'll never find her."

Oscar cursed. Steve was right. He couldn't kill him, and Steve knew it. He released his arm, letting his elbow strike the back of Steve's head as his grip slackened.

Steve got to his feet and stood to his full height.

"Where is she?" asked Oscar, trying to sublimate the pain. At least he knew she was alive, even if the message had asked him to help her. Wherever she was, she was in danger, but if she could use her phone, she probably wasn't tied up, assuming that Hayley had really sent it, and that the message was cut short because her phone went dead.

This was Oscar's fault. Hayley was in danger because of him—because he was Steve's brother. He hadn't trusted in their relationship enough to realize she hadn't returned his calls because she was in danger. That meant Steve had days to hurt her before Oscar figured it out.

Oscar fought the urge to hit Steve, humbled by how badly he wanted to hurt him in that moment. He'd never seen himself as a violent person. He'd always been terrified of what he could be, horrified at the thought of inheriting a temper from Bill.

"I thought you would've realized sooner, but I guess it's easier to give up, right?"

Oscar didn't bother trying to reason with Steve—it was pointless. All he cared about was finding Hayley.

"Whatever you want from me is between us. Leave Hayley out of it and let Verity go."

"She'll go straight to the police, and you still won't know where Hayley is," said Steve.

"Okay. So what do you want?" asked Oscar. If he could figure out why Steve was doing this, maybe he could give him whatever he wanted and get Verity out safely.

"Nothing," said Steve, as if it was a ridiculous question. "There's nothing I want. But there is something you want very badly, and I'm curious what you'll do to get it."

What would he do to keep Hayley safe?

Steve stopped, and Oscar didn't like the way he was looking at him. "Maybe there is one thing you can do to show you're willing to keep Hayley safe."

"What's that?" asked Oscar hesitantly. Steve's games always had a dark edge that surfaced just when you thought things were about to get better. Oscar should've known to tread carefully.

Steve grinned, his mouth thinning to a crack. "Kill Verity. She's dying anyway—you'd be doing her a favor."

Oscar rejected the idea immediately, refusing. If killing Verity meant saving Hayley, Hayley'd never forgive him. He wasn't sure he could forgive himself.

Oscar shook his head as if he couldn't believe they were in the midst of such a ridiculous conversation. "Come on, Steve. You don't really want me to do that. *You* don't want to do it either."

"Are you sure?"

"Just tell me where Hayley is and we can all walk out of here—you're going to be in worse shit if you don't," said Oscar, using the words they used when they were kids, in trouble for breaking a glass.

You're going to be in the shit meant they knew they'd done something really bad. Trouble for them meant first, being sent to their room while their parents decided on a suitable punishment—that was assuming Bill hadn't already taken to them with a belt. When Steve got in trouble, Oscar would walk by his room and pretend to sniff the air, wrinkling his nose as if it smelled horrible. It made the fear of an unknown punishment more bearable and usually got a laugh.

But Steve was really in it this time, and he would have to face what he'd done without Oscar to cover for him.

Steve pressed his knee cap into Oscar's. He'd obviously remembered the old injury. "If I'm in the shit, so is Hayley."

53

Chapter 53

Verity

Now

Maybe I was wrong about dying. When you know your time's almost up, you do what you can to avoid facing it. Listening to Steve talk about me like I'm as good as dead reminds me that I'm alive, that this isn't over yet.

I can't save Ashlee, and knowing the truth about her death won't save me, but when I see Steve and Oscar struggling over the knife, I know I can't just grab another from the kitchen and kill Steve.

Despite all the things he's done, I don't think Oscar wants his brother dead. Just as I love Ashlee regardless of what she's done, Oscar probably loves his brother. There are other people out there who would be affected by Steve's death too, people who don't deserve that kind of suffering, but would have to endure it if I killed him.

The worst part is, I know Ashlee was probably dead because of me, because she was trying to help with my treatment. When I told her I had cancer, she cried. She was scared. She wanted me to explore every possible cure.

Steve's words sting. *She's dying anyway. You'd be doing her a favor.*

Does Oscar agree? Would he take an expiring life to save his own?

Maybe not. But to save Hayley?

I wouldn't blame him. I could see how he might reason it.

Steve has forgotten I'm even here. To him, I'm a slight inconvenience, an obstacle to step around before he can leave.

I notice that Steve has wriggled an arm out from beneath him. The other is behind him, pinned in Oscar's grasp, but Steve's darting eyes tell me he's going to make a break for it.

"Last chance, Oz. Kill her, and I'll tell you where Hayley is. Don't, and Hayley dies."

"Please," said Oscar, sounding worn down. "Just tell me where she is."

"See, this is the thing with you. You think that everything can be talked through and made better." Steve laughs in uneven bursts. "But when you don't get to make the choices, when the situation is hopeless, you get just as frustrated as the rest of us. You get angry."

"I'm not angry," said Oscar, pushing a knee hard into Steve's back.

I look at the door. If I tried to reach it, Steve could probably make it just far enough to grab my ankle and stop me.

I catch him looking in my direction. He shakes his head, giving me a warning. "Don't even think about it," he says. "You won't get out the door."

He pushes himself up, gritting his teeth through the pain as the arm behind him stretches to its limit.

This might be my only chance to do something—if Steve gets out of the hold a second time, he's not letting us leave, and from their conversation, it sounds like there's a good chance Hayley will face the same.

I take a deep breath. It's now or never. "I'm not dead yet," I say before charging at him.

54

Chapter 54

Hayley

Now

The regret is heavy in the silence. I wish I'd never let Steve inside, but everything is clearer in hindsight. There was no reason not to invite him in when he knocked at the door.

When I opened the door he'd looked worried. I asked what was wrong. He said something had happened to Oscar. A jumble of horrifying possibilities played out in an instant as I stood there. Oscar had an accident, but he'd be all right. Oscar had an accident and he *wouldn't* be okay. Oscar had ended his own life—something he didn't talk about, but I know he'd struggled with in the past. Oscar was breaking up with me. The last one feels silly and superficial after the other possibilities, but just as scary, causing a swell of butterflies in my stomach.

To avoid more possibilities, I let Steve in, dreading what he might say. What if it's even worse than I'm imagining?

Artemis barked outside, wanting to be let in—she likes to know who's visiting. I called out to her, telling her I'd be there in a minute and encouraging her to stop barking. She gave a high-pitched whimper to let me know she wasn't happy about it, but the barking stopped.

That was the last thing I remembered.

When I awoke, I didn't know where I was, but I felt heavily fatigued, my eyes and my head weighed down by a foggy sensation. At first, I thought that maybe I'd fallen and hit my head, but as my vision cleared, I realized I wasn't at Oscar's house anymore.

A throbbing in my arms drew my attention. There were cuts like stab wounds all over them, some of them deep enough to need stitches. For a moment I had wondered whether I'd been in a car accident, bracing myself for the impact with my arms, but that didn't make sense.

I didn't remember Steve taking a knife to my skin, but I couldn't think much past the fuzzy feeling permeating my brain in those first hours. I let myself rest, pretending to be asleep until I could figure out what to do.

Eventually I felt well enough to sit up and take in my surroundings, finding a bland room with eggshell white walls. A window—possibly a way out—propelled me from the bed, but even as I tested it, I knew it wouldn't give. A shutter blocked the glass, hiding the outside world, stopping me from knowing where I was. Was there a series of empty paddocks outside, or dense forest? I could be anywhere.

Panic threatened to overwhelm me as I searched for a way out, exploring a house that looked like a minimalist's dream. Each room contained empty closets. One. Two. A third room was locked, and my attempts to open it drew Steve's attention.

He stood behind me, watching like a cat watches a cornered bird struggling against the bars of its cage. I hadn't even heard him there, didn't know how long he'd been observing me, but as a punishment for trying to break into the room, *his* room, he added a fresh cut to my hand, in the crest of my thumb and index finger.

That was days ago—three, maybe four, and the cut needed antiseptic and ached when I moved my thumb. The drugs he gave me made it hard to keep time straight. I'd looked for a way out, but after hours of searching, I realized the front door had no lock, just a pass code to exit. There were locks on the windows, and the glass was reinforced. Steve watched with amusement as I tried each one.

I refuse to ask what he's going to do with me, because if he hasn't said it, hasn't committed to it yet, maybe I can convince him to let me go.

He's not here now, so I use the time to search the house for something I might've missed, maybe a way out. I don't try the keypad again. Last time it resulted in a painful punishment of what felt like hot claws raking my back. My best guess is heated metal, but I try not to think about the pain.

I walk by the locked door, trying to spend my anxious energy. I already miss the sunlight, the feeling of fresh air on my face and sand under my feet. I miss Artemis by my side as we enjoy a walk together. If I ever see her again, I'll never complain about the hundred times she makes me throw her ball into the ocean until my arm is weak and she becomes disappointed that my throws have lost their distance.

Hopefully she's all right. After this many days, she'd need fresh food and water. I can't stop wondering what Steve has done with her, whether he's hurt her.

I can't stand not knowing anymore and I ask Steve if she's okay.

"You're worried about your dog?" he asks in astonishment, as if there are bigger things I should be concerned about.

"Is she hurt?"

"Hurt? No." He puts a hand over his heart as if I've wounded him. "She's safely back at your house. Oscar will think you've gone home without saying goodbye." He smiles, a snarky, mean grin. He's thought this through. He wants to make us suffer, but he's wrong. Oscar will figure out that I'm gone. He'll come looking for me if I can't figure out how to get out of here myself.

Even if Oscar thinks I went home, how did Steve know where to take Artemis? "How do you know where I live?" I ask, a part of me wondering if he took Artie somewhere worse.

Since I've already started asking questions, I ask why he's brought me here. Did it have something to do with Oscar? Had I offended him?

He laughed at that, assured me it was nothing I did or didn't do. "I don't think Oz has figured it out either."

So, it was about Oscar.

"Figured out what?"

"That he'll never see you again."

I do my best not to respond while he looks over my bare arms, which have just begun to scab from the claws he used. It feels like he's threatening me, that I might have to live with something worse than a few scars.

Steve disappears and I try to listen out for where his footsteps go, but my ears lose the trail. I don't follow him—I can use the time to search the house for a way out again.

When his footsteps stop, I quietly begin my next lap, noticing the locked door to his room is now slightly ajar, as if Steve has been inside and forgotten to lock it behind him. I want to push the door open and see what's inside, but it feels like a trap in the silence of the house. What if he's in there waiting for me? I look around for a camera again, something to suggest he's watching even when he's not physically there. I'm sure he must have something for the times he leaves me here, but I haven't found it yet.

I open the door slowly, trying to peek around. It's too easy, but I go ahead anyway.

There's a bed, a side table and some clothes in a walk-in closet that leads through to an en suite. The inside of the room is as basic as the rest of the house. I was expecting more from an occupied area in the house, but it seems like he isn't into personal belongings. I search the bedside table, moving quickly in case Steve returns. I find a woman's bracelet and a couple of charger cables. Digging deeper, I recognize the white case of my phone, studded with tiny fake diamonds along the side.

Hands shaking, I pull it from the drawer and turn it on, praying there's some charge left.

The screen lights up and I hurriedly find Oscar's name on my call list. He's been trying to reach me, and his name is at the top of my received calls, with six missed calls. I hit the green button, but my phone won't let me call, claiming the service isn't available. *What if Steve has already killed him?*

No.

A little line on the phone warns me that the battery isn't going to last, so I type a quick message and hit send, hoping he gets it.

55

Chapter 55

Oscar

Now

Everything happened at once. Verity ran at Steve while Oscar struggled to keep a hold of his arm. It was a move Steve taught him when they were kids. Usually, he'd pin him down and make Oscar agree to something stupid, like letting him have the last piece of candy in exchange for letting him off the floor.

Steve slipped free and took an elbow to Oscar's knee. This blow hit better than the last, and Oscar's knee buckled in agony, so that Steve was on his feet before Oscar could react. Oscar couldn't chase Steve now, no matter how much he wanted to.

Steve had Verity by the throat by the time Oscar was up. "Why did you agree to dinner tonight? Was this a setup?"

"I wanted to find out if you killed my sister," said Verity, her jaw set stubbornly.

"What were you planning to do once you found out?"

"That depends," said Verity.

"On?"

"A lot of things."

Steve pressed for an answer.

"On whether you did it. And if you were sorry."

Steve asked if she planned on killing him.

She didn't answer, but didn't look away either.

Oscar walked slowly toward Steve and Verity, his knee struggling with each step.

Steve shot a warning look, and Oscar backed off—Steve could easily hurt Verity if he chose to.

"That's very Buffier of you," Steve whispered in Verity's ear, wrapping his fingers around her neck. "Confucius said the aim of the superior man is truth. Ancient philosophers are kind of fixated on truth, but the actual, observable truth is how they choose to react when things aren't going so well." He turned his attention to Oscar. "Make a choice, Oscar. If you want to see Hayley again, you'll have to sacrifice your principles. You can't have everything just the way you want it. Nothing in life is that easy."

Oscar would never kill Verity, but he saw fear flash through her eyes at the possibility.

"No," said Oscar.

"If I have to do it for you, you can expect the same for Hayley," said Steve. "You need to take a life to save a life."

At that moment, Oscar wondered if killing Steve would be the kinder thing to do, but then the only person who knew where Hayley was would be dead, and with him, Oscar's chances of finding her.

Oscar considered Kiko's belief that Steve couldn't help what he was. Did she really believe that? The philosopher John Locke had a theory that people had free agency—the ability to choose their actions. He believed that failing mental health was an intellectual disorder, a largely refuted theory, but Oscar had to ask himself what he believed, standing there, listening to Steve's flawed reasoning.

By definition, knowing what Steve had done, knowing he could be experiencing disordered thoughts, Oscar asked himself if Kiko was wrong and Steve was choosing his actions not through determinism, but because it was what he *wanted* to do. Did that mean he had a disorder, or was he that way because that was who he chose to be?

It seemed like Kiko believed Steve was a psychopath, his brain wired differently, perhaps less compassionately, with more of an inclination to manipulate people without realizing what he was doing was wrong. It made sense that Kiko would want to believe that instead of the truth, but Oscar believed Steve was a product of their childhood, and all the things he'd chosen since.

"Let her go," said Oscar, but it was already too late as Steve sank a knife into Verity's side.

Steve retracted the blade, now red with Verity's blood, and Oscar realized he was about to stab her again, looking for a deeper bite.

Oscar slammed into Steve and knocked him off balance, watching his head connect with the hard tiles. He promised himself he'd find Hayley before he released his hold on Steve.

56

Chapter 56

Oscar

Now

Oscar made sure Steve wasn't getting up before asking Verity, "Where's your cell?" He eyed his own cell, cracked on the floor.

She pointed at the kitchen island, blood pooling on her lips. She coughed once. Twice.

Oscar grabbed the phone and went to her, checking her wound and grabbing a throw from the back of the sofa to use to compress the wound. "What's the password?" he asked gently, trying to understand as she attempted to speak, an airy sound escaping.

He looked at Steve lying unconscious on the floor. There was no way of telling how long he'd be out. "I'll be back. I promise," he said, running outside, leaving the door wide open behind him.

A woman frowned as he approached, sidestepping him. She must've been listening to the commotion.

"Please, I need an ambulance. And the police," he said.

The woman stepped away as he drew closer, holding up a hand as a warning for him to stay back.

"Please, I just need to make a call. A woman's been stabbed."

He wasn't sure whether his ears were playing tricks on him, but he thought he could hear the wail of a police siren in the distance.

"I already called them," said the woman, eyeing Oscar warily. "I heard a scream."

Oscar hoped she was telling that truth, that she wasn't just trying to scare him off.

"Thank you," said Oscar. "Make sure they send someone right in, or she won't make it."

Oscar went back inside as a police car turned the corner, lights blazing. Up close, the sound was deafening.

"It's okay," he said to Verity. Blood pooled beneath her, and he assessed the wound closer, trying not to move her and risk Verity bleeding out. From the sound of her breathing, Steve may have punctured a lung.

A sound at the door made Oscar turn. Detective Payneham stood in the doorway, gun out, assessing what'd happened.

"Payneham?" said Oscar, surprised to see him.

"I overheard the call. I just got back from another call out. I recognized the address." The detective spoke fast and frantic, looking around at the displaced furniture, his eyes stopping on Verity who was holding her wound. "Jesus, what happened?"

Oscar pointed at Steve, who was still lying on the floor.

The detective looked from Verity to Steve and back again,

deciding quickly. "Don't know if he needs them, but I'm gonna cuff him anyway, in case he surprises us." He locked the cuffs around Steve's wrists. "There's an ambulance on the way."

Oscar looked at Steve. The man lying there didn't look like the brother he grew up with. This man was a stranger.

Detective Payneham put a call through on his radio, detailing the situation.

"It's okay, the ambulance is on its way," Oscar told Verity soothingly, still holding the throw against her cold skin. She started shivering, which told him that her body was about to go into shock. He went to her room and pulled the covers from her bed, throwing them around her to keep her warm.

Please hurry, he added silently, taking hold of her hand, hoping they weren't too late.

57

Chapter 57

Hayley

Now

I try to power up the phone, but there's no charge. Funny how something capable of so much is rendered useless so quickly.

I set the phone down and rifle through the drawer, hoping to find a charger. I find a number written on paper. Maybe it's the code for the door?

What if it's a trick?

Unless he's becoming less organized.

If he's not here, where is he? I didn't hear him leave, and he would've made some noise by now if he was still in the house.

If he's getting more careless, it probably means he's getting closer to ending my life. I have less time than I thought. I don't know how long he'll stay out, but when he comes back, I know he'll kill me.

I read the number—a six-digit code with a tattered edge.

Maybe it's an old code, the numbers since changed, and that's why it's at the bottom of the drawer.

I try to order my thoughts so I can decide what to do. If I try the pass code and it's wrong, Steve's security system will probably send him an alert, making him come home sooner, but if I can't think of a better option, I'll have no choice but to try the code.

The last time I saw him, he was sitting at the table, muttering something about the truth. The drugs he gave me have made my memory shaky and unreliable. I tried to hear what he was saying, but my hungry belly growled loudly at the food he was eating.

The hunger still grips me as I try to think past it. Since I've been here, I've eaten nothing but a couple of crackers. I close my eyes and try to decipher his words. Finally, I figure it out. He wasn't talking about the *truth*. He said "Verity."

Steve was talking about telling Verity something, but I can't remember what exactly. It's just at the edge of my consciousness, in that special limbo kept for the almost remembered.

Except, it wasn't "*tell* Verity." It was "*kill* Verity."

He's going to kill Verity, and I have no way to warn her.

Gripping the pass code, I enter the numbers, double-checking each one.

Chapter 58

Oscar

Now

"He has Hayley somewhere," said Oscar.

Detective Payneham looked up. "What?"

"My girlfriend. I have to go," said Oscar, already starting for the door.

"You're too late," said Steve.

Oscar wasn't sure how long he'd been conscious, if he was ever unconscious at all, but he didn't have time to think about that. He needed to find Hayley.

"She's already dead," said Steve.

Oscar's breath caught in his throat, but until he saw her for himself, he wouldn't stop. "Where is she?"

"I don't know," said Steve. "But I don't like your chances of finding her."

Oscar kicked Steve in the ribs, the ensuing throb in his knee worth it. Payneham looked away—*he didn't see anything*—and Oscar thought he saw a flicker of respect; Oscar did what all three of them wanted to do but couldn't.

They hadn't spoken in a long time, but Oscar knew his brother. Steve liked things to be ordered and in his control.

Oscar closed his eyes and pretended he was Steve for a moment, crawling inside of his head to explore the crevices of his imagination. He felt sick thinking about Hayley and what Steve might've done to her. He didn't know where Steve lived, but he probably wouldn't have taken Hayley to his home—the chances of someone noticing her were too high.

Steve would take her somewhere where no one would hear her scream. Like the cabin in the woods their family had holidayed at when they were kids. Oscar remembered the quiet—you could hear the birds chattering among themselves, away from the intimidating sound made by humans. Steve and Oscar had dared each other to climb the tallest trees and lift fallen branches to see if the buzzing underneath was a rattlesnake. Once, they'd found a dead white-tail deer and Steve had dared Oscar to turn over the rotting carcass, laughing when Oscar couldn't bring himself to try.

Oscar and Bill didn't go back there together after Kiko left, but it was always one of Bill's favorite spots, and Oscar suspected his father still went there to get away from everything.

It was the perfect place to hide someone, but the cabin couldn't still be there. When they were kids, although it was always scrubbed clean when they arrived, the cabin wasn't in the best condition, which was part of what Oscar had liked about it. It was like a glimpse of another era. He imagined that people might live like that without machines, working with nature instead of trying to smooth it into clean lines and

345

shiny surfaces.

He drove there now, hoping Steve hadn't left Hayley without food and water. He tried to prepare himself for what he might find when he got there. Once he arrived, he'd have to hike the last couple of miles to the cabin—none of the roads went that deep—but it couldn't feel as far now as it did when he was a kid.

Steve hadn't suggested they go for drinks because they were brothers. He was gathering information. He didn't care about Oscar's career—he was trying to figure out what Oscar knew about Ashlee, and how close Verity was to figuring out it was Steve. He must've known Caroline was involved, that she planned to get Oscar to take a look at the case. Caroline would've been at the hospital the day Bill was taken in—maybe Steve heard her talking to Oscar before Steve came to pick him up?

Oscar called Detective Payneham to ask if they could get a helicopter to the site, but he seemed to think it was a long shot. Eventually he agreed to send a ground team to check the area by foot.

Oscar asked about Steve, who was in custody and "not going anywhere anytime soon," according to Payneham.

When the call ended, Oscar tried to remember what he'd told Steve about Hayley. Had he helped Steve figure out what would hurt her?

So far, Steve knew Hayley's name, and what she did for a living. He knew Oscar loved her.

Oscar realized as he drove that Hayley was not at the cabin. This wasn't about warm family memories. This was about Steve and his perceived suffering. This was about being ripped away from everything he knew while Oscar got to continue his life, undisturbed.

He turned the car around and drove just above the speed limit, willing to risk a ticket. He remembered Lila spilling onto the road, the metal flying at them impossibly fast, and took his foot off the gas a little.

What Oscar needed was information about Steve. He wasn't sure the man he'd seen was the same boy he grew up with, but there was someone who could help fill in the gaps.

Kiko had given him her address, asking him to stop by if he could for a cup of coffee. He drove to her house now, a modest place in Bridgeport. He wished he had his phone, so he could call first, warn her he was about to interrupt her grieving and make sure she was back from the hospital, but this couldn't wait.

Kiko peeked out from behind the blind and opened the door for her son, wiping at her eyes. "What is it? What's wrong?"

"Steve has Hayley. It might be too late, but I have to find her."

Kiko nodded. "Of course. What do you need?"

"I need you to tell me what happened after you left. I need to know where you went and where you stayed. It might give me some idea about where he's taking Hayley. You said you thought he might hurt someone again, that you took him away so he couldn't. I need to know how you stopped him. Where did you go?"

Oscar followed Kiko inside and sat across from her at the table. "We stayed in a horrible place. I didn't have much money. All I knew was that I needed to keep him away, so I rented a warehouse space for us to live in."

Oscar assumed she wasn't talking about the trendy ware-house apartments people lived in now.

"He tried to leave, of course. I boarded up the windows so he couldn't get out. It drove him crazy. He didn't believe I was stopping people from breaking in and robbing us. We had nothing to take."

"You locked him in?"

She hesitated. "I know it's cruel to deny a person their freedom, but I didn't know what else to do. He was unstable." Kiko looked down, ashamed of what she was about to say. "I used a sedative to keep him calm. I didn't want him to be locked away in an institution, but I didn't know what else to do with him."

Oscar's hand pressed against his lips so that he didn't blurt out the irony that Kiko had kept Steve locked away anyway, but without the treatment that might've helped him. The sedation could explain how he got mixed up with drugs.

"Take me to the warehouse," said Oscar.

"It was a long time ago, Oscar. They've probably pulled it down."

Oscar asked where it was, not surprised to find it was only a few towns over; if Kiko and Bill had stayed in contact, it made sense she wouldn't be too far. He shot Kiko a look. "She'll be there."

He sent Detective Payneham a message to let him know where they were going. They drove in silence, except for the occasional GPS directions from Kiko's phone. It felt like they couldn't get there quick enough. What if Steve had set an emergency clause in case he didn't return, something to make sure Hayley wouldn't get out of there alive? Oscar was terrified that all he'd find—if he managed to find her at all—was her lifeless body.

He couldn't think about that. Until he learned otherwise, he had to keep going.

Kiko pointed to a warehouse that looked like it hadn't been used in a while.

Oscar parked haphazardly and stepped out of the car, Kiko's voice behind him. "Oscar-kun." She laid a hand on his arm. "Don't get your hopes up."

He turned to meet her gaze.

"If Steve's involved..." She shook her head, leaving the sentence unfinished.

How could she know he was capable of this and not tell someone?

"I'm sorry about Hayley. I really thought I could help him," said Kiko. "I figured he was just jealous of you and Lila, that it would stop if he was away from you both. He always needed to be the best. He was so competitive."

Oscar didn't have time for Kiko's regret. He needed to find Hayley.

He looked at the building—it looked like the front was used to store things people had forgotten about a long time ago. There was a front entrance, but there was also access from the side, and, he was betting, there would be a back entrance. "Where did you stay?" he asked.

Kiko led him to the end, around the back. "We stayed in here," she said.

Oscar rounded the corner and noticed the warehouse door was open. He hesitated—what if he was wrong and Hayley wasn't there? What if this was someone's home he was about to break into?

"Hayley?" he called from outside. When there was no answer, he decided breaking and entering charges were the least of his worries.

Inside, he found the room had been converted into a living space with a lowered ceiling.

"Hello?" he called, louder than before.

Panels lined the wall—soundproofing. The same stuff they used to get the acoustics right in a music studio. Maybe that's why a ceiling was installed, but it made the space feel like a hamster maze.

Paper crushed under his foot. He picked it up and found the pass code for the door.

He peered into the first room, finding nothing but a made-up bed.

Oscar ran outside, calling for Hayley. If she'd been there at some point, she wasn't now.

Please don't let me be too late.

Rushing back outside, he searched the perimeter of the warehouse until he saw someone on the ground, blonde hair cast over their face.

Hayley.

He moved faster, ignoring his protesting knee. "Hayley," he called.

Just a little farther.

"Hayley!"

Please be okay.

59

Chapter 59

Oscar

Now

Oscar reached Hayley and brushed back her hair. Her cheek was bruised and swollen enough to make him wonder if her cheekbone was fractured. "Hayley? Can you hear me?" he asked gently, relief flooding him. "Oh my god. What happened to your arms?" he asked, lifting her gently to assess her cuts.

"I tripped." Hayley didn't seem to notice his question, her voice hazy and dry. "I think I rolled my ankle."

Oscar assessed her face and her neck, which seemed fine. He was drawn back to the cuts across her arms, wondering if Steve had done this to her.

Hayley had the sleepy, slowed veneer of someone who had been drugged. Oscar couldn't be sure what Steve had given her. Oscar berated himself for not putting together that Steve was in pharmaceutical sales—he might have realized sooner what was going on, but he couldn't think about that now.

He wrapped Hayley in his arms. "Can you sit up?" he asked.

"Oscar? Steve was at your house...he..."

"I know," said Oscar, helping her sit up.

"It's all right. Detective Payneham took him to the station. It's over."

"Help should be here soon," said Kiko, circling awkwardly a few paces away.

Kiko had tried to prevent Steve from doing something exactly like this, and he'd done it anyway. Oscar could see the regret in the way she stood to the side, like she didn't know what to say to Hayley; Kiko felt responsible.

"I'm fine. I can walk," said Hayley, struggling on her twisted ankle.

Kiko looked at Hayley and shook her head, searching for something to say.

"What day is it?" asked Hayley.

"Thursday," said Oscar gently. "I'm so sorry. I thought you weren't speaking to me. To be honest, I was too scared to find out why."

Hayley retested her ankle and cried out in pain, shifting her weight to the other foot.

"Are you all right?" asked Oscar softly, really asking how badly Steve had hurt her.

Hayley didn't answer. Instead, she grit her teeth and walked ahead of Oscar and Kiko.

Oscar trailed behind helplessly. Did Hayley blame him for exposing her to Steve, for bringing him into their lives?

60

Chapter 60

Verity

Later

Oscar knocks on the door, carrying a bunch of pink flowers into the hospital room—I think they're cherry blossoms. I wave him in with my good arm, still feeling the pull from the gauze and stitches in my side. His profile looks similar to Wes—*Steve*—and I have to remind myself it's Oscar.

"How are you feeling?" he asks, setting the flowers down so that I can see them, but not making a big deal about it.

"Better," I say. The painkillers take the edge off enough that I've been able to get a little sleep. "How's Hayley?"

"She's good," says Oscar, but I can see from his expression that he's worried about her.

"I know what she's going through," I say, the memory still fresh. "Let her know that if she wants to talk, I'm here."

He smiles wanly. "Thanks. She'll appreciate it."

I smile back. It feels good to reach out. I'd been so busy trying to find out the truth that I'd forgotten that it's important to just live sometimes. For the first time in a while, I really do feel good. I don't know how long I have, but I'm going to spend each moment I can exploring, letting myself be surprised.

"You know," I say, sobering, "I thought I saw Ashlee on the roof with me. It seemed too crazy to believe it was real, but she really was there. I heard her say my name as I was falling. I think she was going to tell me what happened. Oscar, she was only doing what she did to get me the money to help with treatment."

He pulls up a chair and sits beside me. "I'm so sorry," he says, and for a moment I wonder if I should be telling him any of this. Steve is his brother. It can't be easy for him, knowing what he did.

The conversation turns to happier things, the future and what comes next. Despite everything that's happened, I'm still here, and while I'm alive, I plan on living.

Epilogue

Oscar

Later

Oscar waited in the hospital while Hayley slept. He thought about going home and coming back when she woke up, but he wanted to be there when her eyes opened. They had given her something to ease the pain from her broken cheekbone, but he couldn't help wondering if she was still feeling the effects of it, the little crease between her eyebrows making her sleep look fretful.

He went to the foyer and asked a nurse if Hayley might need something more to keep her comfortable. The nurse promised to go and check on her, and Oscar headed for a vending machine to restock his mints and water supply. He didn't see Caroline approaching at first until she called his name.

"Walk with me," she said, and led him out to the hospital grounds. When they were far enough away from the hum of the hospital, Caroline slowed, coming to a stop. "How is Hayley?"

Oscar slid his hands into his pockets and lowered his head. "I don't know, Caroline. She hasn't said much."

"And how are you?"

Oscar shrugged. "I'm fine. I just—I hope Hayley can forgive me."

The lines on Caroline's face sharpened. "Hey. What your brother did was his choice. You couldn't have known he would do this."

"I *should've* known. I should've known from what happened to Lila."

"Oscar, listen to me. If you're going to blame yourself for this, then you have to blame me for making you a part of this case."

Oscar held a hand over Caroline's. "No. Caroline, you've been nothing but kind to me. You and Jane have always been there. You were trying to rescue me. Again. You're...family."

Caroline raised her brow. "If I'd known your brother was involved, I would never have put you in that situation."

"I know." He caught her eye, bringing the point home. "You couldn't have known Steve was involved."

"Neither could you. You need to focus on Hayley now. Show her you love her. Be there for her when she needs you."

He saw her point. Hindsight was a cruel reminder of how little we were aware of while we were in the moment, but as much as it hurt, Oscar was glad he knew the truth, and it meant Verity had some answers about Ashlee.

It meant *he* had answers of his own. The world looked like an entirely different place now that he knew what Steve was capable of, but as he went to visit Hayley, conscious of what she meant to him, he was beginning to see what he was capable of too.

Acknowledgments

A lot goes into writing a book. While solitary at times, it's definitely not a one person job. A huge thank you to the reader for coming on this journey with me.

Thank you to everyone who worked on the book and read the early drafts. Thanks to Beth, and to Alyssa Matesic, who did an amazing job editing the manuscript. Thanks to TBR Press, and to Donald, Angelle, Anna and Tam for reading early drafts. Thanks to my writing group and beta readers for their candor. Thanks to Oni, Zen, Quinn and Xari for your patience.

If you enjoyed this book, please leave a review to help readers like you find it.

About the Author

MQ Webb writes psychological thrillers, suspense, and horror. Their debut novel, *How to Spot a Psychopath,* was an Amazon bestseller. *When you're Dying* is the second book in the Oscar de la Nuit psychological thriller series.

You can connect with me on:
- https://mqwebb.com
- https://twitter.com/marswebb1
- https://www.facebook.com/MQWebbAuthor
- https://www.instagram.com/mqwebbauthor

Subscribe to my newsletter:
- https://mqwebb.com

Printed in Great Britain
by Amazon

21848449R00209